A Séance at Syd's

An Anthology of Modern Acid-Folk-Haunt-Psych-Prog-Space-Kraut-Radiophonic-Rock Etcetera Quotes

Dave Thompson

MEGA DODO
PUBLICATIONS

In association with

Paper Jukebox

© *2015 by Dave Thompson*
Introduction © *2015 by Nik Turner*
Outroduction © *2015 by Chris Lambert*
Front Cover design © *2015 by Dale Simpson*
Back cover design © *2015 by Gregory Curvey*

ISBN 978-0-9544528-6-5

A Séance at Syd's
An Anthology of Modern Acid-Folk-Haunt-Psych-Prog-Space-Kraut-Radiophonic-Rock Etcetera
Quotes

TABLE OF CONTENTS

x

INTRODUCTION

by Nik Turner

Having been stimulated by very experimental ideas, I have always been open to, and very interested in, musical experimentation.

I have also always welcomed the opportunity to participate in, and contribute to the work of young, and up-and-coming bands and musicians, and have always been happy to become involved in their projects, and possibly play on their albums (strictly upon request!). Looking through the artists included in this book, I am immediately reminded of my own past collaborations with Sendelica and Dodson & Fogg, both of whom carry into the twenty-first century the musical spirit that I first discovered in the twentieth.

I was raised on Stockhausen; traditional jazz; John Cage; cybernetic serendipity; free jazz; John Coltrane, (known to have taken LSD) and his sheets of sound; the expressionist music of Miles Davis, Pharoah Sanders, Ornette Coleman, Eric Dolphy, Sun Ra, Albert Ayler, Archie Shepp and Eddie Harris (among many others).

My main influences, then, tended towards jazz, Afro-American music and shamanism, sounds that are driven and fueled by meditative experiences, the raising of consciousness, forms of enlightenment, self-awareness, mind expanding substances, and psychedelic drugs.

So much creativity and wild and exciting visionary magic has been created, and was exhibited, but not only by those under the influence of, or affected by, psychedelic and mind-altering substances.

It is also the preserve of those who might not be personally experiencing the mind alteration, but who are nevertheless stimulated by the ripple effect of those who did fall under the influence of it.

That's why I have always encouraged young musicians to experiment; to explore new territories; and to discover new musical worlds, pushing the boundaries of their imaginations and their music with the attitude of enjoying themselves, and not giving a hoot what anyone else thinks.

Because they are the only ones who actually know what they are trying to achieve.

Them, and all the like-minded souls who join them on their miraculous journeys.

Nik Turner, April 2015

Nik Turner was a founding member of the ground-breaking conceptual art and experimental mixed-media psychedelic musical experience and alternative social phenomenon, the space-rock collective, Hawkwind.

BRIEFLY…

You've seen the title, and you've pondered its scope. Now you're asking—who is here?

Well, not everybody that could, or even should be, that's for sure. From the initial list of names who were approached to participate in this project, around one quarter either could not, would not, or did not take part.

Gratifyingly, the majority of the absentees did send their apologies, and it would be churlish to fault their reasoning. An unexpectedly successful new single; the demands of recording a new album; the chaos of being away on tour; a general reluctance to be interviewed; and so on.

A handful of potential inclusions agreed to take part, but then chose not to, and presumably they, too, had their reasons. And a few didn't respond in any form. Maybe "Acid-Haunt-Folk-Psych-Prog-Kraut-Radiophonic-Garage-Space Etcetera" felt too limiting for them.

Oh, and then there were the ones….

Later in this book, Chris Wade of Dodson & Fogg tells the story here of his encounter with a band who had just received a spin on the Mark Lamar show, and promptly transformed themselves into rock'n'roll stars, *far* too important for the divey club in Leeds that they were playing.
I think I received an e-mail from them a couple of months back. Or, if not them, some other band that had been bitten by the same vainglorious bug.

They, too, were *far* too important to appear in a book; *far* too big to share the page with the lesser mortals that were also involved; and far too busy being untouchable to even care what the Spanish Inquisition thought about them. (Don't worry; it'll make sense when you get to chapter two.)

All of which is absolutely fine, because even without their contributions, it still means that approximately three-quarters of the musicians who were contacted *did* respond, with what you are about to read.

That is, some eighty different bands, performers, artists and label heads, selected not only as representatives of the sprawling mass of musical notions that have made this decade so unexpectedly enthralling, but as its spokesmen as well.

It needs spokesmen, too. Because, despite all the doom and gloom that surrounds the music industry of today; despite the epitaphs that are written almost every day (give a thousand monkeys a thousand typewriters, and forget the works of Shakespeare. They've already given you a billion blogs); and despite the widespread insistence that we've all never had it so bad; the modern music scene is actually pretty darned healthy.

No longer the Anglo-American hegemony that once held all the cards, contemporary music now drip feeds its sonics from every corner of the globe.

This book interviews musicians from Portugal, France, Germany, Finland, Spain, Italy and Sweden, and it might have traveled even further had Google Translate been fit for purpose. Back in the mid-1970s, the *New Musical Express's* Gasbag feature indulged a long-running correspondence from a reader who, if memory serves me well, lived in Accra, Ghana, and was concerned about the lack of coverage for his heroes, Beatles-band. Needless to say, the humor was at least partially rooted in the fact was that his English was appallingly broken. Technology now allows the rest of us to indulge in the same stumbling joke.

(But we digress.)

Once, the major labels held all-consuming sway, swatting aside any upstart indies that might challenge their dominance as though they were less than gnats. Today, it's the majors who are the endangered species, as bands prove they don't even *need* record labels any more.

Self releasing through Bandcamp, spotlighting on the Active Listener, financing via Kickstarter... those three sites (and they are by no means alone) could keep you discovering new music for the rest of your life.

Maybe nobody's making a fortune from any of this, and a few plays on the BBC still count for something, whomsoever you speak to. But Auntie is no longer the be-all and end-all of the pop picking spectrum, and that can only be good.

Besides, the fact that the BBC *does* play these bands, or some of them anyway, is itself an indication of the seismic shift that has reshaped the rock universe. Because even the word "rock" no longer means very much; and, because they are no longer beholden to the powers of commerce, more musicians are able to say more for themselves than at any other time in the history of recorded sound.

A few of the interviewees here acknowledge that. The final question asked where, with a time machine at their disposal, and all of history to explore... where would they choose to go?

More than a couple said they wouldn't budge. Because, in the words of the Owl Service / Greanvine's Diana Collier, "we have so many treasures [today] to mine from... to go into the past would preclude us from so many things." And she goes on to list a handful of current personal favorites, to which everybody reading this could probably add a dozen more.

Yes, we would all like to live in a world where the Purple Gang still take granny for a trip. But would you also want to live in one that didn't have Blue Giant Zeta Puppies? Not such an easy decision now, is it?

Classic Deram or modern Fruits de Mer? The debut David Bowie LP or the first Crystal Jacqueline? *Sergeant Pepper* or *Mrs. Silbury*? *Swaddling Songs* or *Hey Hey Hippy Witch*? *Pick of the Pops* or *The Muffin Junkee?*

Maybe such comparisons are facile. Maybe, if you were selective enough in the things you chose to listen to, the past is always a better place to visit, and (almost) fifty years back from today does seem especially perfect.

Consider the theme music to *Doctor Who*—in the sixties, it was rendered so fantastically futuristically that it could indeed have tumbled half a century back in time. Whereas today's interpretation sounds so portentously toothless that it might as well have been recorded in 1963, as well as written then.

So, by all means set the controls, Mr Wells. But be careful. There may be Morlocks.

Unlike their approach to their music, my approach to the artists featured here never varied. A series of questions was formulated and duly dispatched… general questions, for the most part, aimed at pinpointing the most rudimentary elements of life in and around a twenty-first century music scene that is more gorgeously splintered and specialized than any that has ever preceded it.

Inspired by the interrogations that beguiled pop stars of the early sixties ("favorite color; favorite hairspray; how far would you go on a first date?") a few of the questions were obvious, a few were off the wall.

But I purposefully omitted what might have been the most obvious one of all… if you really were in attendance at a séance at Syd's, how would *you* make the Madcap laugh? What one question would you ask him?

The answers could have been interesting, and I thank Chris Lambert for a revelation that reflects upon a few of them. As curator of the magnificent *Tales of the Black Meadow*, Lambert has already caused us to reflect upon some of the most perplexing mysteries to absorb modern thinking. The discovery that Syd Barrett was as bound up in the mire as Roger Mullins is one that absolutely eclipses any fantasies that the rest of us might have indulged.

Full participation in this book was not compulsory. The questions were to be answered or ignored as the individuals preferred, while other observations were invited, other thoughts were encouraged. Some minor editing notwithstanding, this book represents what was returned to me, by the people who got back to me; and who, by the sheer breadth of their responses, more than amply represent the sheer scope and soaring imagination of the music that this book is intended to celebrate.

And that is despite it being (and this is why we love it so much) an utterly indefinable blend of at least a dozen, and maybe more, musical themes and streams—none of which are going to elaborated upon any further, because really… you *know* what you're listening to, you know what you like, and you know why you picked up this book. And if you don't, the sounds that are talked about, and the people who talk about them, will give you an excellent place to begin.

That said, if we want to be strictly linear about things, you can't find a much better description of the music featured here than Ghost Box label founder Jim Jupp's portrayal of his own company's output. It is, he says, a "not historically accurate, but naggingly familiar… world" in which "pop culture from the mid sixties up to the early eighties is happening all at once." But which could probably be narrowed down even further, as the Rowan Amber Mill pointed out when documenting their current activities in a February 2015 Facebook posting.

"They are currently all at sea in the English Channel existing concurrently in the years 1967 and 1976. They are soaking up the atmosphere and very busy recording tunes in an acid folk-meets-radiophonic stylee."

The years 1967 to 1976. Constantly throughout this book, we find our attention being drawn back to the decade-or-so that, in the UK, was born in Psych and died with Punk, with one truly the logical conclusion to the other.

Psychedelia was conceived when we thought we still had a chance. Punk was what happened when we realized that we didn't. Flower power just doesn't feel quite so alluring when the dustmen are on strike, and the tower block lift is awash with urine. And to all those sixties kids who thought punk was ugly; well, of course it was. Nobody likes to be awoken from a dream.

But, of course, it's also the decade that separated Emma Peel's *Avengers* (1965) from British Rail's *The Finishing Line* (1977); *Cathy Come Home* from *Reginald Perrin*; *Ready, Steady, Go!* from *So It Goes*.

And yes, there's a reason why the reference points are televisual. It's the same reason why almost every reader will smile knowingly as the Hare and the Moon's Grey Malkin affectionately recalls "the era of browns, yellows and oranges…" and how it was so "grim and creepy." How "cinema and children's TV was the best back then"; how "it influences our music more than any other decade."

And why the music embraces that medium so thoroughly that their own natural divisions are thoroughly distorted; which is also why so much of the music is accompanied by the chill of the spine. It's not that singular, of course. Pick apart the sickly earth tones that were so endemic to the seventies, and the composite rainbows of the sixties blaze forth, psychedelia in every known shade and hue, expansive and expanding in equal quantities. Which is why *The Prisoner* and *Python*, *Do Not Adjust Your Set* and *Magical Mystery Tour* are as much a part of our universe as any other show.
But the colors are deceptive all the same, a whiter shade of deathly pale.

Barney Bubbles and Hypgnosis. The Misunderstood and the Fleur de Lys. Daevid Allen's Soft Machine and Nigel Weymouth's Hapshash. "A Day in the Life" and "Death of a Clown." The Apple boutique and the Kinks' "Dead End Street." Carnaby cool with art by the Fool. Brian Jones's Stones and Arthur Brown's bones.

Grocer Jack, grocer Jack, is it true what mummy says?
Take the trip too often, and no, you won't come back.

Because again, do you feel that undercurrent? The sense of something below the surface, a lively writhing beneath the pavement, and by the pounding of my drums, something Wiccan this way comes?

Of all the memories that British TV fans of a certain age hold most precious, the wealth and welter of supernaturally-themed tales aimed at young and old alike stands among the late 1960s / early-mid 1970s most remarkable achievements.

Hour-long scare-athons like *Thriller*, *Supernatural* and *Beasts*; further children's fare that reached ichorous fingers from *The Ghosts of Motley Hall* to *Catweazle*; Doctor Who's encounter with the Dæmons; the BBC's ghost stories for Christmas; and one-off thrillers like *The Stone Tape* and *Robin Redbreast*.

The Blood on Satan's Claw!

"Come Unto The Corn," a cut on the Hare and the Moon's 2015 album *Wood Witch*, opens with an exquisitely well-chosen sample from that movie, and just hearing it scratching from the speakers sends the imagination spiraling back to the first time you saw the movie.

It is often said that you can't capture lightning in a bottle. But you can recapture the frisson of fear that startled you when it struck. And the Hare does.

Holy Behemoth, father of my life, speak now, come now, rise now from the forest, from the furrows, from the field and live.

Hail, Behemoth, spirit of the dark, take thou my blood, my skin, my flesh and walk.

"Holy Behemoth, father of my life, speak now, come now, rise now."

Other authors, in other places, have discussed the reasons *why* a bunch of half-century old kids' TV and Hammer Horror (thank you, Kate Bush) should suddenly be impacting upon our consciousness now, and very reasonable some of their explanations are. There's no need to add to them here.

But the lines blur again as we consider music's own influence on that culture.

Gillian Hills, the star of *The Owl Service*, was a pop star in France long before she found those plates, one of the Yé-yé girls who took that nation by storm, and whose ebullient racket also lives on today.

She returned to England in 1965 to appear on *Ready Steady Go!* and cut one of the most alluring b-sides of the year ("Tomorrow Is Another Day," absurdly relegated behind "Look at Them") ; and then joins Jane Birkin in stripping David Hemmings in *Blow Up*, that most seminal (although, to be truthful, faintly boring) cinematic portrait of Swinging London.

Joe Meek held séances in the same studio that he used to alchemize pop gold; and he taped as much dross as he did dramatic diamonds before he shot himself (and his landlady) on the anniversary of his hero Buddy Holly's demise.

At his best, though, Meek is often still described as the British Phil Spector, although more than one of the artists included here would argue that the compliment should be reversed. Phil Spector was the American Joe Meek.

Quatermass and the Pit, a 1958 BBC TV series that became a 1967 Hammer movie, haunted the imagination for years before it was lionized by Mount Vernon Arts Lab; while Grey Malkin (again) looks back on the late seventies adventures of *Dick Turpin* and insists, "[That] theme music is probably inadvertently influential on, and responsible for, a great deal of the current crop of weird folk, folk horror and hauntology acts.

"There are definitely moments when I listen to a… track I've recorded and think, 'Hang on, that's *Dick Turpin*!' It's not quite as cool a reference as something like *The Owl Service*, but the soundtrack is definitely ripe for reappraisal. And Richard O'Sullivan did look pretty dandy in his highwayman's togs. I reckon so anyway."

The chronology wavers, too. The Rowan Amber Mill medievalized Tubeway Army's "Are Friends Electric," to draw the early 1980s into the web.

Fruits de Mer, another of the labels that has done so much to choreograph the music, has released an EP of fifties rocker Eddie Cochran covers.

The sex-and-death soaps of English Folk reach even further back than that. Drew Mulholland, of the aforementioned Mount Vernon Arts Lab (and much more), recalls his earliest musical memory as learning "Sumer Is Icumen In" at infant school.

It's a thirteenth century celebration sung in Middle English, that you probably remember from Richard Thompson's millennial history of song, but which is also sung in *The Wicker Man*, and it turns up in an episode of Bagpuss too. In other words, it's always been around, and it probably always will be. Neither do any of these ruminations slip so far from all the other musical currents that flash through these pages; and neither do they truly fall so far from one another, either.

Yes, it may look like a long and lonely autobahn that stretches between "Lucifer Sam" and "Come to the Sabbat" (although the titles probably beg to differ); from "Telstar" to "Mysterious Semblance at the Strand of Nightmares."

But it isn't, as the work (and words) of Octopus Syng, the Familiars, the Blue Giant Zeta Puppies and Black Tempest might inform you.

Art does not develop in isolation; and social movements rarely do, either. The same synchronicity that caused punk movements to arise simultaneously and independently in New York and London, in 1976, was at work a decade earlier, when psychedelia first flooded from the American west coast and the English Home Counties.

Maybe a few souls picked up on what was happening in one place, and spread the word in the other. Maybe the occasional rumor reached out across the ocean. But that was all. It was a cultural current, not a newspaper headline, that first encouraged the sixties kids to tune in, turn on… and a cultural current, too, that convinced their own offspring to contrarily tune out, switch off.

Music, movies, mythology, mysticism. The Age of Aquarius dawned in the late 1960s, and the ensuing decade danced to its beat. The fact that history reckons it all went tits-up eventually is neither here nor there. Because it didn't. The journalists moved away, the cameras clicked someplace else.

The freak outs faded, UFO crashed, Middle Earth went overground, the Summer of Love became the season of the money men. The pop charts went to pot, and if you switched your television off in 1977, and haven't turned it on since then, you've really not missed very much.
But the spirits that the era invoked, the dreams it unleashed, and the sounds it created, they are still alive, they are still inspirational. They are still electrifying.

Discussing her own embrace of the music, many years after "the fact," Broadcast's Trish Keenan explained, "I discovered psychedelia, and it seemed to have self-help properties that allowed me to let go of an immobilizing working class pride that was cementing a false identity into my psyche, stopping me from transforming."

Which is why you refer at your own peril to the music as "revivalist." As Paul Weller growled when he was accused of rehashing old Mod, how could he be reviving something when he wasn't even there the first time around?

There's another reason, however, for not attempting to tell you "what" you're listening to. For not answering the age-old question of "I've not heard them. What do they sound like?"
Because we all have different reasons, we all find different focal points, and we all have different ears. Personally, this book was itself ignited by, and in many ways shaped by, the constant presence on my stereo of half a dozen albums, of which only three are the work of the artists included within:

• Current 93—*Crooked Crosses for the Nodding God* (1989)
• Broadcast—*The Noise Made By People* (2000)
• Mount Vernon Arts Lab—*The Séance at Hobs Lane* (2001)
• the Owl Service—*A Garland of Song* (2007)
• the Eccentronic Research Council—*1612 Underture* (2012)
• the Rowan Amber Mill and Emily Jones—*The Book of the Lost* (2013).

To which could be added the various artists set *Songs from the Black Meadow* (2014); the Fruits de Mer tribute to the Pretty Things' *S.F. Sorrow* concept LP, 2010's *Sorrow's Children*; any one of thirty-plus Active Listener download samplers; and, because it's hard to imagine a more delightful scenario from the world of Brit(ish) Pop in the mid-nineties, a mighty debt is surely owed to an untitled piece by David Devant and his Spirit Wife, lurking in lurid wait at the far end of their 1996 CD single "Cookie." It's a ghost story, in which a is-she-really-that-playful spirit hangs out on the narrator's bedroom ceiling, dropping plastic Napoleonic soldiers on his unwary head. Which may sound silly when it's put like that, but wait.

You're a ten year old pop kid (or a mid-thirties music journalist) hearing *that* for the first time, when all you did was flip (or whatever the terminology was for CD singles) your last fave rave, and there's no way your musical taste could ever be the same again. And I don't care how askance Mikey Georgeson, frontman of the Devant band, and a looming presence here as well, looked when I suggested that Cookie the Ghost is probably the queen of Psychedelic Hauntological pop.

It's still true.

As true as the sense that, although so much divides each of those records from the others, just as much binds them as well.

It might a drop of acid, or a nightmarish haunt; a roomful of folk, or a trip with wild psych; the gnosis of prog, or the howls of radiophonics (in which Dylan's ghosts of electricity dance around every face). It might even be a car in the garage, or a craft out in space. It's there, all the same.

It's always been there.

Very early on, the decision was made to focus this book upon artists who are currently… that is, in the here and now… active.

To expand into historical territory would certainly have been enthralling, and highly rewarding, too.

But it would also have ensured the gathering of material might never have been completed; and, besides, that earlier story has already been told in a variety of tomes, most notably Jeanette Leech's *Seasons They Change: The Story of Acid and Psychedelic Folk*; Timothy Gassen's *The Knights of Fuzz: the New Garage and Psychedelic Music Explosion*; David Keenan's unimpeachable *England's Hidden Reverse*; and more or less every issue you pick up of *Ugly Things* and *Shindig* magazines.
And that's without even mentioning a world-wide net's worth of blogs, sites, discographies and webzines dedicated to remembering, and revisiting, our shared cultural past (all hail, here, the now-inactive, but still eminently readable *A Year in the Country*, and so many more besides).

Of course, there is some overlap between those publications and this, most notably among a handful of artists whose careers were birthed in the golden age to which we owe so much, and continue to astonish today: Tír na nÓg, Alison O'Donnell, Comus and Judy Dyble.

The majority of those performers whom we might consider to be the founding fathers of the theme, however…

…from the Incredible String Band, Vashti Bunyan and Pearls Before Swine, to Nick Drake, Al Jones and Anne Briggs…

…from the United States of America, White Noise and the BBC Radiophonic Workshop, to Coil, Sol Invicta and Andrew King (whose monstrous interpretations of the Francis Child songbook defy any attempt to append the appellation "ballad").

…from the Beach Boys, Tomorrow and the Thirteenth Floor Elevators, to Billy Childish, Robyn Hitchcock and the Paisley Underground…

… and, of course, the Pretty Things in their every shape and form; the Beatles, for all that they did for everyone; and Syd Barrett in too many ways to count. *And so on and on and on…*

…they all are here in glorious spirit alone.

But they *are* still here.

It is a séance, after all.

To Trish Keenan

(September 28, 1968–January 14, 2011)

still Broadcasting

INDEX OF FEATURED ARTISTS

Note: The vast majority of interviews featured here were conducted specifically for this book between January and April 2015.

The remainder (noted * below) were excerpted from interviews conducted for either the Spin Cycle blog at Goldmine magazine's website (goldminemag-dot-com/blogs/spin-cycle-blogs/), or for other previously published projects.

For brief biographies of all, see Appendix One. For specific references to individual artists, consult the index at the far end of this book.

Francois Sky
George Roper Noman—the Nomen
Gordon Raphael
Graeme Lockett—Head South By Weaving
Gregory Curvey—the Luck of Eden Hall
Grey Malkin—the Hare and the Moon
Icarus Peel
Jaire Pätäri—Octopus Syng
Jayne Gabriel—Schizo Fun Addict
Jeb Morris—Grandpa Egg
Jed Davis—Eschatone Records*
Jefferson Hamer
Jet Wintzer—Schizo Fun Addict
Jim Jupp—Ghost Box Records (label) / Belbury Poly*
Joanna Swan—the Familiars
João Branco Kyron—Beautify Junkyards
Joel Slevin—Eschatone Records*
John Blaney—Mega Dodo Records (label)
Jordi Bel—Stay
Judy Dyble
Keith Jones—Fruits de Mer Records (label)
Ken Halsey—the Past Tense*
Kevin Oyston—the Soulless Party
Leah Cinnamon—Sky Picnic
Lenny Helsing—the Thanes
Leo O'Kelly—Tír na nÓg
Lorenzo Bracaloni—The Child of a Creek / Fallen
Marc Swordfish—Astralasia*
Marco Rossi—Gathering Grey*
Marco Magnani—Mark and the Clouds
Mark Reuter—Army of Mice
Marrs Bonfire—the Green Question Mark
Maxime Schwartz—Black Psychiatric Orchestra
Mike Stax—the Loons*
Mikey Georgeson
Mordecai Smyth

Narsis Passolas—La Meccanica Sonora
Nick Salomon—Bevis Frond*
Paolo Sala
Pete Bingham—Sendelica
Pete Meriwether—Sky Picnic
Peter Lyon—Palace of Swords
Richard Thompson—Lost Harbours
Roger Linney—Reverb Worship (label)
Roger Wooton—Comus*
Sand Snowman
Simon Berry—Beaulieu Porch
Sproatly Smith
Stephen Bradbury—Black Tempest
Stephen Stannard—Rowan Amber Mill
Steve Palmer—Mooch
Steven Collins—Owl Service, Greanvine, Stone Tape Recordings (label)*
Ted Selke—the Seventh Ring of Saturn
Tom Conway—the Familiars
Tom Hughes—Gathering Grey*
Tom Woodger—Blue Giant Zeta Puppies
Will Z

In which all and sundry are invited to tell us of their earliest musical experiences, either as a musician or a listener.

I remember the parties at my house, organized by my much older brothers, when my parents were out at night. Long hair, flared pants, the smell of patchouli and loud rock music was abundant.

The [entire] scenario was kind of bizarre to me, and I developed an allergy to distortion pedals. At that time, I was a huge fan of sci-fi movies—so, as a reaction, I started to listen to movie soundtracks and other kinds of electronic music.

I also remember recording a cassette with Kraftwerk's Autobahn that was being broadcast on a radio program. It was quite an experience for me at my music fan early stages.

João Branco Kyron

My first memorable listening experience was playing Sam Cooke's "Back on the Chain Gang" single at 78 speed, to make him sound like Pinky and Perky. This was age five, in 1973. Myself and my sister were in hysterics listening to it.

Alan Murphy

Hitting pots and pans with a wooden spoon, as my mother tried to record a Carpenters TV special on her tape deck, was probably my first musical attempt.

For my first gig proper, on the back of a truck with the band Lodern, I thought that being continually mildly electrocuted by the mic was just what happened when you played a gig. One of our songs was called "The Flaming Lipsy One," so I probably deserved it.

David Colohan

As a listener: My mum singing me lullabies every night as a child at bedtime. One of my earliest and happiest memories. As a musician: Singing a solo in church at Christmas, with my Dad accompanying me on guitar. I sang 'Little Donkey.' So cool. I was five.

Ellie Coulson

As a listener, the first thing that made me take notice of music in general was "Money," by the Flying Lizards. I had never heard keyboards like that before. Of course, I've since found it was a prepared piano that was used and no synths were used.

As for earliest experience as a musician, a friend and I decided to form a band so we had two practices with me on a malfunctioning SH101 and him on guitar; we then did our first gig the following

Saturday, recruiting a bass player and a drummer from the audience. Needless to say, we were bloody awful, but we got asked back to play again, so we must have done something right.

Andy Hokano

The first recording I ever did was a cover of Marie Osmond's version of "Paper Roses," on one of those old seventies tape recorders. A few years later, I was multi-tracking between two tape recorders, using biscuit tins and knitting needles for drums, and an electric guitar which I got from my mum's Kay's catalogue for about £2 a week.

Simon Berry

The Hi-Fi used in my family when I was a kid was a reel to reel tape machine (the brand was Geloso), and I first heard a tape my brother recorded from the radio, which included lots of Beatles songs: "Get Back," "You've got to Hide your Love Away," "Lucy in the Sky with Diamonds," "Norwegian Wood" and more.

I felt a special connection with those songs immediately. I didn't know a word of English at the time, but it didn't matter. Having been recorded from the radio, most of the songs had the beginning missing and I still remember where, at least some of them, started: ...…"man who thought he was a loner but he knew it wouldn't last" or ....."small, everywhere people stare, each and every day."

Also, there was the disco version of Santa Esmeralda's "Don't let Me be Misunderstood," which somehow to this day I prefer to the original. And it was from that album that I heard a version of "Gloria" (whose original is by Them) with the first three guitar chords I learnt to play, thanks to my brother patience in teaching me.

Those three simple chords are amazing. I wish I was able to come up with such a strong simplicity. But the first time I attempted to record a song onto our Geloso recorder with my brother, both on acoustic guitars, I had the first shocking disappointment… of hearing my own voice. It didn't sound like I thought it would sound.

So there I was, an enthusiastic twelve year old kid with guitar, going totally whimsical: "what the hell is that? That's not me singing! Come on!"

But then I learned that recording yourself is the best way to learn how to sing, or at least it has been for me.

About a year after, I was getting more confident taping cheap microphones around a chair as mic-stands. Once I called my brother and my mother to sing harmonies while I sang "Twist and Shout" Beatles style. I wish I had kept that tape.

Marco Magnani

As a listener, the earliest music I can remember being obsessed with – and this was as a very young child – was "The Poky Little Puppy" song and the Jimi Hendrix version of "All Along the Watchtower." The former made me feel super happy and the latter just kind of blew my little girl mind.

As a musician, I've been playing instruments since I was eight and joined my school's concert band. My earliest memory of that is being terrified before performing at the Christmas concert because I'd been playing "Silent Night" in some odd minor key and couldn't remember how to play it the way we were supposed to.

Amanda Votta

I have two cousins who are like my brothers, and when I was around six years old, they inadvertently got me into electronic music. They were about eight and ten years older than me, with jobs and money to spare, so they had this attic conversion done to house their new SH101s and Solina string synthesizers.

Because of my age, they kept me at arm's length in case I broke something, so all I could do was stand at the bottom of the ladder to the attic, and listen with deep curiosity to the weird squelchy and intriguing noises that were coming from above.

I made notes of who they were listening to on their record players and went off to "tape" said artists off the radio. Back in those days, it was bands and artists like Kraftwerk and Jean Michel Jarre that totally fascinated me with their pure electronic sounds. As I got older, I demanded my cousins play the above-mentioned on their turntable, as well as other artists… (early) Depeche Mode, Vangelis or Tubeway Army and even Wendy / Walter Carlos. I just immersed myself in it all.

When I was twelve, I managed to save for a second hand Korg Poly 800 synth with reverse colored keys. Many a night I'd tamper with it, not really having a clue what I was doing.

Whatever sounds I got out of it, though, I'd try and record with a cheap tape recorder I had in my bedroom. I had no way of layering sounds, so all I'd do is come up with a ditty and record it for a future time, when I could afford the proper equipment to sequence and layer properly.

Unfortunately, that wasn't to happen for almost another ten years!

Kev Oyston

I remember, as a very young child, visiting my Grandma and "playing" with her upright piano. I remember being totally enchanted by the instrument; the thunder of the lowest notes hammered out, and the light sparkle of the highest notes lightly tapped. Needless to say, my Grandma didn't really like me "messing around" on the piano.

I think this is why I often start with a piano when writing for Army of Mice.

Mark Reuter

I think the very earliest musical experience that blew my mind was a Finnish rock band called Hurriganes. I guess it was 1976. I was five years old then, but I wasn't the only one who got "Hurriganes Fever."   All the kids around my neighborhood blew their minds to the Hurriganes. Especially Remu Aaltonen, the singer and drummer, who was our the biggest rock n' roll idol.

We made "drums" by putting duct tape over the top of empty pickle cans. Then we played them and we played being Remu. Every kid dreamed of being Remu at that time. Albert Järvinen (guitar) and Cisse Häkkinen (bass) were very cool guys too, but Remu was the coolest guy in the world in our minds. It's my earliest musical experience as a "musician" and a listener. I think it was a spark that got me to start my music making later.

Jaire Pätäri

I remember being about nineteen years old and hearing John Renbourne's "Pavane" and Ralph McTell's "Willoughby's Farm."

They seemed to embody an Englishness both ancient and timeless; they were tracks that made me see the guitar in a whole new way.

Tom Conway

I think that my earliest musical memory is probably the sound of my mother singing me to sleep when I was a baby. Another early memory, which may or may not have been formative, was hearing The Beatles' "Eleanor Rigby." (It was the b-side of "Yellow Submarine.") I can remember crying, because it sounded so sad. I must have been four or five at the time.

Peter Lyon

My first ever solo "gig" was playing the sax at an informal concert at school when I was 10. The school had been burned to the ground the night before by an arsonist but the prevailing attitude was that "the show must go on," so we all played our tunes to a completely shocked audience in another building, as the gutted remains of the Victorian school building still smoldered outside.

Chris Anderson

Well, since I was a child there was always a Spanish guitar on the sofa, because my father played in a freakbeat rock and roll band in the sixties, friends of Los Bravos, Los Salvajes, Los Mustangs… the Spanish beat scene of that decade.

Those were Beatles / Stones highly influenced bands that had a great impact in Spain during the sixties as well, and they were really great musicians too. He taught me how to play the guitar as we were listening to the Beatles. He always reproaches me for breaking a Small Faces seven-inch single, "All or

Nothing," and for buying, as my first LP despite all his efforts, (yes it is really embarrassing but true), Rick Astley. A long, long, time ago. (Sorry!)
Jordi Bel

One of my earliest musical memories was thanks to my older brother, who one evening invited me into his room to listen to a piece of music through giant seventies head phones. I'd be about six or seven. He told me that I was going to hear someone being electrocuted; he turned the lights out, cranked the volume up and put on Killer by Alice Cooper.

Fair do's, the album sleeve itself was enough to give you the willies. I remember sitting on his bed enjoying the musical prelude, visualizing the long, slow walk for the condemned prisoner ending in the chilling noise of the electric chair.

A very cinematic piece of rock that very nearly made me shit myself. It didn't put me off Alice, and indeed listening to that song again, now I can imagine us doing a cover version.

I got my own back on brother years later, by getting him stoned on a huge coconut bong.
Sproatly Smith

At bedtime, my dad would sit on the bed singing gruesome traditional folk songs, which were also underscored with feelings of sexual tension, sadness and dissent. I loved his battered old acoustic, which was a sunburst Dreadnought. This ritual seemed like the most natural thing in the world, but now I see how it helped me to think about life and art as unified.
Mikey Georgeson

I remember being profoundly affected by the Beatles' "Norwegian Wood" and "You've Got to Hide your Love Away"—it seemed every Christmas in the early 1970s, Beatle's films would be on TV and my mom insisted myself, brother and sister watched them. Help was a fave as it was a comedy we could understand, plus "I am the Walrus" (from Magical Mystery Tour) we loved, because we thought it was mental!
Alan Murphy

As a child, I was surrounded by my father's music: James Last, Klaus Wunderlich, Richard Clayderman et al., which certainly gave me something to kick against.
Diana Collier

I still don't think I've progressed much. I'm still obsessive and don't know what I'm doing.
Dan Bordello

My dad was a big influence, despite being not particularly interested in music (although he was in his twenties in the 1960s and a Londoner, he admits that any kind of "scene" completely passed him by).

I remember liking his Duane Eddy 45s, and very early on, I discovered some ace tunes on reel-to-reel tapes that he recorded from the radio… stuff like the Small Faces' "Tin Soldier," Dave Davies' "Suzannah's Still Alive," the Moody Blues' "Twilight Time" and, oddly, Pregnant Insomnia's "Wallpaper" (although it wasn't until I was about thirty that I found out what that was). I loved all that stuff.

Jethro Tull and the Pentangle were the first groups that got under my skin though. Dad's fault again, for buying cheap compilations that I subsequently destroyed on my hand-me-down record deck that I don't even think had a manufacturer's name on it.

Earliest experiences as a musician… well, I couldn't play very well, but had a load of fun if given access to an echo box and a tape deck with a stereo input…

Graeme Lockett

Early childhood memories are a fog of enchantment and patchy impressions. I think I remember listening to "Happy Together" by the Turtles while on vacation somewhere, sitting in the back of our Dodge van (full-size). I was staring at my shoes. I also sang the Dead Milkmen's "Punk Rock Girl" a cappella at a school talent contest in second grade.

Jeb Morris

I suppose in a way all the music you take in has some kind of effect. My Mum was a great pianist, and there was always music around the flat as I was growing up. She was into classical stuff, songs from the shows, she loved Sinatra, but when the Beatles came along, she was also well into that.

My earliest musical memory would be going to see Frankie Vaughan with my Mum and Dad at the Theatre Royal in Brighton while we were on holiday. That would be when I was about three or so. By the time I was five (in 1958), I was spending my pocket money on records.

I remember buying "Red River Rock" by Johnny and The Hurricanes, (the b-side "Buckeye" is brilliant), and "More and More" by Johnny Duncan and The Blue Grass Boys, etc etc. And I guess by the time I was seven I could play guitar okay, and I was even trying to write songs.

Admittedly, they just sounded like a kid's version of the stuff I was listening to, but at least I was giving it a go.

Nick Salomon

First musical experience was rehearsing "Sumer is Icumen In" at school around 1967, and thinking all the rounds wouldn't fit together; and, when they did, being thrilled and amazed.

Drew Mulholland

First band gig when we were thirteen taught us the meaning of inappropriate. We were called the Great Unwashed and we played "Cocaine" and "The Needle and the Damage Done" to an uneasy audience at the Mowsbury Park Golf Course Variety Show. They didn't ask us back.
Chris Anderson

When I was about ten years old, our neighbors would often invite us round for the evening and, while the adults talked, I used to sit under the table listening to albums from their son's record collection on headphones.

The one I liked to listen to most was Spotlight on the Moog—Kaleidoscopic Variations by Perrey and Kingsley. This consisted of one or two original compositions and covers of well known tracks such as the haunting "Umbrellas of Cherbourg" and "Strangers in the Night" (complete with weird sound effects)!

I studied the very psychedelic album cover and imagined what what a Moog Synthesizer looked like. From then on, the name Moog represented something magical to me and that sparked my interest in synthesisers and recording. It wasn't until last year that I finally bought a Moog, but it was well worth the wait.
Chris Bond

I suppose [my memories] are the same as most people from my generation and background: aged about five, sat in a class with twenty-nine other no-hopers, blasting away on a recorder. We all made a horrible din trying to play "London's Burning," amongst other children's favorites.

The teacher was also trying to get us to read music, which I just could not get the hang of. I hated it. I hated the shrill, squeaky sounds and I hated trying to decipher these dots on lines. However, a couple of years later, we had a new music teacher who noticed I had a natural sense of rhythm.

She encouraged me to be the percussionist in the school orchestra, which was much more to my liking! I even learned to read music for percussion—it's quite simple: count and when you see an "x" on the line, hit the instrument that line relates to!
Mordecai Smyth

Well, if you want my literally earliest experience as a listener, that would probably be the cassette my mother gave me when I was a small child—of disco renditions of popular classical music! I didn't really start developing my own listening tastes until I was aged about fifteen. The first vinyl I ever bought myself was Flood by They Might Be Giants. Smash Hits magazine had given it a really bad review and I wanted to know what sort of a sound could be so hated by "trendies." I liked it; it was bonkers!
Joanna Swan

When I was about five years old, my dad took me to my first rock and roll concert. The Kinks were playing at the top of a ski mountain in the middle of the summer; it was one of their last US tours as a group. I had to be on top of my dad's shoulders to see the group, and I distinctly remember Dave Davies playing the riff to "You Really Got Me."

I think that triggered the guitar bug in me. My dad tells me the other audience members were pretty stoned and thought it was the coolest thing that he brought his son. I came home smelling like marijuana in my little leather jacket, and my mom wondered what the hell had happened.
Duncan Shepard

James Bond films / Doctor Who played a big part of forming my musical baseplate, due to John Barry / Synth sounds… even though Doctor Who scared the living crap out of me at times. (Jon Pertwee's face used to set me off.…)
Alan Murphy

I remember the first piano lessons as a child, five or six years old. My piano teacher, Miss Giles, was blind and she would place her hands over mine on the keys to position the fingers correctly.
Crystal Jacqueline

I was raised with the Beatles, and I think they've been coloring my view of everything else. Still can't get enough of Revolver or The Beatles, which I had in my walkman when I was seven. All of the Kites have been very into late sixties into the early seventies music… it's the sounds, the words and the vivid feeling of "this is now!" and "we don't know what we're heading for."
David Svedmyr

My first concert was the Jefferson Airplane, the Who and B.B. King at Tanglewood in August of 1969. My brothers were up front, and I sat further back with my parents.

I remember the black and white filmstrip that played over the left side of the stage before the Airplane came out; you can hear it at the beginning of Bless It's Pointed Little Head. The Joshua Lightshow blew my mind!
Ted Selke

Driving on a very, very long journey in our dad's car with velvety seats, with Frank Sinatra caressing our ears as trees and roads and clouds flew past. The world seemed silent, with only Sinatra as the soundtrack.
Angeline Morrison

The first concert I went to was Ravi Shankar—my dad took me. I think I must have been about fifteen at the time.

I can't remember anything about the music (which I'm sure was great), but the one thing I do recall was the huge joss sticks they lit at the front of the stage. Their smoke rose up, then drifted back along the ceiling to the rear of the auditorium on a convection current of warm air.

Steve Palmer

When I was a kid, my grandma had a very good hi-fi system. She always woke me up with Boney M, Queen and other assorted classic records, obviously at full volume.

Narsis Passolas

My parents didn't listen to pop music at all, so my earliest music memories were classical music. But the summer of 1973 changed my life completely: I discovered pop music, although maybe "discovered" is the wrong word; "got obsessed" is probably more correct.

As a nine year old, I couldn't separate what was good and not. I loved it all and this happened to be in the middle of the weirdest time of rock music ever, the heyday of glam rock.

Every artist had their own style (and I didn't necessary mean musically)—Slade, Sparks, Sweet, Gary Glitter, Suzi Quatro, Mud, Alvin Stardust, Roxy Music and, of course, David Bowie.

It was people from another planet, and my fondness for football, fishing etc was totally gone. So here are some songs from the Swedish top ten in July, 1973 and I loved them all (the selective taste came later):
• "Free Electric Band"—Albert Hammond
• "See My Baby Jive"—Wizzard
• "Mama Loo"—the Les Humpries Singers
• "Good Grief Christina"—Chicory Tip (my first two concerts were with the fabulous Chicory Tip)
• "Clap Your Hands And Stamp Your Feet"—Bonnie St Claire
• "Another Town, Another Train"—Björn And Benny, Agneta And Frida (in a few months, they changed their name to the easier and more functional ABBA)
• And, at last, my own favorite, "Lonely Lovers Symphony" by an Italian man called Giorgio. Many years later, I understood that it was Giorgio Moroder. The same man that co-wrote the Chicory tip hits with Peter Bellotti, and of course a lot of other things.

Anders Håkanson

I have a memory of stomping around my parent's house to the Dave Clark 5's "Bits and Pieces." As that was released in 1964, that would make me about five years old at the time.

As a musician, I have a memory from when I was about thirteen, of sitting in a tree with my mates, all holding assorted percussion bangers and shakers and blasting out a version of Dave Edmunds' "Black Bill" (the b-side of "I Hear You Knocking") on kazoos.
Stephen Bradbury

My very first memories are musical. It was me aged three or four years old, executing whirling dervishes during the last part of "I Want You (She's So Heavy)' [the Beatles] or frightened by the crazy laughter of *Dark Side Of The Moon*.
Will Z

I come from a very musical family; most notably, my grandmother is a classically trained pianist, while my father was always in bands (and still is!), some of whom I vaguely remember jamming in our basement.

Needless to say, there was always music around, and I suppose part of what led me to where I am today.

If I recall correctly, the first rock song I really remember hearing as a child (and liking of course) was either "Subdivisions" by Rush or "Another Brick In the Wall" by Pink Floyd, on the radio in the family Chevy Blazer. And I was always fascinated with the record collection at our house.
Chris Sherman

Playing my aunt's out-of-tune acoustic guitar in 1978 and finding the root notes to "Anarchy in the UK," making me think that I like this guitar business, even if the strings hurt my fingers.
Alan Murphy

My mum and dad used to sing to me when I was little. The lyrics ran thus:
"Go to sleep my little scraggy head
"Go to sleep and curl up tight in bed
"Go to sleep my little scraggy head
"That's what Mummy said"
I'm feeling sleepy just thinking about it.
Chris Lambert

I became aware of my love for music in my earliest childhood, when I was about four or five. The first sources of real musical pleasure were my mother's records, which were basically classical music.

As soon as I became able to define my own tastes, my listening took a very odd twist, since I fell in love with both Andean folklore and Krautrock. So my early influential heroes were basically Beethoven, Kraftwerk and Inti-Illimani! Quite a broad range of musical interests, isn't it?
Paolo Sala

I can remember watching my father turn some very interesting shades of purple when watching the Dave Clark 5 performing "Bits and Pieces" on TV. "They're just stamping their bloody feet!"

A few years later, a black chap with huge hair appeared spraying Voodoo blues all over his Saturday night. I can remember thinking as I watched dad's dinner gently slide down the patio windows that this Jimi Hendrix was definitely worth perusing….
Icarus Peel

My dad was really into Bob Dylan, the Stones, the Beatles and, strangely, the Monkees. So I remember being about ten years old and playing a lot of those records and especially digging The Monkees!

Then, in 1977, I got into punk. I used to go to school just over the River Thames from Chelsea and a few of us used to sneak off after school and go see the punks (like going to the zoo) down the King's Road.

That was a (literal) eye opener, and I remember hearing the Sex Pistols on the radio and my Mum and Dad saying how horrible that music was, but there was something about the noise that I liked.
Dave McLean

One of my earliest proper musical experiences was when I bunked off school as a young teenager to go and see Pink Floyd play live at a theatre in Newcastle. I have very vivid memories of it, especially the smells!! A heady mix of patchouli oil and hashish.

It was the dog-end of the Dark Side of the Moon tour, quadraphonic sound system... I felt all my senses being wonderfully overloaded. Life would never be the same again.
Pete Bingham

I don't really remember my first musical experience, but music became important to me when I discovered the Doors, with the Oliver Stone film. It was at that moment that I really discovered music in all its glory. The Doors were my first musical door. Then I discovered the Brian Jonestown Massacre and the psychedelic was in me.
Maxime Schwartz

Crabstock

The Fruits de Mer Records Festival of Psychedelia

April 10 : USA - The Bowery Electric, New York
The Seventh Ring Of Saturn ; Sky Picnic ; King Penguin

April 11 : USA - Outer Space, Hamden, Connecticut
The Luck Of Eden Hall ; Sky Picnic ; The Seventh Ring Of Saturn

April 26 : Wales - The UFO Club, Cardigan
Sendelica ; Earthling Society ; James McKeown ; Crystal Jacqueline ; Jack Ellister

May 3 : Finland - Club Darkside, Helsinki
Sendelica ; Octopus Syng ; The Legendary Flower Punk ; Us and Them ; Jack Ellister

My parents bought me an LP of the *Jungle Book* so I would have played that to death, listening to the story and songs.

John Blaney

Tuning in shortwave radios bought from jumble sales for 10p and hearing signing off tones, then long bursts of silence in the early hours of the morning (I was an insomniac from an early age).

Alan Murphy

I was just about allowed to have a party for my fourteenth birthday which was very exciting. We were in full swing, rocking out to "Let's Spend the Night Together," when a local gurrier shot a pellet gun at the front door because he felt left out.

My parents weren't impressed, although I was quite pleased that news of the party had spread far and wide.

On another occasion, Clodagh Simonds and I were given permission to go to see the Supremes at The Adelphi Theatre in Dublin. She wore a Japanese kimono and I wore my grandmother's ancient Chinese coat. I swanned out the door and although my mother, to her credit, did a double take, she merely remarked, "Is that what you're wearing, dear?"

Alison O'Donnell

My house was always filled with music, though being from a Christian household, there were an awful lot of hymns and praise music. We owned several albums by nun groups (which even now I can hum).

There was very little from the hit parade, so I came to all the groovy young bands quite late, as most of that rock and roll stuff was frowned upon (although I did once catch my sister miming "High Fidelity" from the Kids from Fame, a sight that still haunts me to this very day).

My mum and I often listened to a tape of an American preacher urging us to burn our Queen and Led Zeppelin records due to all of the backtracking. My first experience of "Stairway to Heaven" was many years later (and it was a cover).

I quite liked classical music and was Head Chorister in the church choir for a while. I remember being very excited when I had to sing a solo and absolutely adoring Handel's Messiah. So we were deeply uncool. I was uncooler than anyone I have ever met.

Chris Lambert

My very first time with an acoustic guitar (an Eko acoustic guitar, direct from 1976) was at the age of eight, watching my father fingerpicking and singing for my mother Beatles songs like "Michelle" by the fireplace during the cold wintertime.

It was an absolute revelation to me! In that moment, I realized guitar and music composition would be my love, passion, and devotion all my life long.

I grew up with artists and bands like the Incredible String Band, Tim Buckley, Fairport Convention, Pentangle, Bert Jansch and John Renbourn, Sandy Denny, Anne Briggs, Joan Baez, Mellow Candle, Pink Floyd and Syd Barrett, the Beatles, Jefferson Airplane, Grateful Dead, Love, Ultimate Spinach, Deep Purple, Black Sabbath, Rainbow, Gentle Giant, Yes, Popol Vuh, Amon Düül II, Can, Captain Beefheart, Tangerine Dream, Klaus Schulze, Ashra Tempel, Brian Eno, Arvo Part, Ennio Morricone and more.

Lorenzo Bracaloni

I remember hearing *Low* by David Bowie when I was around six years old and, as a small child obsessed with all things extraterrestrial, finding it fired my imagination much more than *Star Wars* and *2000AD* (my principal twin interests of the time).

It wasn't so much that it sounded "space age," more that it had an otherworldly mystery and a haunting melancholy (it made my six year old self feel both sad and comforted).

It provided, as I believe the best Art does, a window to an unseen world in which we recognize hitherto unknown aspects of ourselves.

Sand Snowman

I remember being too short to reach the record player, but desperately trying to get The Who Sell Out on the platter.

I first played with my Dad's band on stage at age ten; I played "Money for Nothing" by Dire Straits. (Quite prophetic...)

Pete Meriwether

I remember my whole family dancing to "Tiger Feet" by Mud at a New Year party. It looked really exciting, and I still have a soft spot in my heart for it.

George Roper Noman

Watching PiL's "Public Image" video on Tiswas, and thinking it was the greatest, most profoundest record ever made and that they were the most ace looking band ever.

Alan Murphy

I started to record songs with a 4-track tape recorder back in autumn 1998, in Kouvola. It was so much fun that I bought an 8-track digital recorder in summer 1999 and I named my one-man band Octopus Syng. Then I made a couple of little records in Kouvola, before I moved to Helsinki in 2003.
Jaire Pätäri

I grew up in a small, small village up in the north of Sweden, Lapland. I can't remember how old I was, maybe about eight to ten years, but one of my older brothers was a member of a music club where he got a vinyl LP once a month, and he was playing loud music from his room every day.

When he was out meeting friends, I took the opportunity to listen to his records. There was a few bands that I remember I had a special ear for. It was Alan Parsons Project, Styx and Manfred Mann.

I don't remember which singer it was, but I know that I thought "this man must be very good looking." I don't think I ever saw a picture of him, so I can't tell if it really was true.
Britt Rönnholm

My first ever concert… February 1964, arriving at Carlow Town Hall to play with The Tropical Showband, wearing a blue Beatle suit, and size nine Beatle boots (I wore size sevens!), which belonged to the band member who had left.

I hadn't even met most of the much older members before. Getting straight in the deep end, with surf music, "Wipe-out" etc, the Beatles' "Can't Buy Me Love," the Stones' "I Wanna Be Your Man," Jim Reeves, Hank Williams… and so it's been going ever since.
Leo O'Kelly

My earliest musical experiences as a listener were from my brother Andrew, who was a Rolling Stones fan in the 1960s, although he did have the Magical Mystery Tour EP which I loved.

I preferred the Beatles. My first LP was for my tenth birthday (1974), when my mum bought me Rubber Soul. I still love it today. I think the first single I ever bought was "Forever and Ever" by Slik in [1976].   We all have ghosts in the closet.
Marrs Bonfire

One of the strongest memories I have is of me and a pal, back in the summer of 1973 or '74 so I'd be ten or eleven years old, and my pal's older cousin sat us both down and actually said to us "listen to this, it's really great" and put on the S.F. Sorrow album by the Pretty Things.

I found out later (when I happened across the LP for myself in 1981) that it was a US copy that had the cover with the round tombstone design—and I was just totally blown away by that first song "S.F. Sorrow Is Born."

I was already well into Alice Cooper, Slade, Sweet, Mott the Hoople and Roxy Music... but this was something else altogether!
Lenny Helsing

I went to a few folk clubs, and really felt like an outsider—it seemed like some kind of secret society that only accepted you if you came from the right lineage, and I found it all rather hostile.

Although I loved the music (or some of it anyway), I didn't feel the folk club scene was for me, so I began learning folk songs by listening to the key records from the 1960s and 1970s revival.
Steven Collins

I went to public schools in Minneapolis, Minnesota, where music was included in our curriculum. I sung in choir, played drums in band class (which was required), and took piano lessons as an eight-year-old (I could at one point, and still can, make it through about the first page and a half of of Mozart's "Moonlight Sonata"), but never retained much of what I learned in regards to musical theory or reading music.

By the time I was in high school, I was creating very little musically, but focusing very intensely on various mediums of visual art instead. Singing was something I always did in the privacy of my room where no one could hear, but never really realized my potential until much later.
Ellie Bryan

I was turned onto psychedelic music in 1980. A friend of mine had an el cheapo Byrds compilation and I remember hearing "Eight Miles High" whilst playing ping-pong at his house. I found psychedelic music liberating, and it opened up my mind to possibilities I had not considered before.
Dave McLean

Val Doonican had an easy listening program on Saturday night TV and I can recall "Windmills Of Your Mind" and "Scarlet Ribbons" as great favorites. Heard them both by him recently, and was pleasantly surprised at how good they actually sounded....
Icarus Peel

The first music that really grabbed me and demanded I listen to it was the Stranglers. I was sixteen at the time and mesmerized both by their exotic, gothic sound, and by their strong songs and playing—especially Dave Greenfield's keyboards, which at the time were unique in punk.

To this day, I love that band—at least, the Hugh Cornwell years. I think their third album, Black and White, is one of the all-time greats. Released in 1978, it still sounds futuristic...
Steve Palmer

[In] June 2006, I went to see Vashti Bunyan in concert with a friend, and midway through her set he leant over to me and whispered "you could do that."

It got me thinking that maybe I could do it, and for the next few days, I found myself listening to a lot of folk (and folk-inspired) music made by people who didn't follow the folk blueprint, and who hadn't come to prominence by trudging around the U.K. folk clubs night after night.

I eventually ended up with a vision in my head of how I could fuse the folk revival sound that I loved with other influences, and maybe come up with something interesting and exciting."
Steven Collins

Hearing the Stranglers and thinking they sound like a Hammer Horror film; being really transformed by "The Meninblack" song and thinking "How did they make this really weird, interesting song that sounds like Sci-Fi western?" when I was age eleven.
Alan Murphy

I remember listening to the radio as a child. *Friday Night Is Music Night* on the BBC. I don't think I liked it very much, but that was probably the first radio show I can remember listening to.

My nan would have the radio on when I stayed with her, and I recall listening to this big old valve radio, probably on a Saturday morning before we'd go out shopping. Songs like the New Christy Minstrels' "Three Wheels On My Wagon" and "There's a Hole in My Bucket."

Those were the pop songs I remember listening to on the radio. I don't know if they were kids shows or if that's what passed for light entertainment at the time. I certainly don't recall listening to the Beatles or Rolling Stones. I didn't discover them until much, much later.
John Blaney

My first musical experience was as a three year old trying to sing along to the neighbor's Fisher Price Television toy. You wound it up and it would magically play, in a music box style, not only "Row, Row, Row Your Boat," but also "London Bridge is Falling Down." I was a very reluctant singer even then, but I could be tempted to sing for the promise of a Fig Roll.
Stephen Stannard

The first moment that music really hit me was when I was about eight or nine, out on a day trip with my dad, his friend Rappy and his son about my age circa 1973 / 74.

Rappy had a big-ass Cadillac Eldorado convertible. I remember sitting up on my knees, facing out the rear window, wind blowing my hair wildly. "Goin' Out of My Head" by Brasil 66 was on the radio and the moment is pure joy in my memory. I think I've been chasing that feeling ever since.
Jet Wintzer

One of my earliest musical memories is of listening to a cassette copy of Jeff Wayne's musical version of *War Of The Worlds* on a small, old fashioned tape player. To a five year old, it was absolutely real and truly terrifying.

To this day I can't hear the bizarre prog / disco / musical / David Essex fusion that it actually is; I can only hear the sound of impending Martian apocalypse.

I think this might explain my relationship with music, and why the Hare And The Moon sound the way they do. Fear, doom and Justin Hayward suddenly infected everything.
Grey Malkin

I think the first album I brought was the *ET* soundtrack, and the first single was probably "Star Trekkin'" by the Firm. This says a lot about what I had access to. I loved film soundtracks and often recorded TV programs onto cassette, so I could listen back to them.
Chris Lambert

I was playing electric guitar in high school and college and listening to whatever my white, suburban, middle-class American friends were into. It wasn't quite as banal as it sounds!
Jefferson Hamer

[I remember] hearing the Amen Corner and American Breed versions of "Bend Me, Shape Me" played back-to-back on a BBC TV show hosted by Alan Freeman in 1967; immediately knowing the American Breed version was far superior; and realizing I was going to be a music anorak for the rest of my life.
Keith Jones

Back in the 1970s when I was around ten, my dad purchased a Genie organ. It was one of those with the built-in drum beats and colored toggle switches for different sounds.

I would plug in headphones, and then play on that thing for hours on end. Our keyboardist Jim Licka actually has something like it in his vast emporium of keyed instruments.
Gregory Curvey

My parents couldn't afford babysitters, so my earliest memories of live music are of lying under tables in folk clubs as a toddler, drowsily trying to sleep on a pile of coats and looking at the adults' legs, while the musicians sang and played songs from long ago.

This was, of course, great practice for attending future gigs as a drunken teenager, where I often ended up in much the same situation.
Emily Jones

The first experience with music that I can remember was when I was very young, I might have been only three or so…. my mother would stack up their old singles on the auto-changer of their record player and set them going. I would sit totally captivated.

The Beatles, Mary Wells, Johnny Kidd and The Pirates (they were dad's), Millie Small, The Shadows and "Telstar"… "Telstar" fascinated me. All those weird sounds at the start, it sounded like nothing else.

I still have several of those old singles but "Telstar" was played to destruction, probably fatally scratched in some auto-changer related disaster. I recently bought another original copy, although I have it on several compilations. I just wanted to have the original single...
Tom Woodger

Over the years, my musical interests shifted. I went from enjoying pop (or pretty much whatever was playing on the radio) as a child, to heavy metal in middle and high school as an angsty teenager. It wasn't until my first year of college where I began listening to and appreciating folk music.
Ellie Bryan

For as long as I can remember, music seemed to first be a weapon between my parents. I was scared, but fascinated by its power as it was making things and plates [go] flying as they were having verbal fights.
Francois Sky

My mother was a great fan of light opera, so she had a collection of 78s of Mario Lanza and "the Student Prince," etc. Hidden amongst them was a song called "I'm A Ding Dong Daddy from Dumas," which appears to have been sung by Louis Armstrong, but I don't remember it being sung in that distinctive voice.

Also, because my dad had cunningly created a chest of drawers in which the record player was located, the chances of any record surviving playing while the drawer was opened and shut were remote…
Judy Dyble

As a teenager, I was still in the choir and the pop scene generally passed me by. I was off making tunnels in bramble and bracken, while my friends were at discos.

When hormones started calling and I thought I ought to try to be cool, I found myself listening to Bon Jovi, Erasure, Clannad, Steve Vai, Jean Michelle Jarre, REM and two Christian artists called Steve Taylor and Adrian Snell.

It was really only at university that I discovered what others were listening to; I think it's why I enjoy almost all genres now, due to a dearth of experience in my youth. I remember the first time I

heard "I Am The Resurrection" in 1992—long after it came out. I had heard of the Stone Roses, but had been very sniffy about them, but hearing that and a mix tape by Matt Cox containing tracks by Radiohead and Dinosaur Jr opened up a new world to me.
Chris Lambert

I had a rope of 45s about a yard long at that time, that I would bring to school every day to listen to in breaks. I had bought a bunch of promo 45s for a dime apiece at the local Harvest Festival and got some incredible stuff like Sly and The Family Stone's first ("Underdog" / "Bad Risk") and "Time Seller" by The Spencer Davis Group (with pic sleeve!).

And there were the packs of seven for 77 cents where you could see one 45 side on either side. I filled out my Mitch Ryder, Tommy James, Turtles and lots of others with those!

I used to go to the Record Rack, inside Sukel's Shoe Store in Pittsfield, Mass. They had the top 40 singles for 77 cents each and a great selection of LPs for $3.33. I insisted on being taken there from about five years old on, and I would spend my allowance on the latest Beatles single or Stones or Monkees or whatever my favorite song on the radio was at the time.
Ted Selke

There was a bit of a gap before I really got interested in music, and that's probably thanks to my music teacher, Mr. Osmond. He played a Pentangle record one day and I was the only person in the class who said they liked it.

It was "Lyke Wake Dirge." Hardly what you might call a pop song. Anyway, I liked it and the next time I went to London with my parents, I asked my dad to buy me a copy of the album from the old HMV shop on Oxford Street.

The first records (45s not LPs, which were too expensive) I bought with my own pocket money were comedy records. Stuff like the Goodies and I seem to recall a novelty version of "King Of The Road." No doubt my early choices were influenced by my encounter with the New Christy Minstrels and Peter, Paul and Mary.
John Blaney

My father playing records on the weekends (Big Band, Sinatra) and my sisters and brothers playing their records (Crosby, Stills, Nash and Young, Boston, the Beatles and the Beach Boys)
Jayne Gabriel

I remember my father playing folk guitar and singing "Hang Down Your Head, Tom Dooley" to me when I was about four. I totally loved those stories about cowboys and tragic wild west love-gone-wrong songs. Then I remember him playing Jazz on his Tenor Saxophone along to Big Band records while I was trying to sleep, initiating a giant distrust of Jazz in my mind.

When I was ten, *Sgt. Pepper's Lonely Hearts Club Band* came out, then I heard Frank Zappa and the Mothers of Invention, and the Doors. It was all over for me, for I knew music was the thing.
Gordon Raphael

The earliest listening experience I really treasure is getting *Paranoid* by Black Sabbath on vinyl, when I was about eight, from a record fair in Leeds, and freaking out to "Iron Man." I remember opening the gatefold sleeve and thinking they looked really cool.
Chris Wade

I was in the midst of a Frank Zappa obsession when my professor at the University of Colorado handed me a stack of folk records. That was the first time I heard Fairport, Richard Thompson, Martin Carthy, and Planxty.

I liked the haunting, modal melodies and exotic, not-American-sounding lyrics. I was also floored by Thompson's guitar playing.

Later, when I moved to New York City and got more entangled in the East Coast folk scene, writing and recording with people like Anaïs Mitchell and Eamon O'Leary—my bandmate in the Murphy Beds—sharpened my perception of what any song, traditional or not, can and ought to be.
Jefferson Hamer

Amongst my happiest early musical memories was playing with a proto-prog three piece called Edge when I was about fourteen or so. We longed to be Yes.

I remember working out great long concept pieces round Richard the drummer's house, smoking Consulate menthol cigs and thinking we were very cool. We did a gig at a local church hall to what seemed at the time to be loads of people (I guess it was about 100), and we even had slides projected over us on stage.
Stephen Bradbury

My first experience as a listener, as far as I can remember, was my dad playing his old 78s on this really old record player; it looked like a huge piece of furniture, like a sideboard or something. I remember "The Folks Who Lived on the Hill" by Bing Crosby, and "Ebb Tide" by Frank Sinatra being favorites, and they both are still favorites of mine now.
Brian Bordello

Marc Bolan. A combination of corkscrew hair and glam. Wonderful.
Roger Linney

When I lived in Rio de Janeiro, I met a couple of guys who, like me, loved the Smiths, Killing Joke, Joy Division and other eighties bands. They were looking for a singer, because the previous one had left because of a compulsive drinking disorder.

The band was called Último Recurso (Last Resort) and we rehearsed at the guitarist's tiny bedroom, with real lousy equipment and a smelly basset hound It was the best of times.
João Branco Kyron

As a musician, my earliest experience would probably be playing guitar in a duo with my friend Simon (now one of the Trembling Bells) in his bedroom.

From memory, it was a kind of Nick Cave grizzled delta blues "my woman has left me" type thing, which was ill-fitting as we were fifteen year old schoolboys; it also evidenced quite a poor sense of geography, given we were in Inverness.

Many years later, the first the Hare And The Moon recordings were made on an 8 track with no knowledge or experience of how to record, or even play half of the instruments (not much has changed).

Perhaps somewhat worryingly, this then became our debut album.
Grey Malkin

I was bought up in a musical household; my mother sang in a choir, played piano and violin whilst I was a child. I have many memories of sitting in Churches listening to her choir sing, or seeing her have piano lessons.

At the age of four, I pestered her for, and eventually received lessons; although I never practiced that much, I did enjoy the playing and this grounding has paid off.
Richard Thompson

…learning to play guitar on an acoustic made by Parrot, which my brother Ant received as a Christmas present, [but] which he never bothered with, as he wanted a Rolf Harris Stylophone.
Brian Bordello

When I was growing up, there was no music. There was news on the radio, and on the TV it was sports. And unlike everyone I knew, I was the oldest of the kids in my house. No one brought home 45s or announced the Beatles were going to be on Ed Sullivan that night.

That was the news the next day outside of the fourth grade walls. There were newspaper and magazine pages traded among my fellow fourth graders, discussions on the best Beatle, comparisons with rival Dave Clark 5. I read the papers but this was news to me.

They were back on the following Sunday and that was when I saw them.

The Beatles of course changed everything. The sociological impact was monumental, with long hair leading the way. It outraged the norms and blurred the lines. They dressed and looked alike. There was no defined leader. And they were wild. Things would be different. They were for me.

Stu Newman, my friend across the street, had an older brother and sister. And a somewhat normal life, one that included music. Around the block, Lanny Sichel had a sister and she had the new releases. With Lanny lacking a brother, I had to do. Afternoons into early evening were spent listening and dreaming. It was a refuge and it was almost home.

Both Stu and Lanny became early bandmates and lifelong friends. Before a recent move, Stu was a regular on the CBGB's-NYC circuit. Lanny had success with the Berrys, also playing CBGBs and in the area, getting radio play and even appearing on Uncle Floyd. Lanny is the lead guitarist of King Penguin, our band on Fruits de Mer Records. I play bass.

Back in Levittown, what started the idea of actual participation was the Monkees. They weren't in England; they were walking down our streets. Every week. On our televisions. It became mandatory that every American kid had a guitar. Lanny and Stu got nice Hagstroms; I was stuck with a no name import. It was OK, even though it was a six-string and I had to play bass on the "E" and "A."

Back then there five of us and we played on sidewalks and in backyards. Microphones gave us shocks. Police were called on twelve year olds.

We were the Ravens, America's answer to Britain's best. Note the avian angle. We had the Byrds lineup of five with a Gene Clark Tambourine Man / sometimes lead vocalist Steve Towner. We played "Mr Tambourine Man," "Stepping Stone," "A Well Respected Man."

Probably my favorite was "Just Like Me" by Paul Revere and the Raiders. They were on TV not once a week but every day with Where the Action Is.

I would go on to twice see the Raiders' former lead singer Mark Lindsay in concert. The second time was in 2014 in Manhattan.

Two weeks later at a Fruits de Mer show that also featured Sky Picnic and the Seventh Ring of Saturn, King Penguin played on the same stage. The Bowery Electric was a long way from the backyard.

Bill Sweeney

When I was a kid my brother and I would make up songs and sing them into the boom box tape recorder. The lyrics were utterly inane, prurient and scatological. I still remember the melodies to "Guatemala," "Jackass" and "Penis Crusher."
Jefferson Hamer

Improvising on the glockenspiel in the second year of Junior School in front of the whole class.
Aaron Hemington

Mikey Georgeson singing with the Mystery Fax Machine Orchestra

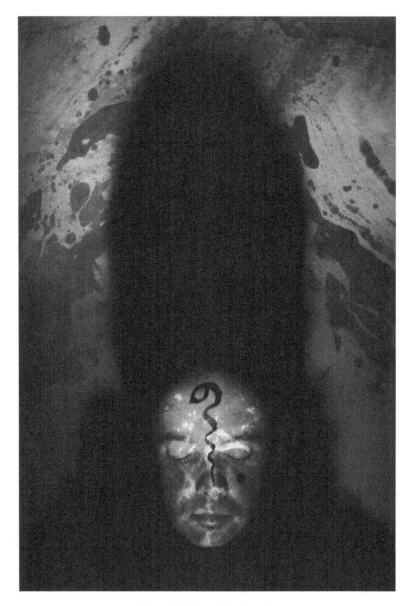

The Child of A Creek

If the Spanish Inquisition came to your house and demanded you give them a description of the music that you make and / or love, what would it be?

Hmm, tricky. Organic, rich, eclectic.
Ellie Coulson

That is incredibly difficult! I know what I'd like it to be; melodic, strange, surreal, sinister, beautiful, kind. Sometimes, I think I might be close to achieving that. Other times, it all sounds like shit.
Emily Jones

I would never tell, even if they poked me with cushions or sat me in the "comfy chair"!
Mordecai Smyth

PsychoPaganKrautEthericSymbolistSuggestiveIntrospectiveImpressionisticEsotericEarlyModernisticDis soHarmoniPhonic Whispers in a World full of shouting
Sand Snowman

I would resist for as long as I possibly could, for fear of sounding like an idiot, but I'd probably eventually say something like "a slightly psychedelic take on the sounds of rural Hampshire played by a bloke who was born twenty years too late and grew up listening to Slayer by accident," but "acid-folk" probably covers it…
Graeme Lockett

Oh God! Then I really would be in trouble! I guess I would try and explain that I wanted to avoid any description that might turn into a pigeonhole. Too often, a label ends up defining what you are "allowed" to play.

My aim here was to just do what the hell I wanted, to bring in elements from any musical style I liked, and mix them up and see what happened, so the deliberate aim was to avoid any label.

Of course, almost the first question you get asked when people find out you are a musician is "what kind of music do you play?" and to say "My music defies categorization, it is a unique creation that admits no boundaries!" would sound like a load of pretentious bollocks….

…probably because it is a load of pretentious bollocks....
Tom Woodger

Nice question, cause I could say we could divide my musical path in two up to 2015. From 2004 to 2014 I was focused on psychedelic folk music mainly, but my music used to sound traditional sometimes (check out my second album, *Unicorns Still Make Me Feel Fine*); and sometimes it was much more experimental and dilated. (There's an appearance from Pantaleimon from Current 93 on the last one, The Earth Cries Blood.)

I could say starting from my fourth record, *Whispering Tales under an Emerald Sun*, the ambient feel has started to play a greater role in my music than in the past. My approach is to not plan anything during the writing and the composition process: I love and I need to be spontaneous.
Lorenzo Bracaloni

Psychedelic Baroque
Aaron Hemington

[Ghost Box] music is largely, although not entirely, electronic, and mainly instrumental (though increasingly less so); its artists share influences in library music, TV soundtracks, vintage electronics, folk music, weird fiction and forgotten films and TV shows.

We think of it as a kind of world where pop culture from the mid sixties up to the early eighties is happening all at once, in a kind of parallel world. Not historically accurate, but naggingly familiar.
Jim Jupp

It sounds like wherever I am between waking and sleeping. Some rain-silvered walk through haunted, ivy covered, spring green and autumn colored woods as night comes on and the blue hour approaches, on through meadow flowers to a deep, flat black lake that mirrors the stars. Or so I like to think.
Amanda Votta

Some other people have described our sound as paganesque, haunting, pastoral, ethereal, bucolic (had to look definition up), trippy and quintessentially British folk. I can't argue with any of those.

Froots' Ian Anderson has called us a "flagship of the new wave of weirdlore" and "shining stars of agri-psych"… gotta admire his skill at labelling (and his finger picking).

I have to draw the line at ghostronica though, and I'm not sure our music is "performed by a motley collection of psychedelic, gothic and experimental musicians," or maybe it is.
Sproatly Smith

We threw a lot of adjectives around for this one! Arcadian; bardic; authentic; ugly-pretty.
Joanna Swan

We concluded that it's "authentic storytelling treading the uneasy edge between the beautiful and the disturbing."

It draws a lot on Jansch and Pentangle…
Tom Conway

But it's not Jansch-lite; if anything its Jansch-heavy!
Joanna Swan

If I speculated we had some kind of translator (I don't understood Spanish and I guess they don't understand Finnish or English), maybe I told them "it's such multi-colored music that lives in the glow of a raindrop when the sun shines in it."

But I'm afraid they would burn me on a pyre after that description.
Jaire Pätäri

It's home-made English pastoral baroque pop-psych.
Simon Berry

Timeless tunes, with shades of Rock, Folk and Psychedelia, with no consideration for what's in fashion.
Marco Magnani

An ululating collage of found sound and unusual semi-organic synthesis
Andy Hokano

This is always a tricky one. Someone once described Palace of Swords as "Pop Art Gothic," which has a certain ring to it, so I'd possibly go for that.
Peter Lyon

You'd have to be careful what you said to the Spanish Inquisition, but I guess honestly is the best policy! We write songs dealing with the standard themes of love, loss and relationships but often from an unusual point of view, incorporating elements of magical realism, art, biography or science fiction in the lyrics.

Army of Mice songs include electronic textures and found sounds, vintage and modern synths, dirty guitars, and gorgeous vocals.
Chris Bond

Experimental music with folk themes.
Richard Thompson

Essentially, what I was trying to do at the start was to somehow capture in sound the feel of some films and TV shows that had a major effect on me as a child—things which, for reasons I can't explain, have always evoked the same feeling in me as my favorite folk music.

Films like *The Wicker Man*, *Blood on Satan's Claw*, and the *Quatermass* films, and also TV shows like *Children of the Stones*, *The Stone Tape* and the BBC's MR James adaptations. But not The Owl Service, funnily enough. I didn't see that until much later.
Steven Collins

Firstly I'd say "No one expects the Spanish Inquisition!." All joking aside, I'd have to say, right now, it's in the realms of potential soundtrack music. It's conceptual as it has a theme to work from, and it's most definitely got its roots in electronic music as well as orchestral.
Kev Oyston

Psyche-folk-pop songs with soul and a strong penchant for the unexpected.
Mikey Georgeson

What psychedelic music might have sounded like, had it been invented by the Edwardians. Post-laudanum?
Chris Anderson

While I am not nearly fluent enough in Spanish, I suppose I would attempt to explain that it is modern melodic psych-rock.
Chris Sherman

Shoegazebossanovadronecore-meets-experimental-emo-Detroit-acid with apocalyptic-psychedelic-Gospel overtones.
Jet Wintzer

Good fun with disturbing undertones, a musical equivalent of a light hearted schizophrenic episode.
Alan Murphy

Tough question. I guess it's an amalgam of all the things I like, a bit psychedelic, a bit indie, a bit punk, a bit pop, a bit folky, always sung in an English accent, with UK place references, plus I'd hope there's a bit of me in there too.
Nick Salomon

It's a mirror of me. There's nothing closed off. It's not fun, but it's full of joy. It's sad and it's fragile, but it's strong and it'll endure.

It's androgynous and purposefully ambiguous: so am I when I can be bothered to shave. I do it because I have to, because it needs to spill out of me. It sounds pretentious, but I'm an artist; if I'm not pretentious, I'm not doing it properly. I'm a conduit for it.
Dan Bordello

I was recently reviewed, in a nice way I hasten to add, as "a Hendrixian wank-off," and "Ritchie Blackmore in a Nissen Hut."

Needless to say, I was delighted with both.
Icarus Peel

Flying Saucer Attack coined the phrase "rural psychedelia," and that's good enough for me. I adjusted it slightly to the "rural arcane," which I'd choose depending on how much coffee I've had when said inquisitors come knocking.

Mind you, I have robes that we sometimes wear at gigs, so I could just pass myself off as a fellow inquisitor and suggest we go and intimidate some buskers instead.
David Colohan

It's a clear picture of the inside of my head, at any given time. It might be very traditional folk, or it might be soul, or doo-wop, or rockabilly, or 1890, or it might be 1975, or it might be 1962, or it might be an imaginary soundtrack to a Thomas Hardy novel. Sorry, Inquisition, if you're looking for something more specific you'll have to kill me.
Angeline Morrison

My music tries to explore simplicity, but often combined in layered and sometimes baffling ways. I'm trying to write less notes these days. A visit from the Spanish Inquisition would be alarming, but no doubt I'd offer them a cup of tea and perhaps some nice chorizo.
Mark Reuter

Melanchodelia ™
Chris Anderson

The most disturbing folk band I have ever heard.
Roger Wooton

I would say that our music (The Owl Service and Greanvine), which I would qualify as being Steven Collins' music, is English folk song set against a backdrop of sound that is influenced by many strands of music from the sixties onwards, including English folk revival, psychedelic, and electronic soundscapes.
Diana Collier

That's a tough one. I don't really like boxes, or being tagged as a certain kind of band. I think it's quite obvious where we come from historically, but I like to think we have added something new to the mix.

A recent review, in Progressivemuso possibly sums it up best: "They make a kind of psychedelic, jazzy, space rock which is completely absorbing, but Sendelica occupy their own unique musical space."
Pete Bingham

If I had to sum up my music I would say it's "Haunted."
Drew Mulholland

Actually it would be more sensible to sit the Spanish Inquisition down, and play them everything I've ever sung, saying "you tell me."
Judy Dyble

It's nervy psych-folk. Loose. A bit sloppy. Energetic though fragile at its core. 100% self-loathing. I'm not sure anyone listens to it.
Jeb Morris

To describe the King Penguin concept, it might be necessary to borrow a line from Gene Clark's most famous (or infamous) composition, the Byrds' "Eight Miles High."

The phrase is "Stranger than known."

King Penguin started as participants in a recording project conducted by the Gene Clark Internet fan club. It would put together an informal salute to the singer with the air of a prophet, a country boy with Shakespearean phraseology and a Prince Valiant haircut. An artist like No Other.

Lifelong friend and sometime bandmate Lanny Sichel was recruited, along with singer / guitarist Gary Moran. We had played together in the high school era. Going back to those days, I had never heard voices that approached their blend. When they harmonized, it was a thrill to be in same room. Gary and Lanny had coincidentally returned from various rock and roll wars and reunited on a casual basis. The timing was right. All that was required was learn to play again, and on a higher level.

I had been in a band at college, and again when I got out. Journalism, however, was the calling and when the phone rang, it meant working nights and weekends. The bass went under the bed.
I had to relearn and step up.

Long Island guitar legend / ace teacher Larry Logeman was recommended. He accepted that the recording took precedence. He gave me everything I needed for that project, and we went on from there. With his premature passing, I lost a friend and a mentor as did many others in the local guitar world.

Ray Lambiase, a solo recording artist and a bandmate of Lanny's and I in the Gabis Bros., another Byrdsian outfit, was recruited as producer. He had recorded us then and would record us now.

The timing was fortuitous. Mary Jo and I had just bought a house, and she had been assigned to a three-month stint in Paris. The new place had a huge living room and it became our recording studio. Ray already had the gear. I was still working nights. I gave them keys. My only request was not to let the cats out.

One day I emailed Mary Jo a photo of the setup and a first mix.

"What is all that stuff in the living room?" she replied from Paris.

"It is a recording studio. We are recording a couple of songs."

"You don't play guitar."

"I play bass ... Did you listen to the song I sent? What did you think?"

"It's fantastic."

"It is, isn't it."
Bill Sweeney

I would describe our band as a mixture of everything we have ever heard, a mixture of Boney M and the Seeds... Throbbing Gristle and the Mamas And Papas
George Roper Noman

I overheard Sonny [Condell, bandmate] being asked "How do you describe your music?" His reply: "I don't." That's good enough for me?
Leo O'Kelly

I would describe the Honey Pot as "Marmalade On An Acid Tab" and Crystal Jacqueline as "Stained Glass Window Music"
Icarus Peel

Intensely mellow and hypnotically psychotic psychedelic pop rock.
Duncan Shepard

Once I'd been strapped into the comfy chair and overcome my initial surprise at being interrogated by Cardinal Fang, I'd have to say that what Mega Dodo releases is melodic music with lots of hooks.
John Blaney

We would tell them the truth.
Narsis Passolas

I think I have got influences from the whole area of sixties psychedelic rock, pop and folk music scene. On some days, the songs sounded so good that they almost made me cry; and on other days, they sounded so bad that I totally lost my faith in what we were doing. But it's always the same with Octopus Syng. It's nothing new for us.
Jaire Pätäri

Black Sabbath and Pentangle having a drunken argument at midnight, in a graveyard. Chuck in some tales of talking ravens, murder, ghosts and the occasional mandolin and there you have it.
Grey Malkin

As an ex-girlfriend used to say, "all your records sound the same… its all 'woo woo yeah yeah baby baby'."
Marrs Bonfire

Popped psychedelic rock and rollisms. I've been saying that for years.
Gregory Curvey

Mexican-bubble-gum! Hahaha. Or someone called us "Pomp Punk – Sid Vicious luvs Greg Lake." But what I really think is the best description of our music unfortunately sounds obnoxiously pretentious, which btw, I am absolutely not, darling—it's "Musical Surrealism."
Dave McLean

I always try to avoid to define my music; to get out of trouble, I used to say that I'm a pop music maker and my songs are just pop tunes. But, I'm afraid this definition won't help appease your anger, Mr. Spanish Inquisitor, so I'd better give you some more in order to avoid your strappado torture.

I've always wanted to be psychedelic. This is what I try to be every time I write and record a song. I mean psychedelic, but I always end up frustrated, because I realize I made another bloody pop song.

In other words, I'd like my music to sound like chiming bells, and my lyrics to speak about physics and metaphysics. Let's put it this way: my songs are "psychedelic wannabe."
Paolo Sala

Inspired, other worldly, Fraggle Rock.
Jayne Gabriel

Eclectic acid world folk rock... with a bit of sitar for good measure. I like to think I'm just a songwriter really, and can hopefully use any style or theme I feel like using.
Chris Wade

Difficult to beat Sophie Cooper's quote on United Bible Studies performing at Woolf Music Festival: "It was like watching Shirley Bassey fronting Black Sabbath, performing Incredible String Band covers."
Alison O'Donnell

Our music is the well-behaved pupil, playing the piano and singing with a clear voice, with puberty knocking on the door with all it could offer of strange dreams and a twisted view of the world. But if we don't overdo it, it could be "baroquefolk with some underlying disturbing moods, but not afraid of putting in a simple pop melody now and then."
Anders Håkanson and Britt Rönnholm

I would play to them our song "Giving Up Hope," track seven from our LP *Passport to Freedom*. We used a Viola de Gamba, a renaissance instrument, giving a very epic flow to the groove, but I'm afraid it wouldn't be useful at all, because the Spanish Inquisition is still alive on the Spanish Government now, actually....
Jordi Bel

The Intricate Mysteries Of The Melodic Explorative.
Crystal Jacqueline

I have invented my own scales, modes and tunings. Rather than modulating from key to key as in traditional classical music, I move forwards and backwards in time.

High pitched fast echoes for forward motion, low backwards sounds for retrograde action. You're going along and you don't know what to expect. You're scared my song will be lost forever, but then it ends. It does not continue forever.

As soon as it's over, water begins to drip from the speakers; then steam, and finally smoke. Diamond stylus eaten through after only one playing of my record.
Gordon Raphael .

I usually say Garage-Psych or Surf-Psych, or maybe Space-Surf, which is probably not a bad label most of the time—although some of our early stuff is almost like rockabilly or blues.

People have said they can hear the influence of Sky Saxon, Link Wray, the Shadows, early Flaming Lips, the Meteors, the Cramps, Man or Astroman? Sparklehorse, Hawkwind and Dick Dale in our music and I am not really surprised, as I really like all of them.

The biggest influences that I see are probably Dick Dale, the Move and the Bonzo Dog Doo Dah Band—particularly the humor of the Bonzos; silly, but a bit dark… very English.
Tom Woodger

Basic rock'n'roll with a few twists here... this is always a broad church to go with, and at least gives a flavor of what might be expected, or possible to imagine, without actually saying "we're a beat group" or "we're a garage band."
Lenny Helsing

I'd probably draw a shotgun without a word, to give them a bit of groove.
Francois Sky

Crow Call… is my original songs written on the banjo, but heavily influenced by story telling, traditional folk, pagan spirituality, and metal music which I refer to as "dark, metal-influenced folk."
Ellie Bryan

new / old / classic / obscure / psych / prog / vinyl / odd
Keith Jones

[With A Garland of Song], sonically, it was always my intention to make a record for people who loved acid-folk and psych-folk, but who also liked heavy, traditional folk records like Crown of Horn [Martin Carthy], Galleries [the Young Tradition] and Love, Death and the Lady [Shirley and Dolly Collins].

Regarding song choice, apart from "Flanders Shore," I selected all the traditional songs—it was basically my own trad greatest hits.
Steven Collins

They would have to twist the thumbscrews hard, because I'd get a little stuck! It alters over time, as I feel I am still not fully formed in my musical tastes. I missed so much and am still catching up.

I would say the music that floats my boat the most at the moment is Jeff Buckley, Fleet Foxes, Nick Drake, Peter Broderick and Wyrdstone. I tend to enjoy music that is evocative, and that feels somehow bound up by history. I really love a mix of music and spoken word—especially if the two combine to create a new world in my head. Moon Wiring Club and concretism are particularly adept at this.
Chris Lambert

Post-Medieval Jesuscore
Ted Selke

An ever-mutating, psychedelic space-brew of melodic, electronic, flowing and flying music that refuses to be pigeon-holed, to an extent where I deliberately subvert my own history, albums and rumor wherever possible…
Steve Palmer

I want to create some exciting new sounds and perhaps flirt with the old Canterbury Sound a bit, as I love the bands who came out of that scene.

I went to college in Canterbury, so I think I'm allowed (the same one as Steve Hillage—not at the same time though!).

I also think some form of tribute to the late Kevin Ayers would be appropriate—along with the late Syd Barrett, another artist whose music I find reaches me deep down. All my heroes are dying out. But they have left us with a fine musical legacy.

Actually, I find the thought of people playing my songs when I have gone quite comforting—to have left a little bit of myself in the grooves of some records!
Mordecai Smyth

Well, that's unexpected. Cosmic electronische acid sequenced synthscapes?
Stephen Bradbury

I would describe the Bordellos as having a slightly out of tune, out of key, very shambolic lo / fi sound , but with very catchy pop songs underneath the ineptitude.
Brian Bordello

I cannot accurately describe my music, because I don't play a particular style.

    Although psychedelia is the main line, rock, post-rock, experimental, folk, etc. are on the same path. To keep it simple, I'll say Psychedelic Rock.
Maxime Schwartz

Aah, the good old need to put the everything on shelves. Well, after being tortured with a plume tickling my feet for about five minutes, I would confess that Beautify Junkyards create something like a kosmische-tropical-electronic-giallo-folk
João Branco Kyron

Woodland Folk, Pastoral Folk Horror or even Radiophonic Acid Folk, depending on what music we're making at the time. It's entirely unhelpful I know. My description may also change depending upon whether the Inquisition were poking me with their soft cushions.
Stephen Stannard

Pink Floyd's younger, less talented, little brother.
Leah Cinnamon

When you have recorded an album called 12 Visions dealing with subjects like alchemy and black masses, or songs like "Satan Girl" on *Dark Tales of Will Z.*, all you have to say to the Spanish Inquisition is "Where is the pyre?"
Will Z

For me, the singer shapes the song, and so working with a different singer gives a whole different vibe to the music... [for example], Country Parish Music is very much about Rosemary Lippard's voice .
Steven Collins

Mystical Mid-Tempo Folk Music. Then again, that might get you burned at the stake. Maybe I'd just say Christian Contemporary.
Jefferson Hamer

In the dim and distant past, a bit American folky, then traveling through folk rockiness to strange and psychedelic, and now it's all a bit singer-songwritery with a bit of prog and a bit of ambient and a bit of whatever turns up and sounds interesting. Not a lot of rap or hip-hop though. But you never know.
Judy Dyble

The right wrong notes.
Chris Anderson

Amanda Votta

Mr. & Mrs. Smyth

Strange Turn

Mark and The Clouds

CHAPTER THREE

A few words, please, on the wonderful music that you love to listen to…. By artists who are not yourself. Obviously.

I love, love, love early Rozz-era Christian Death. When I first heard it, it sounded like something made in some other reality by creatures that weren't entirely, if at all, human. Add some Jesus and Mary Chain to that and you have my idea of perfection.
Amanda Votta

J'Adore; Stereolab, a truly "progressive" band, one that takes unexpected musical and stylistic turns, retaining a melodic presence that is pretty without being twee. Adventurous and charming, with a hint of the Gallic detached yet forlorn beauty of Ravel and Debussy.
Sand Snowman

A melody or tune outweighs every other consideration in music. Without melody, music is fatally flawed.
Steve Palmer

Brainticket…. We owe them a lot
Marc Swordfish

The artists that most influenced me are Brasil 66, the Stone Roses, Antonio Carlos Jobim, and many anonymous electro phantoms. I can't say why I love this music, because it feels like it just connected to my DNA. This is music that created longing within me.

The Roses created longing to be an artist and to feel the love an artist receives... essentially the Roses made me want to be adored. Jobim and Brasil 66 just turned me into a true romantic, and I've really suffered ever since. The idea of true love owns me now, and I have been celibate for fifteen years in search of her...
Jet Wintzer

When we started Lost in Rick's Wardrobe, we tried to play the songs as they were played back then. We played songs that we loved and we wanted to sound like Aphrodite's Child, Focus, Mellow Candle and Curved Air.

We did it for ourselves and to have songs and arrangements to play live. When we started to do songs of our own, we felt a pressure that we couldn't make anything better than the songs we already

played, and that somehow was our identity. Now we have an identity as Me and My Kites and, if we should do a cover, then it should be a song that can be better in a Me and My Kites vibe. A song far away from the sounds that influences us, still close enough to make us love it.
David Svedmyr

Lately I've been really into Nick Cave and the Bad Seeds. I love Nick Cave's lyrics and unique delivery. His music manages to be incredibly dark, but uplifting at the same time. Quite a feat.

Gutted to have missed out on tickets to see him in London this year, but probably for the best given that I have a newborn baby (makes getting out for the evening a bit tricky!)
Ellie Coulson

We both love Pentangle. They're our well-spring of inspiration and our shared enthusiasm for them brought us together.
Tom Conway

We don't agree on everything, though. In fact we've discovered there are bands in the genre Tom loves that I hate, and vice versa!
Joanna Swan

Yes, I've tried to persuade Jo to cover some Richard and Linda Thompson numbers with me, but she's not convinced.

I love them for their yearning quality, their melodies, their passion and their real-world pessimism…
Tom Conway

I countered Richard and Linda Thompson with the Sallyangie and Trader Horne, but you were having none of it.
Joanna Swan

I don't want to sing about a magical king living in a cave with pixies dancing round him.
Tom Conway

So we've agreed not to. But I do love the world of myth, folklore and magic, so I enjoy listening to bands that embrace that.
Joanna Swan

It's the tension between what I like and what you like that makes our music interesting. We're forced to think outside the box in order to create something that satisfies us both.
Tom Conway

I guess the result is the songwriting equivalent of Magical Realism?
Joanna Swan

Bands I love—the Stranglers—musically and sonically intricate, always failing to repeat themselves.
Cardiacs—A liberating excursion from reality played by shit hot musicians that don't mind being really base and basic as well as complex and bewildering.
Alan Murphy

I love Jeff Buckley, John Martyn and I have grown to really like Bob Dylan too.
Roger Linney

There are probably quite a few groups and artists who have influenced me over the years.
One of my all-time favorites, however, would have to be Felt. Lawrence is such a wonderful lyricist, and the band's music is so redolent of various ideas and emotions.
The best Felt songs also seem to transport the listener to a magical realm, which is possibly the sort of effect I'm aiming for with Palace of Swords, albeit with fewer chords.
Peter Lyon

Rowland S Howard is an example of someone I love. Teenage Snuff Film is, to me, the perfect album. The soundtrack to many interesting moments in my life.
He was a guitar hero who wasn't in the slightest macho. His playing was an extension of himself, and sounded as vulnerable, but tough as nails as he looked.
He looked like an androgynous boxer from a Jean Genet scripted sixties French film that was too disturbing to be released into the world. Also a very underrated singer: listen to "Ave Maria" from Pop Crimes. Listen to the crushing inevitability he breathes into the line "History led her to me."
Or when he turns "White Wedding" by Billy Idol into something genuinely sexy and disturbing. I love Rowland. There's a track he did with Lydia Lunch called "I Fell In Love With A Ghost" and that about sums it up.
Dan Bordello

I love the deep, majestic pomp of Procol Harum; the poignant lyrics of Tom Rapp ("Rocket Man", "The Use Of Ashes"); the floating, ethereal wonder of Gandalf's album, for example; and oh, so much more.
Simon Berry

Hendrix, The Shadows, Beatles, Stones, Who, Kinks, Beach Boys, Johnny Kidd and The Pirates, Love, Spirit, Country Joe and The Fish, David Ackles, Patto, Wipers, Damned, MC5, Vanilla Fudge, Joni Mitchell, Dave Crosby, Sandy Denny, Johnny Winter, Beefheart, Gene Vincent, Byrds, Action, Pretty Things etc etc etc
Nick Salomon

There are a couple of older bands I really do love: the Incredible String Band for one. Twenty years ago, when I first picked up *The Hangman's Beautiful Daughter*, purely based on the cover art, it became a slow revelation for me.

Initially, the record struck me as being silly in tone, perhaps frivolous, but as I listened more and overcame that perception, it grew into one of my favourite records of all time, a truly weird and inspired masterpiece.

Then there is Comus, whose first album is masterpiece. I was lucky enough to see them play in London a couple of years ago and I can only describe it as a revelatory experience.
Richard Thompson

I can't stand it when anyone says the Beatles are over-rated or rubbish. I think they are the best thing that ever happened to music. I know it's predictable to say so, but just line those albums and singles up and you're in awe. Endlessly creative and innovative.
Chris Wade

Thinking of old bands, skipping my obvious love for the Beatles, Stones and all that, I love Steppenwolf because they had a perfect blend of immediacy, simplicity, rawness and universal excitement, and John Key's voice strikes me as the guy from the street; maybe a bit rough sounding, but very true and real.
Marco Magnani

I love any band out there working hard, doing it for the fans and the love of the music. Bands that don't care what others say and continue to do their own thing.

I'm a big fan of the local band the Neutinos. They continue to explore new ways of working and recording, but also knock out a fantastic rock song.
Mark Reuter

I love... the Beach Boys, Beatles and Byrds because of the genius songwriting and harmonies.
Aaron Hemington

Too many influences, too much music! Too many years not listening to anything much!
Judy Dyble

Bands that I love would have to include Throbbing Gristle and the whole early Industrial scene (SPK, NON, Z'ev). Those guys were heading out into unknown sonic territory, and didn't care what people thought, a case of "come along for the ride, or fuck off."

Another band I love would be Austrailian band T.I.S.M; again a band who succeeded by not playing the game. Also, I have special fondness for Krautrock, Faust and Amon Düül II in particular.

Of more recent bands, Ulver are pretty awesome, also Sigh have released some pretty interesting stuff.
Andy Hokano

Now I do love the Damned, creators of rich, witty, puzzling, uplifting, imaginative pop music. Plus their very name is a nod to Charles Fort, whose *Book of the Damned* is a beacon to all of us who feel a burning desire to maintain the right to perceive life outside of the framework of the mainstream hegemony.
Mikey Georgeson

I love Love, man. I often imagine myself as a psychedelic kid living in 1967 and enjoying all the musical fruits that period had to offer and then kaboom!!!!...... up comes *Forever Changes*.

It must have really blown peoples minds. In 67, you would have been listening to psychedelic songs with backwards guitars, phasing and songs about "love and peace," and then along comes a mutant Johnny Mathis, singing one part Rodgers and Hammerstein, one part Mariachi pop and one part Classical.

Mix all that up with incredibly original and haunting lyrics, beautiful bass and drums and superbly original lead guitar. It took my breath away the first time I heard it, and it still does today. I have bought or lent this record to so many people from many different schools of musical taste, and they all love it.
Dave McLean

Awful to have to choose one favorite band, but—if forced—I would have to say the Velvet Underground. It's a fairly worn out cliché , I know, but it's true for me that there is no other band like them. They have so many attributes that I love: drones, darkness, experiment, distortion, mesmeric repetition, vulnerable imperfect vocals. They still sound fresh today.
Diana Collier

Ooh… tricky one. The thing is, I can't really think of a band that I can say I love absolutely everything that they've done.

Possibly only new-ish groups that haven't got a huge amount of stuff out there, like This Is The Kit for instance, but I'm always quite nervous about having such high expectations of what they're about to do next.

That said, Kate Stables is an incredible writer and singer, so I trust her implicitly to come up with the goods!
Graeme Lockett

A band I love would be the Jimi Hendrix Experience. I love every song on every album. The lyrics are thoughtful, the production quality was (at that time) only rivaled by George Martin, and the musicianship still inspires me to create.
Gregory Curvey

I loved Mandrake Paddle Steamer and was disappointed that they didn't record more.
Drew Mulholland

The catch is, you can't sound like any of [your influences]. You don't have their voice. So the real, hard work comes in figuring out what you sound like.

I might be influenced by Bob Dylan or Nic Jones or Anne Briggs or whoever, but I still have to be able to stand up in front of an audience and deliver my own rendition of a song, standing in my own shoes.
Jefferson Hamer

Who I absolutely love and admire, and believe it or not it's just for his very first album that I love him the most, it's got to be John Foxx. His debut album *Metamatic* is by far the album of my life.

When I very first heard it, I was still quite young and it never sat well with me, but as I got older, it completely resonated with me and what I was feeling then so I just grew to love it.

It's pure cold, concrete, dark and very electronic. Still stands up massively well today. It's my comfort album so I gotta love John for giving me that album. There are plenty of others I love, but I'd be here all week…

Kev Oyston

Over the course of three years in the seventies, I saw three bands premier three of the biggest albums of all time. In each case the record was unknown to the audience.

I liked two of the groups, loved the third. The latter is still loved, but not the same way.

Jethro Tull arrived in 1968 with a soaring instrumental take on "Cat's Squirrel." Everyone assumed the band's name was also the lead guitarist's. That ended when Martin Abraham was replaced and the sound became a folky / poppy flute thing.

We went to see Jethro Tull at Stony Brook and they opened with the familiar "Teacher." That was the first and last semblance of a song. What followed was a lesson in dynamics. Unbelievably loud roars were followed by one guitar / one voice whispers. This was the formula and this was the show. The album was *Aqualung*. The flute was gone, as were the tunes. As was the *This Was Tull*.

As my friend said, "The first song was good."

This was my initial experience with this sort of showcase but not the last. Tull probably took their cue from Led Zeppelin. Jimmy Page's band produced a wonder with the eponymous debut. The follow up was all noise and clutter kicking aside the classy creamy blues.

So are Van Halen and Boston really worth your breath? Why waste time with the lightweights when you can hate the bands you love?

Speaking of such emotion, there is no act closer to this heart than the Who. King Penguin bandmate Lanny, my brother Bob and I saw the original incarnation, the "I'm a Boy," "Happy Jack" Who in 1968.

No other act will equal the power and genius they emanated from that small stage at the Westbury Music Fair on Long Island. On record, Pete Townshend somehow topped it with Tommy. He sought greater plateaus with *Who's Next*.

Lanny and I went to see them perform that one, before the release of the album, at Forest Hills in New York City.

"Won't Get Fooled Again" was already in the air, so we had an idea what was up Townshend's jumpsuit. Pete made some remark about bring the organ player, but it was evident the synth sounds were prerecorded, and worse, an acoustic guitar was obviously in the mix. Our heroes were practically lip-synching live!

There were exciting moments but the payoff scream of "Fooled" seemed more out the Led Zeppelin book than something the Who would do. And Roger Daltrey's new curly locks and now bared chest appeared embarrassingly Robert Plant-ish.

But to paraphrase "A Quick One While He's Away," "Who are forgiven."

Lanny and I would go to see them again and again, sob at their losses, rejoice in their resurrections. They are still the Who. We will soon see them, again at Forest Hills.

The third in this trinity of disappointments is the holiest cow of them all. Everyone loves Pink Floyd, everyone loves *Dark Side of the Moon*. I see another side.

This 1973 concert at Montreal's classy if crumbling Forum started with promise. I went with a French Canadian friend from our nearby college, SUNY Plattsburgh. We met up with his Gallic pals and they knew the venue. It was open seating and these locals led the way to the second row.

Soon, it was *Zabrieski Point* all over again with Roger Waters shrieking his way through "Careful with that Ax, Eugene." Coming early, it portended an amazing night. Think again. What followed were background singers, cheesy props and prerecorded clocks. Soon, it was time to go. On the way out, one of the French friends sneered, "Preeetentisssh craaaap."

Oui.

Bill Sweeney

Fleetwood Mac. From the beginning, the sound was astonishing, raw and wild with Peter Green's guitar work and vocals.

No passengers in this band and the rhythms are wonderful. Then the band evolved with new members Stevie and Lindsey and the melodies, lyrics and overall sound just got better and better.

Crystal Jacqueline

I just came across David Ackles' debut album from 1968; a friend played it to me and I instantly fell in love; it's like there is no distance at all between the performance and me listening to it now.

It's so together, alive on it's own and timeless, but still in a certain place. Might be one of the best made ever and hopefully more people finds it, "Down River," "Lotus Man" and "His Name is Andrew" should be classics!

David Svedmyr

Well, there are artists and bands that I have absolutely loved for a very long time, like Incredible String Band, Tim Buckley and Tangerine Dream.

I could say I hate everything that sounds new wave, like Joy Division etc. That band has been one of most colossal disappointments in the music biz and they've given shape to a totally unjustified hysteria and clones, especially in the UK... the same for the Smiths.

The eighties were (and they are) a totally different thing to me: Dead Can Dance, David Bowie, Tangerine Dream and Klaus Schulze, as I mentioned before; Edgar Froese's solo albums, the Cocteau Twins, Brian Eno (and many more) and the heavy music scene.

Lorenzo Bracaloni

The first two bands I love that come to mind are Pink Floyd (Syd's Floyd) and the Velvet Underground.

Why? Because, especially Syd's Pink Floyd was such a very revolutionary band with their musical and psychical vibes. Of course the Beatles were a very revolutionary band too, but their psychedelia was very often "happy and innocent," as if it was some kind of dreamlike 3D cartoon music.

Syd's Floyd's music has those the same elements too, but behind these psychedelic, naïve elements, there's very dark and fearsome elements what makes Syd's Floyd's music a little bit multi-dimensional.

It wasn't just a good trip; there was a bad trip stalking around the symbolic corner all the time. So, that's the reason why I prefer Syd's Floyd psychedelia to the Beatles' psychedelia (they both were so brilliant, so brilliant anyway).

The reason why I love the Velvet Underground is how their music was often very rugged and hopeless, but at the same time I can hear some very humane warmth and comforting mood in their music, although Lou Reed wanted to get the image that he is the man who doesn't care a shit about anything.

So, Syd Barrett and Lou Reed, they both were unique songwriters / music makers.
Jaire Pätäri

Well, my influences are well documented—Tangerine Dream being the most obvious. My favorite period is *Phaedra* / *Rubycon*—I don't go much later than that barring a couple of the live albums.
Stephen Bradbury

I've always loved Donovan—I think he seems to get an unfair rap from a lot of folk fans. I probably prefer him to Dylan, although I don't know what that says about me.
Steven Collins

Love—the Pretty Things, the best UK R&B and the best UK psych band ever, no argument; they recorded the best UK albums of the sixties (S.F. Sorrow) and seventies (Parachute); they're still brilliant live and they've recorded for Fruits de Mer—what's not to like?
Keith Jones

Vashti Bunyan! I love her music and her soft voice. Also, I have a very special relation to her music. When our first child was born, I was listening to two artists at the hospital: Vashti Bunyan and Anthony and the Johnsons.

The delivery was really long and painful, and when it finally was over, exactly at the moment when Nelly came out to life, Vashti was singing "Here Before." It was such an amazing feeling.
Britt Rönnholm

Tír na nÓg

Diana Collier and Owl Service

Pink Floyd are a band I have always loved. My favorite Floyd recordings are *The Final Cut* album and "High Hopes" from *The Division Bell*, which probably would get me bullied in the wrong company (of other Floyd fans).

Some friends insisted on playing Led Zeppelin for an entire weekend in the car to make me like them. The tape is probably still stuck in the deck and can stay there. I was more of a Krautrocker than a classic rocker, and still am. Pink Floyd don't count, heh.
David Colohan

I just love music, I suppose. I think it would be unfair on your readers if I compiled a list here, as it would be very long.

But it may surprise you to hear that current favorites are Sly and the Family Stone, Bobby Womack's first two albums, Caravan (*In the Land of Grey and Pink*) Gong (*Angel's Egg*) and Cannonball Adderley (*Somethin' Else*)
Mordecai Smyth

In the psych-oddity music scene today, there are a lot of small independent bands that are awesome and deserve recognition.

Some greats would include the Blue Giant Zeta Puppies, Wooden Thomas, Mysterious George and Eshniner Forest.

My friend Bruce Hendrickson is working on some tripped out sounds in his new project H^2. He's been able to get a really awesome Syd Barrett type of slide sound on his guitar.
Duncan Shepard

Bands we love: Byrds, Byrds , Byrds!
Jordi Bel

I love bands that take chances, stray from the acceptable norm and offer up something dazzlingly different. I'll give two examples of bands that rock my world..... one oldie, the Velvet Underground, one newie, Sigur Ros.

When I heard both these bands for the first time, I was just like "Wow, where has this music come from?" It intrigued me, I wanted to hear more… they just speak to me in ways other bands don't. Sublime.
Pete Bingham

Bands I love? Well, ELP from the Tarkus era, the Rolling Stones (*Beggars Banquet*), Yes (*Fragile*), Colourbox (*Breakdown*)....
Gordon Raphael

Narrowing it down could be compared to choosing one child over another (although actually I only have one). Hmm. Garbage—they rock.
Alison O'Donnell

We love Moby Grape, and feel that they were not only one of the best west coast groups of the period, but also the most underrated.
Tom Hughes

One of my major influences in the beginning was Buffy Sainte-Marie.
Her first album, It's My Way, was introduced to me by my cousin, who had rented it from the library, and essentially played on repeat in both of our stereos, computers, and cars for a year.
Ellie Bryan

Lots of loves: the Velvet Underground, Love, the Doors, Jimi Hendrix... everything from 1967... I even married a woman who was born that year! New loves: Anna Calvi... she's scary! Daft Punk... I just love Random Access Memories.
Leo O'Kelly

There are so many special groups for me, and so the likes of Love, the 13th Floor Elevators, the Byrds, the Seeds, the Downliners Sect, the Music Machine, Donovan, the Chocolate Watch Band, the Dovers, Buddy Holly, Kaleidoscope, Howlin' Wolf, the Beau Brummels, Bo Diddley, Wire, Bob Dylan, Our Generation, Chuck Berry, the Incredible String Band, the Sorrows, the Damned and the Ramones ... are all major inspirations for me wanting to make some kind of music!
Lenny Helsing

Original songs let you get away with more on the performance end, because there's no definitive recording of the song to compare with your own rendition, not yet anyway. But you might get called out for shoddy writing.
Traditional songs give you the great lyrics up front. But you've got to differentiate yourself from your heroes who've already set a high-water mark.

There's no shortcut to figuring out how to do that. You can try and have it both ways, and work with the lyrics and melody, until the words and dialect feel good coming out in your own voice. You can sift through the books and all the existing versions. Shop around, just try not to break anything.

That was the goal of the *Child Ballads* album.

Jefferson Hamer

The Fuchsia album was the main reason why Me and My Kites happened. My friend Reine played me the album.

I was stuck with it, couldn't get enough. For the next few weeks it was the only thing I listened to and it's been like the soundtrack of my life since then.

When we started recording an album with my songs, we named the band after a Fuchsia song. "Me and My Kites" suited the concept well, and it felt good to honor the band that have given me so much. It was like my album, it played to me.

The song "A Tiny Book" was the catalyst, it's like a "Heart of Gold" for the doubtful. I listened to the Fuchsia record almost every day for a year and then we started to record our music.

Not sure if there are any audible Fuchsia influences though, but they were very close in the process.

David Svedmyr

What is it about Fleet Foxes I love so much? Is it because I had their album on repeat while I was insulating the loft?

Yes!

Is it because they appear to have captured something utterly ancient and yet totally new at the same time?

Yes!

Are they influential?

A little, except I find them hard to replicate, so I love them all the more.

They also remind me of Simon And Garfunkel at times, which is no bad thing.

Chris Lambert

I deeply love The Hammersmith Gorillas. They played at our club in South London around '76 and we chatted with them before and after the gig, totally unaware that we were about to see the equivalent of Steve Marriott channelling Jimi Hendrix, backed up by your best mates.

Icarus Peel

There are so many bands I love that I can't narrow that one down, even at gunpoint (in case anyone was thinking of drawing a weapon—don't, it would be useless).

So I'll just mention a band I remembered again today, and remember every now and then with huge affection: The Pale Saints. They are very underrated. And very beautiful. Their album *The Comforts of Madness* ought to be on every list of classic albums. So delicate and powerful.
Emily Jones

The B52's, because they never take themselves too seriously, and still manage to make great pop songs, plus have a good time doing it.
Jayne Gabriel

I am a very big fan of the Brian Jonestown Massacre and Black Rebel Motorcycle Club. For me, these two groups are extraordinary, both in the studio and on stage, the show is magical.
Maxime Schwartz

Everyone always mentions influences of Syd Barrett / sixties Pink Floyd in Octopus Syng's music and I can't deny it; they are right, but it's not the whole truth. We wanna create our own personal unique sound in the music we make.
Jaire Pätäri

I love Guided by Voices. They have a lot of great songs and they put on a kick-ass rock show. Bob Pollard is a melodic genius, a top-tier singer and an enviable wordsmith and song craftsman.
Ted Selke

I love Les Rallizes Denudes from Japan, an almost perfect band.
George Roper Noman

I love Cardiacs! Of course there are other bands I love as much, but, hey, this is my statement: I absolutely love Cardiacs! Tim Smith and his crazy band mates, I feel deep and unconditional love for them.

It was really unfortunate to discover this band only recently (about 2008 or so), as Tim Smith's illness had already put a full stop to their musical activity. Very sad!
Paolo Sala

Bands I love? Loads, loads and loads…. The Move. I really like the Move, that combination of wacky-baccy whimsy, great guitar and thundering rhythm section is just brilliant, and the song writing is superb, and very distinctive.

I like Dick Dale for his energy and killer guitar sound; and Sparklehorse for his lyrics, and, well, pretty much everything about his music, really. And Grinderman. I love Grinderman…. and Graham Coxon… and Buddy Holly…

Tom Woodger

Love the Beatles because of the varied styles. Love the Small Faces's first LP for its raw smash it up modism. I don't dislike any music, as its people trying their best.

Marrs Bonfire

I absolutely love Black Sabbath. In many ways they are totally ridiculous, and became increasingly so as the years went on (much of *Sabotage* and *Sabbath Bloody Sabbath* is brilliantly bonkers and that's before even considering *Technical Ecstasy*), but that is why they are so good.

Either they had a very acute awareness of how silly it could be, or they had none at all and both approaches are perfect.

It allowed them to do whatever they wanted, to be genuine and, in all seriousness, to be one of the last great folk bands.

Plus, I do like a good heavy metal mustache, and they had those turned up to eleven.

Grey Malkin

Love—Kate Bush for letting us into her world, and for showing that everything is possible and for writing such beautiful songs. (I could be very long-winded here, so it's better to stop now.)

Anders Håkanson

A band I love would be Renaissance, the mystical and wonderful purveyors of part-classical, part-folk progressive rock during the 1970s. Gifted with a wonderful vocalist (Annie Haslam) and three other outstanding musicians, the heart of the band was songwriter Michael Dunford, whose beautiful melodies powered every song. The Cornish poetess Betty Thatcher was their lyricist. I never tire of listening to their classic albums.

Steve Palmer

I found Alison O'Donnell on MySpace; we exchanged a few messages and, before I knew it, we were writing songs together. She needed no persuading at all; I've spent a fair bit of time with Alison since that first encounter, and I can honestly say she has more energy and enthusiasm than anybody else I've ever worked with.

Our first batch of gigs together included a show in Manchester and, as there was so many of us, only half the band stayed together in a bed-and-breakfast, and the rest of us made other plans.

We'd driven up from Essex that morning, it took hours, and the gig ran on quite late; I think we left the venue around one or two in the morning. Even after all of that, Alison was still up trying to get a jam session going in the B&B at 3am. That's what she's like—this ball of creative energy that never sleeps. She's amazing and inspiring.

Steven Collins

[Clear Light] … looked great, it was on Elektra… [and it all sounded] kind of other worldly and exotic, but very psychedelic and musical. It has remained one of my favorite U.S. albums right through, along with things like Ultimate Spinach, Savage Resurrection, Mad River, Country Joe et al.

Nick Salomon

I'm a huge fan of the Beatles, particularly their records from Rubber Soul onwards. They certainly nailed it with *Revolver*; "Tomorrow Never Knows" still sounds fresh, new, exciting and shocking.

Nobody's making music as original as that today. And I suppose it's that kind of psychedelically tinged pop music that has influenced the choice of music I've released on Mega Dodo.

John Blaney

Early Pink Floyd (pre-*Dark Side*) is what [Sky Picnic] initially bonded together over, so I think that will always be our greatest love of the genre.

The middle and late period Beatles. King Crimson… which is where our prog leaning influences come from. As for modern bands, Dungen basically has the sound I strive for.

Chris Sherman

Well the band I most love, which is not a very original choice, is the Beatles; my first musical love and the reason I started to play and write songs.

I can still remember when they split up… I was only four at the time, but I can picture my brother and me talking about it with my dad around the red kitchen table. My dad was not a fan, which probably made me love them even more.

I recently bought the CD box set of all their LPs and they still blow me away; so much humor and mischief in their music, and Paul McCartney—what a bassist!

I remember when we were recording the Bordello's Debt Sounds LP, and Dan was going out with a cousin of Paul McCartney's, and she was singing a duet with me on a ramshackle Velvet Underground feedback drenched thing called "Honeypie," and I was thinking "who would have thought it… Beatle blood line on a Bordellos LP."
Brian Bordello

Bands we love: Pink Floyd, Stone Roses, Primus
Pete Meriwether

During the last two years, I have been listening to a lot of old French stuff, especially France Gall's sixties stuff. I love it so much. Then I have listened to Edith Piaf, Erik Satie and Claude Debussy too. I think there might be some influences of sixties France Gall and Erik Satie in Octopus Syng's music in the future!
Jaire Pätäri

The Pretty Things are the best group that ever was. However, I'm pretty passionate about lots of groups from a vast array of different genres.

The Pink Floyd's psychedelic phase is one that never fails to challenge and inspire. Glasgow sixties group the Poets are also true champions, both in my heart and in my mind. Likewise, too, Dutch groups such as the Outsiders and Q65.
Lenny Helsing

[It's not music, but in terms of my writing], I have been very influenced over the last few years by Phil Smith (aka Crab Man) and his work on *Mythogeography*.

His book Counter-Tourism encourages the reader to play with heritage sites and their experience of the landscape, that was big drive to essentially play more in my writing.

In terms of fiction I am influenced by Richard Matheson (because he is / was a genius), Lovecraft (for his documentary approach), John Wyndham and John Christopher.

In the case of the last two, I have been struck on recent re-reading on how they both essentially re-write the British landscape encouraging the reader to re-view the familiar through a distorted lens.
Chris Lambert

If you were looking for a single artist I love, I'd have to say Bjork or Kate Bush, who are both true musical geniuses. But if it has to be a band, I'd go for Orbital.

Their music might seem to be based on repetitive patterns, but there's an incredible amount of variation within the sounds they use, all being constantly tweaked as the track progresses. They actually improvise a lot live. They cover a wide range of feelings from fun to very heavy and have some really sublime tracks like "One Perfect Sunrise."

Chris Bond

I've tried hard to like the Incredible String Band; we have been compared to them, but I find their voices hard to swallow, and some lyrics too. I can see how they revolutionized folk, and indeed music in general.

However, original ISB member Clive Palmer has been one of my favorite musicians, songwriters and inspirations for the Sproatly sound.

He played one of my least liked folk instruments, and made it sound so beautiful and joyous. (That'll be the banjo, not the sax). We usually play one of his songs in our live set.

I can't say I hate ISB, I don't. I have quite a few of their LPs, they just don't get played that much. I prefer the similar sounds of Dr Strangely Strange.

We had the pleasure and honor of Robin Williamson supporting us when we played at Chapters in Cardiff, and he was wonderful and spellbinding, and his singing, storytelling voice was lovely.

Sproatly Smith

I love the Grateful Dead. The songs have beautiful words and melodies and there's plenty of space to settle into the music once you've actually committed to listening to it. Plus I find it unthreatening.

I don't care much for the calisthenic obsession of contemporary bluegrass. Any music that I'm watching while holding my breath, hoping that nobody makes a mistake: that's not really the emotional experience I'm after. Then again, there's something undeniable about flawless execution, like in virtuosic violin music. You got to get down on your knees for that.

Jefferson Hamer

The Familiars

…and a few more on the bloody awful rubbish that you hate. Because… well, it's not really music, is it? It's just a bunch of long-haired apes shouting and banging, and you can't even understand the words…. What a racket.

"Hate" is too strong a word, brother, I don't really hate any band. I suppose what mildly irritates me is some of the new wave of psychedelic bands / individuals… lets call them "academic psychedelicists"… who seem to be doing "psychedelia by numbers."

Like they have taken a masters degree in how everything should sound "just psychedelically so."

Psychedelia is all about expression, going further and freedom. Not a contest to see who can sound the most like July 3, 1967, Decca Studios.

Dave McLean

Bands that I hate…. I don't know. I really hate most bands.

George Roper Noman

In Sweden, we have music that is called "dansband." If you translate it into English, it will be dance band. I don't know how to describe the music, more than it's really awful and terrible. The lyrics are so full of clichès.

Britt Rönnholm

"Hate" is a big word. I cannot say I hate people who use a crappy computer software to make money, sorry, music—I just don't care. Assuming hate is close to love, I could hate musicians I love when they disappoint me.

For example, I could hate Pink Floyd for having a new release out with bad outtakes from their previous album. Imagine if Paul McCartney does the same and releases an album with outtakes from Anthology sessions, and claims it's a new Beatles album…

Will Z

I can't stand the music on the radio, or "artists" [who] sing just because they have a good physique, and to do a monster profit. Advertising Artists, I call them (Pharrell Williams, Katy Perry, Taylor Swift and all that shit.)

Maxime Schwartz

Those bloody nuns.
Chris Lambert

As for bands I hate, that's a tough one. I generally despise all this manufactured TV show created bilge that fills the airwaves with no innovation or any attempt at originality; songs churned out as an amalgamation of what was popular last week, gradually getting more and more sanitized.

One band I hate for good reasons is Inade, I had a solo project called Zoophyte in the late nineties, releasing tapes through Matching Head and Destroy All Music, and I bought a copy of their Alderbaran album and I just thought "you bastards, you've gone where I was heading and beyond."

So it made me go back to the drawing board in my sound creation.
Andy Hokano

Really, what I wish would go away is modern pop music. Autotune and all that digital crispness have this unpleasantly sharp edge to them, like listening too long will cut your ears to pieces. It does much more damage to the idea of "good sound" than some particularly awful classic / prog rock - a band like, say, Rush, for instance.
Amanda Votta

I hate any band out there for the money and glory, [who] fill their cover sleeves with endorsements telling us all what trainers they wear. I don't care.
Mark Reuter

I seem to have an aversion to most things called Bob. I never got the whiney mumblings of Bob Dylan, couldn't stand Bob Marley, and never found Bob Carolgees very funny. I'd make an exception for Bob's Gaudio and Crewe, though.
Simon Berry

I really don't get the David Bowie thing. I like *Hunky Dory*, but other than that, I just can't stand to listen to him at all and I think he's a vampire chancer who went with whatever was popular.

I know that sounds rich coming from a relatively unknown guy talking about one of the most influential artists of all time, but it goes totally over my head.

Maybe this statement will come back to haunt me one day, when I get beaten with rounders bats by the North Wales' David Bowie Appreciation Society.
Chris Wade

I hate, despise and loathe the Smiths. That whining pathetic streak of self-pity with the tree in his arse makes me want to break windows. Miserable, over-rated ostriches wearing the king's new clothes. Shame, 'cos the boy Marr seems a decent lad….
Icarus Peel

I find Abba's tweeness very irritating.
Roger Linney

In terms of bands I hate, I'll just leave it as Mumford and Sons. Their waistcoat wearing, over-privileged, plump faced brand of watered down nu-folk makes me ill, but they are an easy target.
Richard Thompson

It is the ubiquitous Gallagher-related "career bands," who irritate me, with their career chords and lazily penned "rousing" anthems whose banal sentiments are cynically aimed at working on the level of some kind of warped idea of lowest-common-denominator Universality, where maybe if they make it vague enough, it might get used on a Tescos advert.

Music without magic or a sense of wonder, with an eye on the bank account. For a list of bands I despise for this reason, look no further than this week's *NME* front cover.

Artless wankers and all of them male.
Chris Anderson

A… band that I'm not big on is Fairport Convention. I love their first three or four albums, but their branch of folk rock kind of leaves me cold. Is that too sacrilegious?
Sproatly Smith

I don't really hate any bands, as even the worst example of a band points you in the direction away from them to do / make something interesting, in my experience.
Alan Murphy

I hate Coldplay and most of the stuff in the modern charts, because it's boring, has rubbish chord changes and little imagination.
Aaron Hemington

There are very few bands I hate—mostly, if I don't like something, I'm indifferent to it. Those musicians have put a bit of their soul into their work, and someone, somewhere, probably likes it, so why be nasty?

However, there is one exception to this rule, and that is musicians who behave badly because they think it's cool or "rock and roll." There's never any excuse for being what my friend Angeline would term (with great relish) an Utter Tool.
Emily Jones

A band I am not so keen on is Mumford and Sons. Dressing like a farmer is all very well if you are a farmer (Ian Anderson from Jethro Tull was a fish farmer, somewhat confusing the whole argument), but being Coldplay with a banjo and a bonnet doesn't make you a folk band. Not in my book, anyway.
Grey Malkin

I think Genesis (post-Peter Gabriel) are a very easy band to loathe. I can't quite put a finger on why, every time I see any footage of them, my blood begins to boil. It may be how incredibly seriously they take themselves; it may be all those endlessly bland songs that seem to be made purely with the aim of selling the most records possible; or it just might be the fact that they were originally (with Peter Gabriel on board) an innovative and really interesting band.
Stephen Stannard

Hate—manufactured pop acts churned out by the sausage factory which is the X Factor. An easy target, I know, and I think it's really more that the whole process is a soulless commercial juggernaut which has no regard for individuality and creativity. The acts themselves are a tiny cog in the larger machine so I can't really hate them as individuals / groups.
Ellie Coulson

Hate Satanic metal scream match music.
Jayne Gabriel

I don't like Iron Butterfly much (though I only had the In-a-gadda-da vida album) because I can't stand that overdramatic tone on Doug Ingle's voice. But they have great instrumental riffs.
Marco Magnani

The band I most hate / detest is post-Syd Barrett Pink Floyd. I just cannot stand them; they remind me of an old woman walking upstairs on a shag pile carpet.
They really annoy me so much… that bloody guitar sound and the way "Money" is always played on really boring TV programs about finance… why can't they play the Beatles' "Money" instead? Bloody morons…
Brian Bordello

The Clash, whilst clearly being very nice, empathetic people, produced… predictable protest pop which somehow propped up the binary thinking of the patriarchy.

I do like "Tommy Gun" as a song, though.
Mikey Georgeson

Well, there are a lot of bands we hate, not all their music but most of it. In our country (Spain), there is a big school of really bad music: there are loads of bands that sound awful, and they get success despite all common sense.

Unbelievable.

I could mention several names, but one of the worst bands I've ever heard is Manos de Topo. No tunes, no sound, no show, no groove, no voice, just disgusting. Judge for yourself.
Jordi Bel

Bands I hate: anything that lacks groove, such as classic Billy Joel, new Billy Joel, Billy Joel Live, etc…
Pete Meriwether

To be honest, I'm a bit of an old fuddy-duddy. As a dad of young children, I can't stand anything aimed at kids that is overtly sexualized.

However, I can't think of the names of any of these, as I tend to switch them off. And it tends to be the videos more than the music that is the problem.

This is a really boring answer.
Chris Lambert

I can't say I hate any bands. A bit of a dull line to take, but everything has its place doesn't it? That said, I've yet to hear a Yes album that I want to hear again…
Graeme Lockett

We don't hate anybody. But the list of bands we don't like is one hundred times longer than the list of bands we like.
Narsis Passolas

The Moody Blues. I grimace if I'm caught somewhere when "Nights in White Satin" comes on (sorry Justin). Just find it poncey.
Alison O'Donnell

If I had to name one band which I hate, it would have to be Marillion. When I was a teenager, all of the prefects at my school were progressive rock fans. They also had their own room, which was covered with Genesis and Marillion posters.

Script from A Jester's Tear, if I remember correctly.

So it was perhaps not entirely unnatural that I developed a particular aversion to these groups. In fact, it's only in the last few years that I've been able to listen to anything vaguely progressive. And it's only recently that I've come to realize that (early) Genesis were actually quite good.

I still hate Marillion, though.

Peter Lyon

I will pluck out of the air Kenny G as an artist I hate, but it could equally well be many others like him, who churn out bland, inoffensive (but actually deeply offensive to my ears) music that is instantly forgettable and horribly slick.

Diana Collier

I had seen Bruce Springsteen and the original E-Street Band open for Anne Murray (!) in Central Park. This was the group with David Sancious on keyboards and "Mad Dog" Vini Lopez on drums. Steve Van Zandt was not yet eating up all the available air.

They swung. They rocked. It was joyous. They tore down Central Park. The PA announcer had to beg the fans to allow the Snow Bird take the stage.

Soon, old pal Rich Sobocinski and I had a band with horns and growly lead singer named Bob Seidel. We did a lot of soul, Van Morrison (the artist Springsteen brought to mind when still writing catchy, clever songs) and the Destined-to-be-Boss. We still did "Rosalita," but the author's changing image seemed to pull the magic out of it.

The band was [no longer] around by *Born in the USA*, but I did see a show on that tour. Never have I witnessed a [more] joyless episode.

Fred Goodman examines the old Boss / new Boss dichotomy in the book Mansion on the Hill. He draws a parallel with Neil Young. Both formed associations with big name producer / managers. With the former it was Jon Landau, the notorious boss of the Boss.

Neil Young took David Geffen's money, then thought better of it. Goodman looks at how these relationships, and others in the business, are handled on personal, financial and artistic levels.

A friend said, "It's a great book if you love Neil Young and hate Bruce Springsteen."

I think it's a great book.

Bill Sweeney

I usually don't use time to hate; as soon as something is not [to my liking], I just step aside to keep going my way, because I'm more interested by what I like, and to discover things old or new. For example, a band I really like a lot that I could mention is the Beatles.

But I do carry a heavy grudge for the post Brian Jones Rolling Stones….
Francois Sky

…and really crap muso bands always play their songs when you are trying to have a quiet pint, and instead you are treated to wit and wisdom of post Syd Barrett Pink Floyd… when they have neither.
Brian Bordello

I can't say I hate any band. There are lots I don't understand and some genres I don't like to listen to, like Country or Death Metal. I've a friend who's into Metal and often he plays me tracks which start out with me thinking "these guys are really great musicians," but then the machine-gun-like kick drum starts and someone starts screaming in that "devil-voice" they use, and I can't listen any longer.

Doesn't mean it's bad music though!
Chris Bond

Instead of aimlessly slagging people off, I'll just talk about characteristics I hate: machismo, musical conservatism and playing dumb.

First, machismo: we should have evolved past this cock-rock behavior by now, as a species. Writing about booze and birds and stuff because you're thick, and you think your audience is too, is utterly pointless and regressive.

Musical conservatism is another one: I could mention loads of bands I hate that fall into this category but instead I'll boil it down to this. The Beatles were influenced by music hall, Little Richard, Indian Classical Music, the Byrds, Karlheinz Stockhausen and Motown. Oasis were influenced by the Beatles.

Post-punk, before I was born, drew not just from other contemporary guitar bands and some who—shock horror—abandoned their guitars, but from other forms of art (visual art and literature chiefly) and other forms of music i.e. the dub fetishism that went on with PiL and Gang Of Four. Post-punk as an umbrella encapsulated not just PiL but Scritti Politti, Throbbing Gristle, Delta 5 and the Fall.

The modern definition of post-punk is posh kids of all ages with nice neat haircuts and offensively expensive pre-worn outfits, playing "angular" riffs to people who won't dance because they're not sure if it's allowed. It's all so hopelessly "white," too: to be a proper post-punk band, true to the original spirit now, you'd need to draw from grime or something. Do it properly.
Dan Bordello

A band I hate would be Lover Boy. God, I loathed having to sit through their four minutes of sonic excrement on MTV. I remember the first time I heard their horrible saccharine pop, and saw their red fashion hippy bandanas. I wish I didn't. Ahem.
Gregory Curvey

The two bands I hate the most. Actually I don't hate any band, but if I have to name a couple of bands I really don't like, maybe they could be Toto and...the other band could be Mötley Crüe.

Why don't I like Toto? Because, they're the band whose album was promoted with the words "the first rock album ever where is not white noise at all" (or something like that).

What a fuck! Have you ever heard any rock record that has been ruined by white noise? Their music, it's so boring and flavorless.

As for Mötley Crüe, they had the worst songs ever made; and, in addition, they were very lousy players. They were just one bad Hanoi Rocks copy with very bad and brainless (in a bad way) songs.

That's all.
Jaire Pätäri

I struggle to hate a band. I hate the homogeny that so many bands and artists now represent, but they are all so homogenous that I can't pick one out to especially hate!!
Crystal Jacqueline

Boston, Journey, Styx, Foreigner and Toto.... Utter tosh. It's the kind of lowest common denominator, music by numbers, radio-friendly, bland, insipid pop that's made for people who don't like music.

Phil Collins is another one....
John Blaney

Like many others, I have noticed with dismay a growing tendency towards the twee in current folk music. This is a big concern for lots of us, but luckily I've come up with a sure fire way to diagnose such things before they go too far: simply avoid any event in which the word "boutique" is used as an adverb.

As well as music, this also holds true for absolutely anything else. There is a lot of it about— indeed, I would not be surprised to come across a "boutique boutique" one day… or if there was a twee estate agent that specialized in renting tiny twee shops, it might in fact be called a "boutique boutique, boutique boutique."

There's probably a legend somewhere that should this ever happen, it will be the first sign of the coming Armageddon—or as it will be termed by then, the "pop-up apocalypse."
Emily Jones

I don't like badmouthing bands and instead tend to think that certain artists are simply not for me.

Except Creed, of course. They're shit.
Jeb Morris

Hate—pretty much every band that started out in the eighties; a lost decade for me, and looking back, I still find very little to like musically, although that's my loss.
Keith Jones

Hate-wise, it's gotta be bands like U2, Coldplay, Simply Red or Bon Jovi—absolute dull pretension of the highest degree. Or, to be more current, every track played / spoonfed and churned out on commercial radio, which mainly seems to be overly manufactured, overplayed R&B tripe. Talentless and degrading to music in every way.
Kev Oyston

Here is a nice heartwarming anecdote. Once upon a time, a mate of mine worked in the kitchen of a very expensive hotel. One day, a member of a band who shall not be named, but it rhymes with Oasis (...oh alright, it was Oasis), came to dine in said hotel and generally acted like an Utter Tool to all the staff.

Suffice to say, their soup, when it was served to them, had several fluid additions of a bodily nature in it. And I do like to think that everywhere that this Tool dined and bullied, something similar occurred. By now, it may even have happened so often that they probably think soup is supposed to taste of wee.

That's a lovely story, isn't it?
Emily Jones

I am so happy to tell you that 99.99 percent of the music I have heard out in public, and on the radio, has infuriated me, and enflamed me with delicious hatred!

I can't stand any music from modern era that uses a vocoder or auto tune on the vocals—for example! Except for the Tempers from Seattle, cos they do it in a fabulous innovative musical way.
Gordon Raphael

As for the bands I hate... er... well, there are far too many. It would be very unfair of me to name one. Really. Let's say that 98% of the bands on this planet, I hate them. Haha.
Paolo Sala

I don't hate any bands. I don't hate. I don't want to say anything negative about a specific artist. The times I've done that have haunted me, and I deeply regret them.

I will say that in today's app fast-forward world of quick files mixed with the religion of celebrity culture... it is more apparent than ever that marketing sex and arrogance have taken the place of true talent and real art.

There is evil in the music scene. Keith Jones of Fruits de Mer said once that his competition is not other record labels, but rather the technology of downloads, as well as general apathy. I am proud to be on a record label that creates art rather than commerce.

Jet Wintzer

Aerosmith. Maybe it's more about people who like Aerosmith than the band itself. They are just a band that have never done a good song, and didn't even sound good in the seventies. But they are not alone in that vein. It's more about the talking that they rock so hard, and are so rebellious, and such a good rock'n roll band, when they are no more rebellious than the average Swedish dance-band.

Anders Håkanson

There really isn't one band that I believe we hate, but any lyrics that are super saccharine and just cliché s from the "flower power" era kind of hurt the genre's respectability. That, and anyone who is trying too hard to be weird (current Flaming Lips for example) for the sake of being weird.

Chris Sherman

J' Not so adore; All cynicism and cliché ; pandering to an "audience" one presumes to know the limitations of; "prog" as a musical style to be emulated / recreated rather than (pace Robert Fripp) a way of doing things; the ongoing triumphant rehashing of Classic Rock (the equivalent would be all those sixties / seventies icons refusing to budge beyond Glenn Miller); and most Metal.

Whilst some of the most daring, innovative and brilliant music currently being created comes from the Metal camp, I think it would be a damn sight more daring, innovative and brilliant if it dropped the dull dead- handed clunkings of Metal, especially that bloody guitar sound.

Sand Snowman

I get covering a song if you bring something new to the table with it, like Jimi Hendrix covering Dylan's "All Along The Watchtower," This Mortal Coil's sumptuous version of Tim Buckley's "Song to the Siren," or more recently Earthling Society tackling Alice Coltrane....

But this epidemic of covers and tribute bands doing the same old stuff.... does the world need to hear another dodgy version of "Summertime," "Stormy Monday," "Brown Eyed Girl" blah, blah, blah.

And, worryingly, it's killing off new talent. Tribute / cover bands are keeping new, original talent off the stages of venues in this country... if it keeps on going, there will be no new talent to cover.

Pete Bingham

No real hates… but I did walk out during Rush's set at Holland's Pink Pop Festival!
Leo O'Kelly

I hate Graham Coxon, for being such a great guitarist, and making me feel like I should just jack it in. And Pete Doherty, for writing such brilliant songs… bastard.
Andy Hokano

I've heard Col. Bruce Hampton quoted as saying "there's nothing worse than a good band." I think about that a lot.
Jefferson Hamer

Beautify Junkyards

Alison O'Donnell

If you could record a cover of any one song from the past, what it would be—and why? (And if you've already had the chance to record it, tell us about that.)

I was really taken by Bob Dylan's recent quote about not covering, but uncovering, songs. How come no-one ever thought of that before? Because they're not Bob Dylan!
Leo O'Kelly

Tough question! I don't do cover versions. My music has to come from inside, inside me, and the idea of doing a cover version isn't part of my musical vocabulary.

But, I suppose if I did, it would be some super-melodic track from the 1960s or 1970s—maybe "Everlasting Love" by the Love Affair.
Steve Palmer

Barry Gray's theme music to the Gerry Anderson TV series 'UFO.' Because it's one of the grooviest TV themes ever!
Chris Bond

[Tom and I] agreed early on that we wanted to cover Pentangle's "Trees They Do Go High," and really that was the starting point for our first album, CunningFolk, which is a collection of covers and rearrangements of our shared favorites.
Joanna Swan

I'd love to do a cover of Brian Jonestown Massacre or Black Rebel Motorcycle Club, but I'm too afraid not to do justice to the original, because the bar is set very high. I did a cover of Johnny Cash's "Long Black Veil"—I find that this music to a great soul, and very telling.
Maxime Schwartz

There are so many great songs! It is almost impossible to pick just one….

We have a few we are cooking, even now. One idea we are very taken with is to produce our version of the Joe Meek and *The Blue Men I Hear A New World—Part Two* EP.

Meek recorded the whole *I Hear A New World* album, but only four of the tracks were released during his lifetime as an EP entitled *I Hear A New World—Part One*.

Another EP, *I Hear A New World—Part Two*, was planned, with even a sleeve designed and sleeve notes written by Joe himself, but it was never released. We would really like to produce our own version… maybe one day.

But one song?....Probably "Telstar." It's become sort of a Zeta Puppies anthem, and while its been covered by loads of people by now, I think I'd like us to take a crack at it. That, or the theme to *Doctor Who*.

Tom Woodger

I am admittedly something of a covers junkie. I could do albums and albums of nothing but covers, just because it's a fun break from working on your own songs.

If I had to pick one that I have not had the chance to do, it would probably have to be my old favorite "Black Girl" / "In the Pines" / "Where Did You Sleep Last Night?"

There are so many amazing versions of this out there though, from Lead Belly's on up to modern versions like Nirvana's, that it's always been intimidating to do.

Amanda Votta

Probably "The Herald" by Comus, simply because I'd be impressed that I'd managed to play the guitar to that standard.

Richard Thompson

"I am The Walrus," in part because it would be a blast to sing. And the breaks in between Ringo's godlike drum parts would present some interesting opportunities.

But it's not as much fun to do a cover when there's no way to improve on the original.

Ted Selke

I recorded a quick demo of Nirvana's (UK) "Tiny Goddess" a couple of years ago. My guitarist at the time was a friend of Patrick Campbell-Lyons and sent him the demo.

He appeared to like it, and messaged me saying he'd like to get it released as a single. He also came to Salisbury to watch us play it live in a tiny pub.

I was hoping that it might provide some kind of breakthrough, but nothing happened, despite unsuccessfully trying to contact him for a while.

Simon Berry

We're not averse to playing cover songs; we generally end our set with "Late Night" by Syd Barrett. We've performed versions of the *White Horses* theme tune, and "Price Tag" by Jesse J.

The Sensational Alex Harvey Band song "Isobel Goudie" was quite a tricky song to record and then play live.

One day I hope to play "Light Flight" with the band; we started practicing it once. I often hear a song and imagine playing it live: "Bat Out Of Hell" would be interesting, and this week in the Co-op I was listening to Hot Chocolate's "Every1's A Winner," mentally working out how we'd arrange it. Great guitar riff. But of course, what everyone really wants to hear is our version of "Everyone Says I Love You" by the Marx Brothers.

Sproatly Smith

"What a Wonderful World"—because, far from accusations of being sentimental, I find Louis Armstrong's version so heartbreaking.

I do tend to plumb the dark tragedic depths, but then set that feeling alongside something which contrasts, so I always wanted to give this song an olde world Christmassy feel—probably because, in my mind, I will always have its title muddled up with It's a Wonderful Life.

Chris Anderson

Narrowing down one in particular is tricky. There's a project I've had an idea for, for ages. I really like the concept of Tori Amos' *Strange Little Girls* album. I'd like to do the male equivalent of it, taking songs which my masculine voice (the only thing masculine about me, really, thankfully) would give another dimension to.

Dan Bordello

I've just covered the Fall's "What You Need," as I've always loved the repetitive, hippy riff… plus I wanted to see if I could re-make it in a purely electronic context.

I'm working on Buzzcocks' "Fast Cars" at the moment, to see what that would sound like as a purely electronic exercise.

Alan Murphy

I'd love to do a translated and Westernised version of "Pyar Kiya To Darna Kya," from the film *Mughal E Azam*.

I found this song late at night a few years ago, whilst on a random YouTube crawl, and was immediately struck by it—there was something sweet and fragile, yet commanding, in the melody. I must have listened to it five or six times over and over… you know how you fall in love with a song.

I had no idea what it could be about at the time, and there were no visuals to help on the version I found first, just a picture of the singer (the wondrous Lata Mangeshkar), but to me it seemed to be beauty and goodness singing defiance to a cruel world.

Which, as it turned out, was pretty close; I later read the story, found the film version and discovered that the title roughly translates as "I have loved, so why be afraid?" or "I have loved, so what is there to fear?" And yes, yes, that is important. The world is a terrifying place. To give love is the biggest thing.

So, for various reasons, that song has a personal resonance with me and I've always wanted to make my own version of it. It would be very different, but keep the bones of the melody and the sense and the soul of it. I'm not sure that I'd be up to the challenge, but I'd like to try.

Emily Jones

We still want perform covers in a live setting, but as far as recording goes, we've now got a backlog of original ideas we want to prioritize.

Tom Conway

Since we recorded *Martyred Hearts* last year, I've continued to write lyrics faster than we can find time to set them to music!

For starters there's a ballad called "The Witch of Torryburn," and something a bit more free-form about the ancient spring at Knaresborough.

Joanna Swan

"Arnold Layne"—Pink Floyd… I have always loved this song. Reminds me a lot of an old friend of mine named Brendan who is the official Poet Laureate of Wednesbury. He loves Pink Floyd.

Roger Linney

The *Doctor Who* theme. Delia Derbyshire committed to tape an absolute masterpiece when she put the original version together. Granted not written by her, but she will always be more associated to it than Ron Grainer, due to her lightning-in-a-bottle brilliant innovation.

Just amazing what she did with that track. It can never be bettered. Others have tried and failed, including myself. My wish would be to better it, as I'm sure others would want to, but what she came up with is beyond perfect. I will never try to cover it again.

Kev Oyston

We've just finished recording a heavy psychedelic version of Del Shannon's "Runaway."

We interpreted it in a way that Vanilla Fudge circa 1969 would have. We are currently located in Michigan and Del was from Western Michigan. We thought it would be the perfect time to record a tribute to him.

He had a psychedelic album in 1968 called the *Further Adventures of Charles Westover*, that was very influential on the Striped Bananas.
Duncan Shepard

I would record "Beechwood Park" by the Zombies, because it personifies the Psychedelic Baroque sound we seek.
Aaron Hemington

"Wow" by Kate Bush. In a previous life, I used to sing opera and I would love to give my high notes a workout again!
Ellie Coulson

I only tend to do covers live, or when I'm asked to participate in some project. I guess I might choose 'Waiting For The Moving Van' by David Ackles because it's such a sad and poignant song. Beautiful lyrics which actually bring a tear to my eye every time I hear it. I'd never be able to do it justice.
Nick Salomon

When a band plays a cover during their set, I usually tune-out for a couple minutes and wait for it to end. I'm not against the idea entirely, I just somehow lose interest. It feels like a commercial break during a television program.
Jeb Morris

I / we have not much interest in recording cover songs, because we have so much of our own material.

Actually, we have a different kind of problem; we write more songs than we [are able] to record and mix. So, we have about thirty songs that we should record and make ready some day, but more songs comes out of our heads all the time.

But about our cover songs. We have recorded two for Fruits de Mer: John's Children's "Midsummer Night Scene" and Pink Floyd's "Flaming."
Jaire Pätäri

I first encountered the ballad "Sheath and Knife" through sheer luck and coincidence. Through the endless Googling of "public domain folk songs" and clicking of links, I somehow ended up learning of the Child Ballads.

I briefly read about them, Francis J Child and his work, and wanted to actually hear some, so I went back to Youtube. I found a playlist that someone had compiled, clicked on a few links, and eventually landed on "Sheath and Knife." The version that was uploaded to the playlist was by Broadside Electric, who had a modern folk-rock approach.

The song's dark and tragic nature instantly appealed to me, and with another quick search, I found the lyrics.

Ellie Bryan

My friend, the animator Martin Pickles, suggested I listen to "The Visitors" by Abba, which turns out to be a genius piece of permafrost psychedelic new-wave built around the Indian raga featuring microtones and sliding between notes.

The lyrics are an unblinking look towards the cusp of insanity and embracing one's shadow.

So, "The Visitors" it is.

Mikey Georgeson

It'd be "A Day in the Life" by the Beatles, because to me it's the closest thing to the sound of a dream. It doesn't sound like something from this planet, and it's more songs in one.

Marco Magnani

I played in a funk band that covered "Superstition" by Stevie Wonder. This makes me very happy.

Mark Reuter

If I could cover one song, it might be "Under No Enchantment" by Alasdair Roberts, because it is a work of great beauty, and is at the same time cerebral and deeply affecting at an emotional level. Although I would probably never cover it, as his version is already perfect.

Diana Collier

I would love to try the Stones' "Moonlight Mile" or Bowie's "Heroes" but I just can't find a way of adding anything worthy of the originals.

I think the cover that I most enjoyed creating was "Grantchester Meadows." [Crystal Jacqueline] had never heard it and I had seen it on TV one evening, and thought "great tune, but could sound better."

When she heard it, she wanted to do it immediately.

Icarus Peel

A few years ago, a label asked me to record a cover and I sent three songs: "Orange Skies" by Love (the Bryan MacLean original version); "Saler Man" by Ramases; and "Day-Dream" by Ash Ra Tempel, crossed with "Planet Caravan" by Black Sabbath. But the result wasn't really good, so hopefully the release was cancelled.

Will Z

In my project the Psychgeographical Commission, we released free downloadable mini album of covers and I insisted we do a Moody Blues cover just because(the Dickies aside) who does a Moody Blues cover? Especially in the post industrial scene.

We meander about in it, admittedly; it was the song "Cities," which is a pretty obscure b-side.
Andy Hokano

I have done it, I think. "C'est la Vie," Greg Lake and Pete Sinfield's song. I always wanted to sing that. And I have.
Judy Dyble

I have made very few attempt to cover anything, but I've made a shorter, three-and-a-half minute, cover of the Velvet Underground's "Sister Ray," with my wife [Nicole S] singing. The Velvets are among my top five bands.
    Maybe someday I'd cover Spacemen 3, because not only am I a big fan, but we do have some mutual gear too; therefore the sounds are all there.
Francois Sky

We have a lot of titles on the list of songs that we sometime in the future would like to do a cover version of. These last days, I have thought about doing a ghostly version of Kevin Ayers's "Lady Rachel."
    When I'm in my most optimistic mood, I'm thinking of Us and Them doing Kate Bush's "Under the Ivy."
Anders Håkanson

I would cover Lodestone's tape loops from 1972-74, and possibly one track by the French Rhythms.
Drew Mulholland

Some years ago, I recorded Pink Floyd's "Breathe" for a compilation in a magazine who wanted to tribute the Floyds. I tried to let "Breathe" sound folky, but keeping its legendary mood at the same time.
Lorenzo Bracaloni

Beautify Junkyard's debut album was entirely made with covers of songs from the past, so we chose a set of songs that excited us to transform.
    I can say that working with Nick Drake's "From the Morning," Vashti Bunyan's "Rose Hip November" and Heron's "Yellow Roses" was a real mystical experience; we recorded the base structure

Thanes

The Chemistry Set

of all songs on the fields with a mobile studio, and when it came the time to record, we felt that the music we were producing and the sounds of the surrounding nature were part of a whole, a unity.

It was a wonderful and special moment to do what we did in that place, and I think it transmitted those vibrations to the record.

João Branco Kyron

I'd love to record a cover of Derrick Harriott's "Loser" I've never done it, because I don't think I could ever improve on its perfect combination of melancholy and sweetness.

Angeline Morrison

The Bordellos are really bad at cover versions, as the ones out there prove... apart from our version of the Bo Diddley classic "I'm a Man," which I love (although I am probably in a minority).

We find it much easier to write our own songs, but the one I think we could do very well is by the much underrated Liverpool songwriter Jimmy Campbell.

It's called "In My Room," a beautiful and slightly disturbing song that lists all the things in his room and how he may burn them all now he's on his own. Billy Fury recorded an ace version as well. The subject matter and the darkness appeals.

Brian Bordello

My ideal cover version is a song that I don't know yet. It's brilliant if someone says "can you work out a version of this?" and I think "I've never heard it before, but I'll give it a go."

That's what happened when Alison (O'Donnell) and I did "Frozen Warnings." At the time, the only Nico stuff I knew was the *Velvet Underground* album and *Chelsea Girl*, neither of which I was particularly taken with, but after Alison suggested it I had to go and find *The Marble Index*, which led me to Desertshore, and I now think they're two of the most remarkable albums I've ever heard, so it's a great way to discover new stuff.

I like the challenge too. Listening to "Frozen Warnings" for the first time, I couldn't even hear any notes, let alone work out what they were. I'm very proud of the end result though!

Graeme Lockett

There is a recording of us playing "Little Miss Strange." It may be the most suitable Hendrix song for us to play.

Narsis Passolas

I recorded a cover of Nic Jones' "10,000 Miles" with Michael Tanner during a week where we also recorded in a smugglers' cave in Mupe Bay, Dorset, keeping an eye on the incoming tide.

It has finally found its home on *The Ale's What Cures Ye*, a title which may or may not be misleading.

David Colohan

In rock music, there are the Beatles, and there is everything else. Any description of a top group, song, influence has an understanding of "besides the Beatles."

There is nothing like them. Even David Crosby realized the Byrds were never going to be Fab.

Read *Can't Buy Me Love: The Beatles, Britain and America* by Jonathan Gould, and begin to have an understanding of the impact these four had on the society we live in. The world of music is the one we are concerned with here, and that world remains much the same as it has been since the "Love Me Do" days.

There are the Beatles and everyone else. And although their hairstyles and clothing matched, and songwriting was shared, there was only one Big Beatle. There is John Lennon and everyone else.

So John is the genius, and "A Day in the Life" is his masterwork.

"I read the news today, oh boy." More chilling words never opened anything. It is difficult to imagine them without his inherent sneer. And without checking Google, it seems impossible to remember someone even trying (OK, Miley Cyrus did it on the Flaming Lips' Sgt. Pepper tribute and scared nobody).

Another tribute has Barry Gibb doing a straightforward version. If it's true the Bee Gees actually were the Beatles, that doesn't count.

Another one who attempted this one—at least live—is Paul McCartney (who co-wrote the song). He keeps it pretty close to the Beatle boots. So it would not be the one millionth cover of "Yesterday" or "Michelle."

We are trying something here, we are accepting the challenge. We are doing what everyone says can't be done, what shouldn't be done.

The two things you hear when attempting a classic are a) You can't do that one and b) That's one song you can't change.

As far as a) goes, the one "you can't do" is the one you must. Because it's there. The Himalayas are not going to climb themselves. Somebody has to go to the moon; it might as well be you.

And b) Fruits de Mer issues mostly covers. I still think, despite the great reviews we received for 7 & 7 Is, the best track we have recorded for the label is still the first one by the Byrds, Chris Hillman's "Thoughts and Words."

Since it was not that well known, we were not concerned with messing with preconceived notions. We did it almost as if we had written it, and in small ways, for this version, we did.

That's what we do with "A Day in the Life." We make it ours. What do we bring to it? Everything. We went kitchen sink on Roger McGuinn's "5D." There was talk that one was too personal, sacred. We heightened the Holy and it took it other places. There was spoken word (forwards and backwards), surging strings, Mop Top harmonies. We gave it everything. Not bad for the Levittown Lads.

One thing worth saving is a two-voice approach of "A Day in the Life." We have two leads in Gary Moran and Lanny Sichel (the Walrus is Bill Intemann).

They both went to Levittown Memorial High School and its initials signify Lennon, McCartney, Harrison, Starr and in the right order. So it is written.

As always, our secret weapon is Ray Lambiase. He spins the knobs and this one would need some tricky twirling for our version of the signature crescendo. We would all chip in, fight it out, wrestle with the Sacred Protectors of Liverpool Lore.

I've been there, Liverpool. The first thing I'm always asked is, "Did you walk across Abbey Road?" Duh, that's in London. Everything else—Penny Lane with its roundabout, bandshell and barber shop, Strawberry Fields, the Cavern, the lads' childhood homes—remains a lot like it was when they were told "You Can't Do That."

Somehow they did. For one song, we can too.

Bill Sweeney

It would be "Silver Birch," by Del Shannon from his *The Further Adventures of Charles Westover* album from 1968, and we have recorded it.

The album is a wonderful, spooky, beautiful record. To me, it sounds like his take on *Forever Changes*. It's totally unlike any other Del record, and has some truly psychedelic songs. I urge your readers to go out and purchase it.

For our version, we take Del's song and mix some *Forever Changes* acoustics and general vibe; we take a section of "Sanctus" from David Axelrod and the Electric Prunes' *Mass in F Minor*, then add some mellotrons, backwards guitars, drums and monk-like backing vocals.

That's us… mix it all up and produce some "symphonic psych- pop."

Dave McLean

I would love to do a cover of "Creation" by the Incredible String Band, but I would make such a berk of myself trying to do Robin Williamson's voice.

Other than that, I would like to cover "Hurricane" by Bob Dylan. I had the honor of having the violinist on that track, Scarlet Rivera, appear on one of the Dodson & Fogg songs. I have always loved that gypsy violin sound. I enjoy playing along to "Hurricane" on the guitar; I just love the chords. So it'd be great to do a cover of it.

Chris Wade

Nico's "Frozen Warnings" in 2008. It's glacial. A musician friend of mine said my version sounded "unhinged." I like that. I don't come from a covers-of-any-kind background, but that song was an exception.
Alison O'Donnell

Tír na nÓg recently recorded Silver Apples' "I Have Known Love," and it will be on our new album. Great duo, great song, great lyrics… a lot of people seemed surprised, but delighted when they heard our version.
Leo O'Kelly

Peggy Lee's "A Taste of Honey." So sexy and soothing.
Jayne Gabriel

"Supper's Ready" by Genesis. That would sort out the men from the boys!
Mordecai Smyth

It would be something from Love's *Forever Changes*; possibly "You Set The Scene."
    I would sound absolutely daft singing this in my Scottish accent, and it would be the oddest the Hare And The Moon song ever, but it would still be splendid. There has never been a finer song that so ably covers every possible emotion that a person can feel.
    Failing that, something by Coil or Swans; you know, something nice and cheery.
Grey Malkin

I love playing "White Rabbit" live; it is always an adventure, and always well received.
Icarus Peel

Probably "Candy And A Currant Bun," the 1967 flipside of "Arnold Layne," the debut single by the Syd Barrett-led Pink Floyd. Before we were called the Thanes, we were using the name the Green Telescope for a few years—an EP and a single in 1985-86—and an idea we had was to record a version of this, and release it under the name The Purple Periscope.
    Alas, nothing came of that idea. One day, maybe who knows?
Lenny Helsing

My favorite songs change all the time, so trying to pick one is almost impossible. And to be honest, I'd rather listen to the original, because it's rare that a cover version improves things. Although there are always exceptions. So I'm talking rubbish really, aren't I?

But if you're going to push me, I'd like to hear "There's Nothing Shaking (But The Leaves On The Tree)," because it's a lovely little rock 'n' roll song, and I'd like Motorhead to record it.

Not the current Motorhead line up, but the one with Phil "Philthy Animal" Taylor and "Fast" Eddie Clarke.

John Blaney

"Lilac Wine"—Jeff Buckley version. I do try this one occasionally—I love that it contains a real sense of magic, is utterly ethereal and harks back to ancient times.

There is an element of *Midsummer Night's Dream* in there, a mist on the grass, as well as an extreme sense of longing. I also get a real thrill attempting to emulate Buckley's vocals, as it gives me something to aspire to.

Chris Lambert

Being involved with Fruits de Mer Records has given me the chance to record more covers than I ever imagined, but I have to say it's a blast! I think the latest one I've completed was part of a childhood dream.

I did a version of "Starship Trooper" by Yes, and played all of the instruments, save for a few wonderful guitar tracks that my friend Vito Greco played.

I wanted to have an old fashioned guitar battle at the end, and Vito was great. [Chris] Squire's bass parts were fun to learn, as well as the drums, but I didn't even try to attempt Steve Howe's licks. Besides, I wanted it to sound like the Luck of Eden Hall.

The reason I wanted to record "Starship Trooper" in the first place, was to see if I could pull it off, and as part of the rules were to stretch the length of the song into an entire album side, I had a lot of fun reworking the original arrangement.

Gregory Curvey

Choosing a cover is just as important as recording it.

When I pitched the idea for Schizo Fun Addict to cover "Theme From Suspiria" to Fruits De Mer, I sort of knew it was gonna happen... like it was fated. Suspiria was a film that contributed to my becoming a feature filmmaker.

It is simply a dazzling film, with the best horror soundtrack ever. But the film has a happy ending as well. It's not so obvious, but it does.

I don't know if we will ever cover another tune again. I'm not sure we can top Suspiria. But if we do, the one I want to cover is "Don't Worry Baby" by the Beach Boys. To think this was on the b-side of "I Get Around" in 1964 is incredible. This is a masterpiece and, like Jobim, Brian Wilson makes me want to be in love.

Jet Wintzer

We recorded "Guess I was Dreaming" by the Fairytale, and Molly Rabbit, the original songwriter from the band, contacted us to congratulateus for the version.

Hope someday we can meet him in London for a gig, as he promised that. We like to take brilliant tunes from the bands we love (generally from the past), and make them more understandable to our times.

We have recorded "Chicago" (Graham Nash), "Rainy Day Mushroom Pillow" (Strawberry Alarm Clock), "If I Needed Someone" (the Beatles), "2,000 Light Years From Home" (the Rolling Stones) and "Tomorrow Never Knows (the Beatles), with great feedback from people and labels.

Jordi Bel

I've already had the opportunity to cover a few of things that I never thought I'd get away with! I've done a seven minute version of [Tangerine Dream's] *Rubycon Part 1*, and a version of Klaus Schultz's "Bayreuth Return."

Less obviously, I've done a guitar-based cover of Spirit's "Nature's Way"—something way off piste for Black Tempest. Gotta love Fruits de Mers records for giving me the opportunity to release all of these flights of fancy!

Stephen Bradbury

I love lots of Steve Treatment songs, and not only did we get to cover him, he also got in contact with us and now he sends us his new songs which is the reason we started in the first place....

George Roper Noman

Oh, I'd love to record a version of "Frownland" from Trout Mask Replica by Captain Beefheart and His Magic Band.

Well, for one thing, I'd gather some of the most sweetly insane players I know from around the world, and dress everyone up in mental outfits before we went into the studio.

The lyrics and attitude within that song are so compelling and otherworldly that we could really induce an alternate state of mind making such a chaotic rhythm. For extra fun, I'll put a strong ARP Odyssey synth-solo all through the 45 seconds.

Gordon Raphael

I don't know, but I'd avoid any song called "The Power Of Love" (of which I can think of three) or "Come Together" (of which I can think of four) like the plague
Sand Snowman

"I Walk On Gilded Splinters" would be a good project. So many terrific versions have been done, so it would be fascinating to discover what we could do with this incredible song.
Crystal Jacqueline

Whenever we are approached with the idea of covering a song, we would always need to give it a twist, re-interpret it, add a certain Sendelicaness to the pot.

I really enjoyed our pastiche / homage to Pink Floyd with our track "Set The Controls For The Heart Of The Buddha."

I always loved that riff, which is actually based around an eastern scale, so we took it further and made the track almost dub like, and draped it in eastern tinged embroidery, which I think worked really well and took it somewhere new.

Our most recent challenge has been tackling Donna Summers "I Feel Love," which for me is classic Krautrock. It was great to add twists to this iconic classic and take it somewhere very new.
Pete Bingham

I was always excited to work up a version of "Tam Lin."

I knew the Fairport version from way back, and I knew our [Hamer and Anaïs Mitchell] version would be completely different, otherwise we wouldn't have done it.

We made up—bushwhacked—a lot of lines for this one, and the melody sounds pretty original to me, although there's traces of Sandy Denny in there for sure.

I don't think we set out at the beginning to take the fairies out of the story. But at some point we realized we were way more excited about the strange love affair between Janet and Tam Lin than the specific supernatural details of his curse.

I understand that the sub-plot of the Fairie Queen enriches Tam Lin's character with a specific motivation to impregnate the heroine Janet, thereby ensnaring her as a reluctant partner in his only shot at freedom. [But] those details didn't fit into the arc of the song we wanted to sing. People meet, fall in love, get pregnant, and fight it out under strange circumstances, fairies or no fairies.

I love singing this one. It's been the best-received track on the *Child Ballads* record. Although, early on, I gave up reading the on-line commentary; some people were getting pretty hostile!
Jefferson Hamer

It has to be the Pretty Things recording the Beatles' "Helter Skelter" for Fruits de Mer's White EP ("a bit like the *White Album*, only smaller"); check it out, it's bloody immense (it's also on their new box-set retrospective Bouquets from a Cloudy Sky).

I'm still waiting for Todd Rundgren to get in touch to ask if he can record a couple of tracks for the label, and for someone to volunteer to cover something from the LP Touch on Deram from 1969.
Keith Jones

Done it. "Pegasus"—the Hollies… for its quaint Englishness
Marrs Bonfire

"You Enjoy Myself" by Phish, because it would be impossible for any band to cover, and it will never, ever happen.
Pete Meriwether

The first time I heard "Midsummer Night's Scene" by John's Children, I loved it at once. It's a lost classic psychedelic song. Also, I'm a big fan of Marc Bolan, but because his voice is so unique, I wouldn't ever dare sing a song which he has sang. No one has a such voice that he had.

But Andy Ellison sang with John's Children, so now I could sing one of his songs. Which doesn't mean Andy is a bad singer... no! He's a great one. But he doesn't have Marc's voice. And John's Children was a brilliant band!
Jaire Pätäri

I would love to cover "Golden Brown" by the Stranglers. It is one of the best songs I have heard, sounding at once absolutely unique and then also practically effortless, all with the complexities of the harpsichord going on underneath.

The thing that holds me back from doing a cover of it is the fact that the original is perfect, and any cover would be a pale and feeble imitation.
Stephen Stannard

I've recorded a few covers from the past. Out there in the Internet you can find my version of "She Said She Said" (the Beatles) and a literally slavish cover of "Matilda Mother" (early Pink Floyd) and some others.

But the most "successful" effort I made was on the rendering of "The Everso Closely Guarded Lines," an epic and intricate song released in 1989 by Cardiacs.

That was the most challenging recording I ever made; I think it took me a couple of weeks to finish it. That song has always haunted me, because it seems to match perfectly a dream that I made one night.

So, in 2010, I decided that I had to cover it, or I would never get rid of the obsession. The highlights are for sure the presence of a charango (a ten stringed Andean instrument) and of three guitars played with scissors in order to emulate Bill Drake's keyboards.

I also made a video collecting some shootings from the recording sessions and, as I uploaded on Youtube, it ended up in a little triumph in the small community of Cardiacs fans. I was delighted.
Paolo Sala

How about "The Lusty Month of May" from Camelot? A friend of mine just sent me a clip from the film and I thought it would be really fun to work up an arrangement for a folk band.
Jefferson Hamer

We are preparing a Kinks cover: "Where Have All the Good Times Gone?," and we are going to rename it "Where Have All the Good Bands Gone?" Ha ha.
Jordi Bel

Drew Mulholland

Emily Jones

Tell us one amusing / horrifying / interesting story concerned with a live performance… not necessarily onstage, either—getting there, getting home, backstage, suffering the support / headline band, absolutely anything as long as it happened on the road.

I could tell you about the time that three of my backing dancers transformed into horses when we did that gig just outside RAF Fylingdales one October….
Chris Lambert

When I was with Instant Flight, we played the El Canuelo Festival in Spain with Arthur Brown for the second time.

John Povey from Pretty Things agreed to play a song on harmonica with us on the last number. Then to cut the story short, at the end of our set, we were having some wine and John appeared asking me "Marco, do you know where Arthur is?" so I said: "he was here a second ago. I'll go and get him!" then when I reached Arthur, I said to him:"John Povey was looking for you" and there was a pause….

Mr.Brown, contained, relaxed, simply said "Oh yeah! I was supposed to call John on stage….I totally forgot about it!" and, after that, John Povey was nowhere to be seen.
Marco Magnani

Where do you begin? Losing our drummer in Moscow, half way through a Russian tour, and knowing he had no money on him.

Luckily he sold a mobile phone to a passing stranger to buy a train ticket; unluckily the phone was not his, it was his girlfriend's.

Picking up a giant spring that was caught under our car in London and wondering if it was our spring (it turned out it was when, five minutes later, the car collapsed on its wheels).

Fighting Druids at a Stonehenge benefit gig….

Every day is an adventure on the road.
Pete Bingham

Given that most of the music we listen to was made by people who [allegedly] take / took drugs, I suppose it was only reasonable to expect the police to stop our keyboard player's big white Transit van… he had this, as he had a Hammond Organ, two Leslie rotating cabinets and various other synths, then the rest of our gear.

Coming back from a gig at two in the morning, we were driving round the M25 to get home.

We get pulled over by the police.

We have this scenario down to a tee. Papers at the ready—the keyboard player always carried them, as he was getting a "produce" ticket on a weekly basis and was sick of it.

Our patter was always, "Yes sir, no sir, three bags full sir"—simply because we were tired, and wanted to get home. On this occasion, the rest of the band were traveling behind us in the bass player's car.

Stupidly, when we got pulled over, they stopped behind us. The police were giving the keyboard player and myself the third degree—him outside the vehicle, me inside: each being questioned by a different cop. Then they compared notes.

It checked out. They then proceeded to check the tires, headlight beams, everything. I even remember being asked "Do you have receipts for this equipment…."

Then one officer said, "I can smell cannabis!"

"Oh dear," we are thinking…..

"I've just done a course on detecting it" the nice policeman said proudly. Next: pockets turned out, dashboard, seats, mats all turned over. Thankfully, before they made us take all the equipment out the back, the keyboard player said, "You are wearing patchouli oil Mordy."

"That's it," I gleefully said, "Smell my neck officer."

"Hmm, I don't know what the lads at the station would say about that" he replied.

I said "Well you wouldn't want us to think The Force are homophobic, would you?"

"Very well then sir" (he called me sir!").

This, much to his annoyance, was the truth. Then they moved on to our bass player's car. The drummer (wearing sunglasses) opened a window, which let out a cloud of smoke.

"Yes officer?" he says.

"Are you traveling with the vehicle in front sir?"

"Yes officer."

"Very well then, drive safely sir."

I was astounded. The irony being that as well as looking pretty freaky, with smoke billowing from the window, the passengers in the car were carrying varying amounts of hash, ecstasy and probably LSD.

So much for the "Cannabis Detection Course!"

Mordecai Smyth

…or I could tell you about the time that our stage lights were extinguished by giant floating spheres...

Chris Lambert

My first ever gig more or less set the standard for me. I was in a scrappy punk band. We all wore long white hospital coats and silly kid's sunglasses.

My drummer had a massive Plaster of Paris cast on his broken leg, and had to have his hi-hat tied down. The singer got terrified and ran off during the first "song," leaving me to take over the vocals, with no idea what the lyrics were. I hadn't learnt to play guitar by then (this was punk rock !), let alone know what singing was all about.

My amp kept cutting out, and during one frustrated kick, I got my foot stuck in it. The whole thing was eventually abandoned when a mad girl threw herself out of a window (we were playing on the first floor) and had to be taken away in an ambulance. We thought we'd cracked it !

Simon Berry

Thinking "this is it, we're going to die" as the driver we've never met hurtles along country lanes but being too polite to say anything.

Thinking "this is it, we're going to die" as the ferry is tossed around like a old shoe in a night storm in the middle of the Irish Sea.

Thinking "this is it, we're going to die," as the plane hits severe turbulence over the Atlantic.

Chris Anderson

There isn't one story that over-rides all others, but there is a list of experiences which is ever growing, some good, some bad.

Almost getting snowed-in at a promoters house in Leeds after a gig; we had to dig the car out and carefully guide it down the road whilst snow clad statues in the nearby graveyard looked on.

Drinking home-made vodka in the backwoods of Latvia after an amazing house-show.

Playing a home town gig to absolutely no one, not even the sound engineer; the support act went outside to drink the booze they'd brought along, and the barmaid vanished.

The situation was only saved by our friend cycling past the venue, hearing a familiar sound and popping in to see what it was.

A few years ago, we played a family-friendly Sunday afternoon show. The room was full of parents and excitable children waving coloring books. As soon as our set had finished, one small girl who had been watching promptly vomited everywhere and burst into tears.

Richard Thompson

We were playing in a bar in Dubai for three months. The most uplifting time was when we played "Freebird" to the entire ship's company of USS Independence on the eve of their departure on a three month voyage with no shore leave.

We could not hear ourselves for the whooping, whistling and cheering. "If I leave here tomorrow, would you still remember me?"
Crystal Jacqueline

Horryifying : I went to see Budgie at Dudley Town Hall. That night, towards the end of the gig, Burke Shelley the bass player was electrocuted on stage via faulty gear. He had to be rushed to hospital.
Roger Linney

I remember we played a gig in Morecombe during the Icelandic ash cloud drama, watching the setting sun with Ellie and Chris while waiting for our slot. I don't know if the volcanic ash or the adrenaline of waiting to perform made that particular sunset resonant, but I'll not forget it soon.

This was the second gig we performed in our Steampunk 'cos-play' outfits. I remember sweat dripping off me; thick coats, PVC gloves, and stage lights don't make a happy combination. But all in all, very memorable gig.
Mark Reuter

After a dreadful performance at New York City's famed anti-folk haven the Sidewalk Café, I sat down dejected at the bar next to a musician friend of mine from the area.

We knew each other loosely; I'd met him at least once prior. Anyway, the conversation began ordinarily enough, a few generic inquiries from either side about recent shows or common acquaintances.

Then he starts, "I'm just going to address the elephant in the room here," and proceeds to tell me about the time I fucked him over in Nashville (where I was living at the time) when he and his label manager came through to play a house show I set up for them, and I wasn't even there (opting to go to a wedding instead). Not many people were at this house show, it seemed, which resulted in a pretty pitiful outing.

According to him, at least. I somehow had no recollection of the incident whatsoever. I was too embarrassed to confess this fact of course, so I just went along with his story, nodding solemnly and trying to apologize as sincerely as I could for something I didn't even remember doing.

He accepted my apology and offered-up a hug before leaving me there at the bar, where I sat feeling all the more dejected.

Isn't it enough that I fucked him over? Couldn't I have at least had the decency to remember doing it?
Jeb Morris

One night, I had terrible feedback, and not the good kind, from my borrowed mic and was turned down so low that my flute was pretty much inaudible.

Apparently, though I just carried on and tried to work with it, I looked so annoyed that several people in the crowd came up to me afterwards and apologized.

Not for the sound, but because they thought I hated the attendees that much.
Amanda Votta

One of our loveliest gigs with the Owl Service was supporting Martin Carthy at Canterbury, in a lovely Georgian building.

It was very meaningful to be singing songs we got from his repertoire, and from Anne Briggs who he knew, and then to sit and share wine and food with him. A proper gent.
Diana Collier

I could tell you how we rescued an old lady who was lying in the road, and how she then stalked us for the next three years, before one of our number succumbed to her charms and ran off with her to Grimsby... .
Chris Lambert

While I could tell the story of the time I touched an ungrounded microphone, and got a tinge of electrocution (it was horrible), I will flashback all the way to high school, when I was the drummer in a punk band.

As a drummer, you know you are supposed to bring a drum key with you on stage, as any number of things can go wrong. At one particular performance, I neglected to do so, and sure enough, mid-song, my kick pedal loosened, and eventually totally loosened, and the beater flew across the stage.

No one else in the band saw this, and it was close enough to the end of the song that the lack of kick wasn't that noticeable. Anyhow, the second that song ended, I had to run backstage to get the key, and all the while the band is making wisecracks about my sudden disappearance.

Order was restored shortly thereafter, but that taught me a valuable lesson that I still think about every show now—make sure all of the important equipment pieces you may need are with you on stage!
Chris Sherman

One interesting story I could be telling you is about the dinner I had with the lovely Larkin Grimm during an Italian tour in 2007.

I remember, after the soundcheck, the Italian agent brought us to his own home just to relax for a while, before having dinner all together, and then going on stage. He offered us a smoke and we refused instantly.

Instead, he smoked a lot… so, after a little while, he started to feel really bad, and asked me to entertain (what a stupid weird way to speak, don't you think?) Larkin at the restaurant until he was feeling better.

The dinner was fantastic, and Larkin and I had a very long talk about everything—New York City, recording with Mr. Gira, our mutual friend Devendra Banhart, playing on stage, Indians, ancient history etc etc.
Lorenzo Bracaloni

Supporting Blancmange at the Norwich Arts Centre. Just cause it was pretty cool to be invited to do it!
Ellie Coulson

I don't know what year it was; a hot one, one of the World Cup years at Glastonbury. We were due to play at the notorious Lost Vagueness tent at midnight on the Saturday night.

The band I was in played ska / latin Mexican folk songs, the infamous Los Squideros, "probably the best Mexican band to come out of Hereford in the last 100 years."

The gig was running behind schedule, so we waited back stage, the crew keeping us happy with bottles of champagne, and more bottles of champagne and anything else that might keep us awake.

It was about six in the morning when we got on stage, and the place was packed. By this time most of the band were quite merry.

We'd acquired a bigger brass section, inviting Tragic Roundabout to join us. There were around fifteen of us on stage. I was playing mandolin, so I knew I was never going to be heard over three guitars and two or three drummers, so I could relax and mime. It was enjoyable chaos.

During the short soundcheck, our singer had been shouting down the mic (and off mic) that the sound man was shit, and he'd nearly pulled the plug on us.

The bass player and percussionist, two generally quite gentle characters, had been squaring up to each other all through the gig, and off stage were coming to blows. The female singer was pulling punches on the guitarist.

It was a great punk gig, crowd and band going wild. Against all odds, they invited us back the next year.
Sproatly Smith

Getting home from a gig and finding we have been burgled, and someone had taken our *Pet Sounds* box set!
Aaron Hemington

Apart from going off stage to pee against a castle wall in the middle of our long set, during a gig with Italian band Avvoltoi?
Marco Magnani

Last year, we were touring with a poet friend of ours, Gareth, and after one of the gigs we stayed the night at his cottage in this remote North Norfolk village where he lives. We drank rather too much red wine…
Joanna Swan

Nothing unusual there…
Tom Conway

No, but then we decided to listen to some music, and earlier on in the car, Gareth had been humming "Come to the Sabbat" by Black Widow, so I put that on, and we had all my percussion instruments out of the bag, and before we knew it, the whole household, including the cat, was hopping and jumping around the dining room bashing and clanging and rattling and chanting, and it seemed to go on and on for several hours, even though the track is just under five minutes long. It was all rather jolly and primal.
Joanna Swan

We were playing at a club that had a small wooden stage, raised about a foot above floor level. We did a soundcheck and went for a beer.

I'd left my keyboards on stage set up ready to play with, my laptop open on the upper tier of the keyboard stand.

After the support act had finished, we went back to the stage to find my laptop hanging by a USB cable just above the floor. The audience told us the singer of the support act had jumped up and down so much during his set that my laptop had been bounced off the keyboard stand.

We had five minutes before we had to start playing and the laptop was dead, the USB to MIDI cable's plug was bent at a right angle, and the left hand side of the laptop casing was completely warped where the plug had taken the weight of the fall.

I managed to get the laptop to turn on again after the third attempt, and I just bent the plug back into shape through brute force and jammed it back into the socket. Amazingly it all worked and we had a great gig, but the laptop case is still warped and the lid will never close again. After that, I put strips of velcro on the bottom of the laptop!
Chris Bond

Very early on in the history of David Devant and his Spirit Wife, we played at a charity concert in a marquee in a village field.

Some of the local jazzers were not keeping quiet so Dennis (landlord of the pub where we rehearsed), who had driven us there in a tiny sushi van, told them to shut up so "these boys can play," which became our slogan.

At the end of shows, we always finished off going through the audience in pitch black, making spooky chanting noises and holding torches up to our faces. That night, we lifted up the side of the tent and ran with our torches for what felt like miles into the inky blackness of the village green. We ran back and played our encore to rapturous applause.

Mikey Georgeson

Amusing / Embarrassing : I chatted to an American guy at a gig one night. It wasn't until the band came on that I realized I had been talking to Steve Wynn…. Eek.

Roger Linney

Does almost getting shot for blasphemy count? I was on tour with the Dead Flowers in Italy and we were sunbathing on a small grassy hill in Rome. The next thing we know, some guy in jeans and a t-shirt is screaming at us in Italian and then starts waving a handgun about.

There we are, thinking "shit, we are going to die." Turns out they have strict clothing rules in the Vatican, and we had taken our shirts off in sight of the Vatican (over a mile away).

It's a strict no-no, so if the Pope happened to be using his binoculars that day, he may have been offended by our pale English chests.

Andy Hokano

Playing a set at SXSW, which was messy, crazed and great (we thought). Our American big shot manager phoned later in the night to say we'd embarrassed him in front of all his major label cronies by our performance; cancelled the rest of the tour there and then; and sent us home like naughty school kids.

I was relieved—I thought he was going to find and shoot us, such was his anger.

Chris Anderson

My favorite is the time that the band I was playing in nearly had to pull a gig because, an hour before we were due to play, our drummer sliced his hand open on the lid of a can of Heinz spaghetti, whilst putting it in the recycling bin.

That's about as "rock 'n' roll" as my tales get.

Graeme Lockett

I briefly experimented with using a loop pedal, accompanying my acoustic guitar in the vain hope of making the live spectacle of "a bloke sitting on a stool twanging a guitar" vaguely more entertaining.

At a gig in Germany, I had a bad case of nerves and mis-twanged repeatedly; however, where one's mistakes normally dissipate immediately, I had to suffer the indignity of having them loop around each other ad infinitum, with me sitting there trying to make it appear deliberate.

For some time afterwards, my motto was "Never Do Anything In Front Of Anyone Ever Again."
Sand Snowman

During a gig I played with Arthur Brown (it must have been in 2006) this big, middle-aged woman jumped on the stage to dance, while lifting her shirt up and showing her huge tits to all of us.

Arthur was waving at her to come towards me; it was funny, as he clearly didn't want her around, so he was trying to persuade her to bother the others in the band. I think she must have thought she was Stacia from Hawkwind. Or maybe she was, and I didn't recognize her.
Marco Magnani

We [played] with T. Rex… it was the new electric T. Rex, after they had the hit with "Ride a White Swan." There were lots of teeny boppers shouting throughout our set for T. Rex, and Rob shouted back. I liked that.
Roger Wooton

One time, we had a guitar neck broken after the concert; another time we played with the bass amp not sounding at all….

But the funny one was a gig in which we really weren't paid very well; after the concert the promoters wanted us to have a dinner with them. We spent all the money we had earned in that dinner. The funny thing is that the owner of the restaurant was the promoter's brother.
Narsis Passolas

Schizo Fun Addict have been around since 2000, but we've only played about ten gigs. Two of them were as part of a mini tour set up by Shane from Unpeeled magazine in the U.K..

We played the Freebutt in Brighton, and the Hope and Anchor in London (were supposed to do third date in Manchester but it didn't happen).

The Black Tulips were support for both gigs. They were from Brighton, and had a following, so the place was already getting crowded before soundcheck. Totally psyched for this. But we had to use power converters for our effects and... that didn't turn out so good.

Before playing a note, we blew the circuit breakers and the whole club went dark. Looked like it wasn't gonna happen. Stupid Yanks.

Somehow, they got an electrician in and power back, but we had to borrow effects pedals and for a band like us... effects pedal set ups were like religion! We sucked that night. The Black Tulips blew us away.

Jet Wintzer

Accidentally driving to Canada once (not from Ireland, mind).

David Colohan

When playing guitar with Betty and The Id onstage in a pub cellar in Bradford 2007, myself and Jim Smith (currently of the Nightingales) played at such a loudness that at exactly the same time / chord sequence, it seemed as though the room had gone silent.

I remember looking at him, he looked over at me and we both started to pass out with the sheer volume created—very disturbing and we were both deaf for about four days afterwards.

Probably the first experience of a standing wave?

Alan Murphy

Interesting: I have always loved Ben Chasny's music. So I went to see Rangda at the Lumiere in Kilburn. I suddenly realized whilst we were talking that he had really bad body odor.

Roger Linney

I was once in a band with a female vocalist who *Melody Maker* once described as "a diminutive blonde tigress."

Indeed she was a predator: a sexual predator! One of her favorite things to do at a gig was to get off with a handsome victim from the audience, drag him off to the disabled toilet and shag him into the other side of next week.

I wonder if the journalist was one of her "victims," given his description of her?

Mordecai Smyth

The next day, we took care of business, got the effects right, proper power converters. However, we rented a really posh condo on the waterfront in London, had the Black Tulips over for dinner... got drunk and hit terrible traffic into the show, missed the soundcheck and had to play it raw.

A band from Nottingham that I adored agreed to open the show and they were amazing, put us in good spirits. The Black Tulips were again on fire.

But when we hit the stage that night, we destroyed everything in sight and absolutely killed. Tris from The Black Tulips came running up to me after the gig, looked me in the eye and said, "I didn't understand why your band was headlining last night in Brighton... but now I understand."

And we've been friends / collaborators ever since. That one comment made the whole trip worth it because he had won my respect big time with his band.

Jet Wintzer

Back in 1987, I was working at the Scarborough Mod Rally weekend, where I ate a rather exotic cake and decided to go out of the venue for a walk.

Big mistake… walking around the town in a paisley shirt and hipster trousers at lunchtime, taking verbal abuse from the local trendies.

I got completely lost and was gone for hours. I quite by accident was just about to walk past the venue, when one of the Mods saw me and helped me back in. Thank you, who ever you were.

Marrs Bonfire

It happened almost twenty years ago, when I played drums in a grungy, noisy, psychy band called Age. We had a planned gig in Turin in the evening, and a local radio interview in the afternoon to promote the concert.

We departed from Genoa early in the afternoon and felt very confident and optimistic about the night. It ended up in nightmare.

One of the two guitarists started to feel sick during the soundcheck. He had caught a viral gastroenteritis and couldn't stop throwing up.

We were far from home and we phoned the emergency medical service to get some anti-emetic suppositories. Around ten PM our mate finally stated he was unable to get on stage and forfeited.

The rest of the band decided to play anyway, in an improvised three-member line up. But, as we got onstage, we faced an horrifying discovery: the venue (which was quite big) was completely empty.

No one came to see us, despite the promising radio advertising. The concert started anyway, and at a certain point, in the darkness of the hall, we finally seemed to sight an audience of one.

It was our sick guitarist who was feeling a bit better.

Palo Sala

The first thing that comes into mind is when we were on stage and we had a guy named Ylli, who made our lights. Then came the last song and he had a fog machine.

He put so much fog on the stage that I couldn't see even my hands. It felt like I was in some transition state between life and death, because everything I saw was just bright white light, nothing more. And the guitarist and bassist should sing backing vocals, but they couldn't find a mic in that thick fog.

Jaire Pätäri

The Hare and The Moon

Striped Bananas

United Bible Studies were on our way to be Damo Suzuki's backing band in Galway… [when we] noticed a distinct rattling in the car.

We weren't long out of Dublin, and pulled in at a service station where we were shown a back wheel holding on by a solitary worn nut.

Having been informed of how close to death we had come, we all freaked out in our own way, before heading to the gig and playing a blinder.

Solitary Worn Nuts would be a good description of most of those inside the car that day.

David Colohan

In 2011, during one of our first outings as the Striped Bananas, we were without our fab drummer, Andrew. We had arranged for someone to fill in behind Chantelle and I, but the concert ended up being pretty strange and surreal.

I was electrocuted by an acoustic guitar through a microphone that was shorting out. The drummer was literally insane—he was stoned beyond cognition and was swallowing mouthfuls of pills to top it off.

Fortunately, there was another drummer in the audience, who actually came up to the stage and jumped on the second drum kit. We trudged through our set with sundry audience reaction.

Needless to say, we don't play gigs when Andrew isn't available anymore.

Duncan Shepard

We did a gig with the Who, in Liverpool c.1972. In those days, there was almost always just one dressing room for all the bands playing that night. We were already in the room when the Who arrived.

Feeling a bit awkward, we said we'd clear off and leave the room to them. Pete Townshend said "Not at all, guys… you stay here and we'll just use the corridor."

This, incredibly, is what they did, except for Keith Moon. I was walking by in the corridor, when someone opened a small closet to reveal Keith crouched inside, in fetal position!

Fussy bastard, needing his own space like that!

Leo O'Kelly

Seeing Faust on-stage in the early seventies getting loud, explosive electric shocks from their gear (I assumed it was part of the act), walking off-stage, getting booed (we weren't very forgiving in the Midlands in those days), and coming back on to do an amazing acoustic set

Keith Jones

One time in the late 1990s, I think, we had a gig in Middlesborough in the north of England and so some of us traveled down from Edinburgh in a van belonging to one of the other bands who we were playing with.

We soon realized, however, that the van had only one fully functioning gear, which, as it happens, was third gear... and so it was a pretty tortuous, grinding and fairly intense time wondering if we were actually gonna make it not only to the gig, but even round the next roundabout ,or be able to get away successfully at the next set of lights.

We made it, albeit just, stopping a few yards short of the venue and with smoke and flames belching forth from the vehicle's exhaust pipe, ha ha, and so of course some of us had to make alternative arrangements for getting home.

Lenny Helsing

After a show in a town in the middle of nowhere, with almost nobody in attendance, the local promoter took us to his home, a strange flat with ugly paintings and a gas mask placed in front of a picture of his grandmother.

He put on a porn movie and took off his pants: he was wearing a leopard thong.

We quickly pretended we were very tired and we decided to barricade ourselves in our room. The next morning, the mother of the thong guy was there, cleaning the flat and cooking hot dogs for us.

We said goodbye and ran away. This was the strangest way to end a tour ever! A few days after, we were in studio recording "Ego Ritual" for *Dark Tales of Will Z.*, trying to express all the craziness we found on the road.

Will Z

Ah yes. Trader Horne. 1970. Supporting the lovely Richie Havens at the Royal Albert Hall. Now, you may not know this, but backstage is a vast amount of circular corridors with swing doors separating each section.

Picture me wearing a very long-skirted Tudor-style velvet gown, realizing that it was time to go on stage and rushing through the swing doors. Yes. That's right… the train of the dress got caught in one set of the swing doors and rrrrrippp! The back of the dress tore.

Oh well. There was no audience at the back of the stage, and so as long as I stood still, there would be no problem. But in my hurry to plug the electric autoharp in to the amp, I managed to get tangled up in the lead.

So there I was—in the iconic setting of the Royal Albert Hall, in a torn dress and tied up in knots with a lead. I did the set like that. I don't think anyone noticed.

Judy Dyble

Back in the mid 1980s, I formed a covers band. Our first gig was in a wine bar supporting some ropey old soul band. Because it was our first gig, the place was packed, and because it was our first gig, I had a few drinks to steady the nerves.

We went down a storm, and finished our set with a rip roaring version of the Icicle Works' "Understanding Jane."

To add to the excitement, I'd already decided to smash a guitar. However, I hadn't really thought about how I was going to do it. We were playing in a fairly confined space and as I brought the guitar up, it caught the vocal microphone which landed on the nice hard tiled floor a fraction of a second before I brought the guitar down upon it. In my drunken stupor, I didn't notice this and continued to pummel the guitar onto the floor and what remained of the microphone.

There genuinely were shocked faces in the audience, but none more so than that of the sound guy who was left with a very mangled microphone.

Needless to say, our fee for the night went towards paying for his microphone. We didn't care, we'd had a great time and secured another booking to pay for the damage I'd caused at the first.
John Blaney

Here is a tip for any gigging bands (well, it worked for us).

We were often the support band at some nice venues such as the Marquee etc, and lots of gigs on the college circuit. Usually, the headlining band took up most of the soundcheck time, so we were always on the shitty end of the stick, with the PA man / woman rushing us through part of a song and that was our lot.

In order to remedy this situation, you need the PA person on your side, so you need to impress them. We managed this by soundchecking with a Led Zeppelin song—usually, "Misty Mountain Hop" or "The Ocean."

I don't think there is a PA person alive who doesn't like Zeppelin, so if you have a band that can really rock one of their songs, it is a sure fire way to get the PA person on your side and win a bit more time and get a much better sound.
Mordecai Smyth

My dad came to see me play at a cafe in Cincinnati once. I was doing a vocal exercise before my set and I guess he couldn't make out what was going on, so he walked up and said, "Are you fuckin' around with drugs?!"

Aside from that, he's been very supportive of the whole music thing.
Jeb Morris

Because we are just two people and there's a lot of instrumentation on our recordings, we don't play live so often. So we haven't the usual set of bizarre tour stories. Our stories are mostly based on loud sounds that hide our "delicate and sensible" music. It could be everything from a soundchecking hardcore band at an outdoor festival, to the opening act's drunk and loudly talking friends.

But one story that happened before the Us and Them days that I like is this one.

The band I played in at the time were out and playing in towns in the south of Sweden. We did the gig, and then we borrowed an apartment where we slept. Around eight clock in the morning, I woke up and saw that our bass player wasn't in his bed.

I woke up the others, and we wondered where he could have gone. We went out and looked for him with no result. Then we went to the place where we played last night to pick up our instruments.

There, on the stage floor, we found our bass player sleeping. He had managed to climb into a small window, placed so high up that we didn't understood how he did it. He couldn't remember why he left a cozy bed to go out in the middle of the night, climb into a window and sleep on the stage. It must been a sign of love for the performance. Probably something symbolic, and very deep.

Anders Håkanson

....looking out and seeing the motionless line of dim figures, just visible on the edge of the pool of light spilling out onto the very empty looking dance floor in front of the stage, staring out at them, willing them to move…

…and then a very sharply dressed young gentleman burst through the line, bounded to the front, dropping onto his hands as if about to do a press up, springing himself back to his feet, into a fantastic series of dance moves…

…the motionless line breaks like a landslide, becoming a wave, crashing and breaking into the front of the stage… in a second, the pool of light is full of whirling, leaping bodies… it was a magical moment….

Tom Woodger

TSROS did a trio tour in August of 2011, and we weren't able to book anything in D.C., although we had a great turnout there a few years earlier at the Electric Possible.

They had been blown away because it was a monthly improv night, and we brought out about a dozen kids, mostly girls.

But that didn't lead to any club gigs, so we booked a show at the 14th St. Cafe where they were starting up a weekly band series.

We got there, and there was no stage, no PA system and nowhere to set up drums. We decided to improvise an acoustic set and brought in a guitar and bass. We squeezed into a corner and started playing, but no one paid any attention and everyone talked loudly during our entire set.

I started singing stupid stuff to crack Jacob and Jeremy up, before giving up on singing altogether. On the way out, a lady said that she enjoyed the set and we laughed. We went out to our van and there was a parking ticket on it.

But, on the bright side, we walked around before our set and went into a record store and met Kid Congo Powers!

Ted Selke

One time in the mid-1990s, Mooch were playing a tiny gig at a venue in Cambridge. It poured down with rain and almost nobody turned up; the dressing rooms stank of urine and we got paid virtually nothing.

But the worst eventuality related to Cal Lewin's bass synth, which I suspect damaged the PA—he was an expert at getting those sub-bass parts, was Cal…

Steve Palmer

The Brighton gig, when my bass refused to work and I had to replace it with our gig mates'. The strap was so long, it was practically to my knees. Pretty comical.

Jayne Gabriel

When I was in a band with my brother Andy and sister Lisa in about 2007, we supported a band who I won't mention.

It was at a dive in Leeds, but because Mark Lamar had played them that week on his show, they were jumped up and arrogant to the point of not wanting to even look at us, never mind talk to us.

They demanded the abandoned bog out back be converted into a dressing room, so they could seemingly cool off and not get hassled by the twenty people who'd come along to see them, half of whom were members of my family there to see us.

They were horrible to the bar staff too. I really hope they haven't made it, because if they were arrogant then, in a wee wee stained hell hole, what would they be like if loads of people were gushing and fussing over them?

They demanded that a pizza be delivered to them too, very rock 'n' roll. While we were playing our set, the guitarist of the band came out, stood behind us and started tweaking with his amp.

We stopped the song and me and my brother called him various names rather loudly, before carrying on. He scurried off sheepishly. This kind of thing just put me off doing gigs; that's partly why I keep Dodson & Fogg as a recording project.

After we played our set, I went in to see the "stars," and was delighted to see the five or so people who'd bothered to stay and watch them them all chatting to each other. There were more members of the band than there were punters!
Chris Wade

Or I could tell you how un-rock and roll I am. I work full time and then did a gig in Brighton. We had a lock in, and were asked to play past 11.30pm. I tried to do another two songs, but was too sleepy, so my band mate's girlfriend took over and I fell asleep in the bay window.
Chris Lambert

When you are start out in a band, especially in a very non-musical area (in this case East Devon), at a very non-musical time (mid-noughties), you end up playing some very crappy pubs to hugely non-sympathetic / oblivious drinkers, doubly so if you play original material.

At that time, there was a very small pool of pubs that put on original bands (they much preferred Karaoke or Celine Dion or Shania Twain tribute bands).

At one pub we badgered into letting us play, we were made painfully aware on the night that we were taking up prime drinking space, as we were crammed up against the punters. In a tuning lull between songs, a drinker edged into us for more arm room and said to his friend "Band's a bit shitty tonight."

This got picked up on the vocal mic and through the speakers. He got the only cheer of the night. I would have been more miffed if he hadn't have made such an extremely valid and piquant observation.
Stephen Stannard

I used to own a great big purse, shaped like a ladybird. Once, at a gig, the organizers gave us chocolate cake before we played. I was too nervous to eat my slice, so went up on stage, leaving it with my friends. Whilst I was playing, my very kind friends had an idea for a lovely surprise for me.

They knew I really liked snails (who doesn't?), so they secretly shaped my slice into a perfect model of a snail, with feelers and everything, and placed it carefully in my purse, with a napkin around it so that it wouldn't get damaged. After the gig, we packed up in a hurry and I roughly threw my purse in my bag without opening it.

It was only later, when we stopped at an all night garage for pasties, that I dragged out my purse from the bottom of the bag, where it had been sitting under lots of heavy stuff. I got to the counter and opened the giant ladybird to pay, stuck my hand in, and drew out a brown curled gooey thing that looked exactly like a lump of dog chod. The garage attendant's jaw literally dropped.
Emily Jones

Fruits de Mer
the sleeves that didn't quite make it
(early designs and rejected ideas)

(7 and 7 is)

new and classic psychedelia,
krautrock, acid-folk, spacerock,
progressive rock, kosmische sounds
and more ...on vinyl
www.fruitsdemerrecords.com

Fruits de Mer
the sleeves that didn't quite make it
(early designs and rejected ideas)

('7 and 7 is')

new and classic psychedelia,
krautrock, acid-folk, spacerock,
progressive rock, kosmische sounds
and more ...on vinyl
www.fruitsdemerrecords.com

Above: Rejected Fruits de Mer album sleeves.
Below: Early Fruits de Mer single sleeves

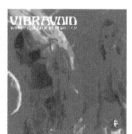

Above: Rejected Crystal Jacqueline artwork.
Below: Ivan Ivanovich and The Iron Curtain single.

Above: Green ?uestion Mark EP.
Below: Rejected Octopus Syng label artwork.

Seventh Ring of Saturn

Grandpa Egg

Mooch

Icarus Peel

I remember traveling to a gig when I played in a Scottish band called Brouhaha. I think there was a fight between a couple of friends, and one of them was thrown out of the van. Then the van broke down.

When we finally got to the old 101 Club in Clapham, the guitarist Bill had such a bad case of stage fright he went stiff as a board. We had to carry him on stage and sit him on a chair...
Stephen Bradbury

It was two years ago, when we were going to Germany to play in the psychedelic festival Stoned Karma, organized by the great band Vibravoid.

We were getting there via Switzerland, just to see my brother who lived there. Irra, our keyboardist, were rolling a joint and thirty minutes later, we arrived at the German border.

I don't why, but our van is a magnet for policemen (maybe because it is totally wrecked?) and all of a sudden, a policeman put his head inside the van from my window and said something like "it smells like...."

They made us put the van in a special garage and two policemen started to search all our objects and instruments looking for more drugs, but Irra told us we weren't carrying anything.

When they finished searching our things, I suggested that we were going to be late at the festival, and then they told us that that they wanted to search all of us, one by one.

They made us get naked. I went first, one by one , and Irra was the last. He has never told us what exactly happened inside the box. We spent more than an hour at the border, but we got to the fest and it was superb.

And yes, Irra lied to us, and we were bringing more drugs...
Jordi Bel

Mellow Candle played at Durham University, driving up there in cramped conditions in a transit van. Genesis were the main attraction. I think we went out to peek at them from afar, but spent most of the time engaged in "other activities" in some kind of green room area. While we were packing up the gear afterwards, a catering van nearby was stacking up crates of booze, getting ready to depart.

While the guys were inside, they left the van with the doors open and I think the lads nipped in and robbed a few bottles for our return journey.

I've only ever flirted with hard liquor, but we gave it a good go on the road back to London. Then Frank came down with some ghastly stomach bug and a lot of vomiting went on, not all of it due to his gastric problem.

I suffer from emetophobia (fear of vomiting) so being squashed at interludes in the back and having to stop to let Frank out onto the side of the road was absolutely no fun at all.
Alison O'Donnell

The first time we played Cameo Gallery in Williamsburg was a disaster. The sound guy didn't show that day, so someone was filling in on the fly, and while we were playing, everything on stage started feeding back. At first we just kept going, but the feedback got so bad that Pete had to get up and leave the stage.

The song we were playing is the one and only song I have ever written, and after the feedback stopped, we just scrapped it and moved on with the set. As soon as we got off stage, I ran outside and proceeded to cry my eyes out saying it was "the worst show I had ever played."

If that wasn't melodramatic enough, the same night, a woman who was dating my friend began planting seeds (i.e. lies) of what would turn into a huge fight between me and my boyfriend.

This was the first of many red flags about her, and we found out later that she was a coke head and just an all around bad person. I wasn't too surprised to hear a few years later that she was in rehab and had to call my friend to apologize as part of her recovery.

Leah Cinnamon

I had a band in London called Black Light (circa 2004). The Strokes were kind enough to get us an opening slot at V-Festival. Like, my life's dream… they were so kind to do that.

It was the end of a four year marijuana relapse, and I was really dwelling up in my mind. I had this twenty year old guy from Liverpool named Paul "helping me out" with my Shoplifter Record label, and ha ha ha, managing things.

Well, through a combination of my obliterated sense of distorted reality, and his management skills, we arrived at the festival exactly when our stage time was meant to begin, and were slowly driving through the parking lot hell for the duration.

It was one of the tuning points that got me off drugs finally. That, and losing my record label after only one release.

Gordon Raphael

We were once playing at Nero's Club in Okehampton. It was just after the first Gulf War and 200 paratroopers / commandoes were allowed a night out from the army camp to let off steam. At one point, the crowd parted to reveal two of their number bollock-naked dancing to Crystal Jacqueline's soaring singing.

She stared straight at them with glacial disdain; they stared back through laughing beer glass goggles, and the moment passed. An old, fat, local bouncer surveyed the heaving muscular throng and whispered to me that any trouble he would sort out. I had already sorted out my quickest route to the fire exit.

Icarus Peel

We went to London to play in the Fruits de Mer gig at Borderline with The Pretty Things and, despite warning Irra not to carry anything, he told us in the middle of the motorway in France that he had forgotten to throw away a bit of hash he had on his luggage.

Thirty minutes after that reflection, a French policeman on a very big motorcycle made us stop on one side of the motorway. A van with more policemen and dogs came to us.

We were definitely going to kill Irra, but the dog had a cold that day.

Jordi Bel

The weirdest performance I have been involved in was The Watchman, which was a culmination of two years tinkering with drone and loops. The piece was a mix of music and theatre.

We decked the room out in builders polythene (so it looked a little like a Dexter kill room), then we filled it with sound making objects.

The audience of about ten at a time would enter and would fiddle with these objects, which would result in either an actor performing something or a musical cue. These things would then combine and run over each other, depending on what the audience touched next. It was about the apocalypse and was as confusing as the audience made it...

Chris Lambert

We have vague memories, that we complement among ourselves, of playing in a festival inside a castle, north of Portugal, an instrumental concert with short movies being projected while we played, a constant flow of flashing lights, sound echoing from the walls, a kind of cosmic jazz being produced on stage, total chaos in the backstage and at the end of the night, we got lost in the woods on our way to the hotel. Fortunately, one of us was able to find the way….

Beautify Junkyards

One day in the late eighties, I was in the South of France, where I come from. I was rather deranged on a daily basis, but I gathered a band together to play mostly whatever I had in mind, and whenever, and I guess they were calling me a Hitler sort of guy for some reasons, (but none political).

Also, I messed up with a chick and became rather unpopular …. I found us a gig somewhere in the nowhere, but some haters and that chick's arse-lickers teamed up to boycott me and my band. We played three songs for an audience of two, then I sent it all to fuck.

The owner got mad, of course, so we finally played for a pizza each, and then we were thrown out on the road at night with our gear. We managed to get back to where we came from, and I really don't remember how. At that point, I could feel somehow fragile, and very upset. Never cheat.

Francois Sky

We were chased out of a frat party once, because they hated us so much. They were booing us and yelling "you suck!" during our whole set. So, as a joke, we started Michael Jackson's "Beat It."

The frat guys flipped out and started cheering. But then we started singing Weird Al's "Eat It" instead.

That was the last straw: the frat guys threatened us with physical violence, and pulled our power from the sockets. We packed up and got out of there fast. Fortunately, we found the guy who booked us passed out on a couch with a pizza all over him, and he had a wad of cash for us, which we took… and drove fast.

Pete Meriwether

The Luck of Eden Hall was in London. We arrived at the gig a bit later than we were supposed to, so we didn't have time to check in to our hotel until after the evening's performance.

We were in Soho, and it took quite a while to make it through the throngs of people and traffic to our hotel, so when we arrived, a couple of the boys put down their luggage and started playing frisbee to blow off some steam.

We all checked in, and some decided to go out to celebrate until the wee hours. Upon returning, it was discovered that one of our troopers had left their luggage out on the sidewalk in front of the hotel after tossing the frisbee, and never brought it in. The suitcase was long gone. A pain in the ass for sure, but not such a big deal, unless your passport happens to be in that suitcase.

In the morning, we called the front desk, who in turn called the police. And to our luck the police, I assume in bomb squad attire, had taken the luggage from the sidewalk. To our surprise, they kindly offered to bring it back to the hotel. Everything intact. I was completely impressed by this act of kindness. If that happened in Chicago, the luggage would have been history.

Gregory Curvey

We were playing in France, and thought it'd be a friendly gesture to learn some French songs. My autoharp and I played Serge [Gainsbourg]'s "La Javanese," and the entire audience joined in the chorus. It was just so moving, my eyes filled up with tears.

Angeline Morrison

Well, it didn't start off too well. Four days before the show, our long term bassist informed us that he was leaving the band and wouldn't be playing the gig.

As this was on December 23, and the gig was on the 27, we really didn't have the time to look for a replacement and saying the bass at the time was our lead instrument only made things worse. Plus, he was the only member of the band who could drive, which only added to the problem.

But being either stupid or carried away by the gung-ho spirit of "the show must go on," we thought we could work around these problems. So we decided to meet up at Ant Bordello's house early on the afternoon of the gig, to rearrange our set as we no longer had the bass.

We were forgetting that Ant has his legendary boxing night parties, so turning up at four in the afternoon to rehearse, we find Ant not hung over, but totally pissed.

The party had only just finished, and he had been up for nearly twenty hours, drinking. But again, foolishly or in the gung-ho spirit, we thought "well, we can work around this; we will just pretend he isn't pissed and work on through this, no problem."

This proved more difficult than first imagined, as Ant opened another bottle (vodka, this time). He then poured some into the glass. knocking it back in one go and throwing the glass over his head to smash, and said "that's better," while falling into a chair.

At this point, I suggested maybe we could do this gig without Ant, but Ant would not have this. But as this was going on, Dan decided that if it was alright for Gary our ex-bassist to leave four days before the gig, and it was alright for Ant to not even be on the same planet as the rest of us, then it was okay for him to swap from playing keyboards to playing violin (although he couldn't actually play violin) at the gig.

Getting carried away, again, with the gung-ho spirit, we decided this might work, and it would also mean we could just walk to the gig, and not bother with the black taxi we planned, as it was only a fifteen minute walk. Plus the coldness of the outside world might bring Ant back to planet Earth.

So, with Ant now in his stage gear (a very loud Hawaiian shirt which he was very pleased with), and refusing to wear a coat although it was actually minus two outside, in case he creased his shirt (even when totally pissed he was conscious of his status as fashion icon), the journey started—me with my semi acoustic, Dan with his violin and Ant with his loud Hawaian shirt and his small bongo drum hanging around his neck on a piece of lace.

We were right about the fresh air revitalizing Ant, as he set off running down the street in a strange… what can only be described as a Cossack manner, but lifting his knees up as close to his chin as he could manage, not even stopping when he got to the busy road and carried on in the gung-ho spirit which we now getting a little tired of, with the cars swerving to avoid the bongo necked vision in green.

We caught up with him and managed to slow him down, reasoning with him that we didn't want to get there too early, and we needed him and his bongo in one piece. But as this was happening, Ant spotted that Mass had finished and people were beginning to leave a nearby church, so he thought it would liven up proceedings for them if he pretended to be an aeroplane.

He ran through the throngs of Christians, arms outstretched making neee-owwww and mmmmmmuum and other plane noises, with the odd "Roger, Roger, God is in my sights" comment, and the flight continued until we reached the venue.

Entering the venue, we thought it would be a good idea if Dan smuggled him as quietly as possible to the back, while I introduced myself to the soundman.

Reaching the back of the room, Ant put his feet up and fell fast asleep, while I was explaining that we no longer needed the D.I. for the keyboards, as the keyboardist was now playing violin.

Suddenly, the sound of what sounded like a pig in a bad mood started to emerge from the back of the room; actually it was Ant, now in full snoring mode.

"At least the room has good acoustics," I said to the sound guy as I excused myself.

After about twenty minutes fine sleep, Ant awoke with the immortal quote that has passed down into Bordellos legend and is used at every opportunity—"have we soundchecked yet?"

The night was only young and, believe me, it got a whole lot stranger.

Brian Bordello

The Rendezvous gig mentioned above has got to be a winner: it did include Ant dancing around and pointing at my dad's face in a weird pixie manner, and singing a medley of Frank Sinatra songs in Bob Dylan's voice, which was eerily prescient given what Bob Dylan's gone and released. Some would call him a visionary, I'd just say he was pissed: all roads lead back to Jhonn Balance.

I also played a Longdrone Flowers gig where we didn't play, as an Irish folk band simply refused to get off the stage and played for four hours. They were still going when we left. Again, pissheads.

Dan Bordello

Just recently my folk duo performed an entire set singing into the wrong side of a large-diaphragm condenser microphone. The sound person never said anything, we had no monitors on stage, and the room was a black box theater so the audience could sort of hear us. A couple of people commented afterwards that it "could have been a little louder."

Jefferson Hamer

We did a gig with Hawkwind at the Brixton Academy, and came on stage looking like a Persil advert. We were all wearing white jeans and white Moroccan embroidered shirts (don't ask me why, we thought it was cool at the time).

When we walked on stage we could hear an audible groan, and thought "this ain't gonna be a very good gig." Anyway, the first song we did was a cover of "Soul Kitchen" by The Doors, and we won them over and got to keep our clothes Persil white.

Dave McLean

Schizo Fun Addict

Judy Dyble, 1964

Chris Lambert and Kev Oyston

Army of Mice

CHAPTER SEVEN

And more of the same, please, about the studio… recording mishaps or triumphs

Since I didn't speak for the first seven years in the band for spiritual reasons, recording and getting my thoughts out was pretty frustrating and taxing. Definitely puts life in perspective. We take a lot of things for granted in this world.
Jayne Gabriel

I rarely go to recording studios. On the rare occasions I've visited them, I have found them to be rather shabby places run by ego maniacs, who insist on telling you that what you want can't be done, despite you knowing full well it can.
John Blaney

When recording for *Ronco Revival Sounds*, Ant Bordello behaved oddly, to say the least. He asked questions including "Can I not just sing, and you do the music later?," and went through a phase of silently handing McDonald's chicken burgers out during recording.

We were often banished to the kitchen when he was recording his contributions, usually prefaced with "You bastards go in the kitchen and stop fucking laughing."

His contributions included a strangely hypnotic repetition of the phrase "Nurse the Screens" ("Nurse The Screens"), horse noises ("Ronco Revival Sound") and a slow motion rant about beach holidays as a child ("Move Sideways," not featured).

One track had to be removed from consideration due to him walking in, putting shopping bags down loudly and coughing into the sink in the background; he has a talent for being quiet until the time you're actually recording, at which point he will, without exception, make an unholy racket.
Dan Bordello

I like the Black Sabbath story of when they were recording the *Born Again* album. The door was open in the studio and the local vicar came in and asked them if they could "turn it down a little please, it's a bit loud."
Roger Linney

Nearly everything I do when recording is a mishap that happens to turn out well for what I'm doing at the time. Or so I tell myself.
Amanda Votta

Only once have I ever thought my fingers were going to bleed; that one time was while recording a song during the *Her Dawn Wardrobe* sessions that ultimately never made it to the album. I think that was in the same session that Chris accidentally deleted an entire song we had just finished recording….
Leah Cinnamon

I once went to Radio One to record a song and an interview with their news beat team. I remember sitting in the darkness of the studio and seeing The Professor (Rimschott the drummer) in the control room, and waving.

I had done a bit of press before but was totally unprepared for the interviewer (Mathew Bannister?) going on and on about what my real name was. In the band I am The Vessel, and it seemed completely normal to refuse to discuss or reveal my real name.

It was not relevant and I felt that revealing it on air would have been a betrayal of the allegiance to outsider reverie and wonder the band represented. They were not happy not to get their scoop.
Mikey Georgeson… oops! The Vessel

Just managing to get anything finished feels like a triumph, and as a lot of our records are home-recorded, there are always a lot of minor disasters, but rarely any anecdote worth noting.

When you're recording in your bedroom, wearing a dressing gown and drinking endless cups of tea, nothing untoward is likely to happen, plus major errors are purely on your own head. The worst that can happen is that your computer crashes, losing the files you were working on.
Richard Thompson

When we got back together in 2008, we hired in an original 1960s Farfisa organ and were so excited, but when we plugged it in, it sounded like a demented mosquito on acid, with the same audio frequencies to boot and no, that wasn't the sound we were looking for.

Can't beat the original gear eh?
Dave McLean

Recording can be a stressful experience, as all your wonderful creations are suddenly put under the microscope.

Timing becomes critical, tuning imperative and a whole world of other things. I remember a first session with a new bass player, where we are putting down backing tracks live.

We get half way through the first number and he makes a mistake. The next thing I see is his bass guitar flying through the air and smashing against the wall! I'm thinking, "What should I do? Carry on, or stop?"
Mordecai Smyth

After a long recording session at a friend's studio, I somehow managed to get a tape machine to turn about twelve inches of tape into a four-foot piece of plastic string. I'm sure there must be some sort of failsafe on the multitrack to prevent this from happening, but I hit rewind and, when it got to the start of the tape, one reel kept spinning like a flywheel whilst the other, with the end of the tape still attached, stopped dead, resulting in the tape between the two reels being stretched to a thin thread before it snapped.

We rethreaded the machine and found we'd left just enough blank space on the beginning of the tape so that the song started just after the stretched section. We spliced on a new bit of leader tape and were able to carry on. Disaster narrowly averted!

Chris Bond

Recording is always in Mr Collins' kitchen, and we are usually interrupted by warring pets. They have no respect.

Diana Collier

All bands have that story in the recording studio of the incredible and unrepeatable moment of magic / inspiration which made everyone's jaws drop as it went down to tape. The warm glow emanating from the hearts of those present and the shivers down the spine when that undefinable thing of wondrousness occurred.

Then you discover the 'Record' button had not been pressed and spend the rest of the day unsuccessfully trying to recapture it all. In our case, the part was indeed recorded, but the engineer later erased it when recording something else over it, the bastard.

Chris Anderson

Due to the highly technical nature of my recording set up, and my vast knowledge of the intricacies of making music, there are several unintentional noises scattered throughout the Hare And The Moon's songs.

During a lull in one of our quieter, more delicate numbers, you can clearly hear the sound of the scrapyard near my flat (all recording had to be abandoned on occasion, until the yard workers went on tea break, when it would then furiously resume). It's really a case of what hasn't happened.

Entire songs have been erased by accident, tears have been shed and sweary words sworn. Being the musician, mixer and producer does mean often emerging blinking into sunlight after several hours in a dark recording "cupboard," with hair askew and wild eyes. I'll bet that never happens to Prince.

Grey Malkin

Recording is a cooperative process, but sometimes it amounts to who happens to be in the studio. When we got to *7 & 7 Is*, and "5D (Fifth Dimension)" I decided to be the one on hand to conduct an experiment in psychedelia.

Tom Cabrera, another high school bandmate, was again called upon for Indian percussion, in the form of tablas, doumbek and zils. Lanny provided electric sitar and tamboura.

It was magical, it was mystical, but it needed something. And I knew what it was. I found it in a bookstore, Bhagavad Gita: A New Translation, by Stephen Mitchell.

I brought it to practice and threw it at faithful drummer Bill Intemann.

The response was a "No" that was somewhat lacking in drama. As mentioned, we all went to different schools together, and I knew Bill had greasepaint on his soles if not in his blood. He was great when the curtains opened, if only because his natural voice is a theatrical one. Nothing seemed forced. He even took the calling to college, before eventually realizing this was a stage he would not be going through.

Still, even though he was just what we needed, he flatly refused. He would not even look at the nice new book.

When we to the studio the following week, I picked up the volume and took it along as an afterthought.

Then we reached the space for the solo. I pulled the book out of my bag.

"I already said 'No.'"

"Just look at it."

"No."

It was my turn to get theatrical. I worked myself up, put a catch in my voice. This was my role.

"I think we know it needs something. This could be it. Look, I tracked down the book, I bought it, I brought it here tonight."

Pause. Drama builds. And then …

"What do you want me to read?"

I hadn't thought of that, not carefully. But I knew it got better as it went along, like any good play.

I looked at the second to last chapter, talk of "man's higher (and lower) nature." This was the stuff.

"Right here," I said, handing over the open book.

He quickly read it over. Looked up, down and then over to engineer and Tiki Studios owner Fred Guarino.

"Let's go."

One minute later, he was ending with "I am the sacred syllable om in the Vedas … the sound in the air."

It was perfect. One take. We cheered and howled. It was stunning.

"How did you do that?"

"I looked at the passage, figured out how many words would fit and read them."

Take a bow.

It was amazing and maybe a little mystical. It prompted more ideas and angles. It made the track, and the project.

Bill Sweeney

When I was in Instant Flight, we recorded the *Colours and Lights* album in the studio of Gary Ramon (Sundial) in Hastings. We were often doing two days in a row, then nothing for a few days, then back to the studio the weekend after.

Our keyboardist Lucie Rejchrtova had a Casio keyboard, which we used to record a song with the mellotron string sound. Before leaving the studio a week before, we recorded a track with the Mellotron imitation sound from the Casio and one with the real Mellotron from Gary studio.

The idea was to then delete the track with the imitation sound, and use the track with the real one, but it took Gary and us a bit of time to figure out which was which. Eventually we realized the real Mellotron sound was the one with that distinctive clipping sound at the start of every note.

So, never judge cheap keyboards too harshly for expensive ones. But the real triumph for us on that album was to have Arthur Brown singing on "Freeway," as he originally agreed just to get there to sing "Kites," which he did, so it was definitely a super-plus to have him on two songs instead of one.

Marco Magnani

All my "proper" studio recordings have been a bit disappointing, probably due to the fact that I'm a belligerent egomaniac and I've always had to compromise when it comes to the involvement of other human beings. I've recorded all my current albums on a little box in the corner of my bedroom, using battered, old, half-broken instruments, Sellotape and Blu Tack, and naïve optimism.

Simon Berry

My major studio disaster has to be doing a live recording for the BBC. I was using my rather temperamental Mini Moog.

We soundchecked, and then went off for food, arriving back just before we went live, at which point the sound engineer came up to me and said "I hope you don't mind, but I had a quick go on your Moog."

I could have killed him there and then. With a ten second count down, and this guy has rearranged all the dials; so instead of a perfect anologue sweep to the start the set, the world's most horrendous squelchy bass fart was broadcast to the nation.

Not my finest hour.

Andy Hokano

We are lucky enough to have Chris' home studio at our disposal, and I love recording random stuff. I remember throwing a Ping-Pong ball at my acoustic guitar, and recording that.

The recordings of me scribbling on paper made for an interesting percussion instrument. These subtle touches often get a bit hidden in the final mix, but we know they're there.

If I'm in someone's kitchen, I tend to go around picking everything up and flicking it to see what sound it makes. I even monitored the pitch of the work microwave with my tuner; it microwaves at a steady Ab.

Mark Reuter

We were at the now defunct Seagrape Studio in Chicago, recording tracks for *Belladonna Marmalade*. Our cellist, Eric Remschneider, had finished up his parts, and went out to his car to discover someone had crashed into it, smashing the back.

I felt bad, but there wasn't really anything I could do about it, and at least his cello wasn't in the trunk.

Right after that, he went on tour with Smashing Pumpkins and we never played together again. Hmmm, I wonder....

Gregory Curvey

The band from Texas sounded insanely great in the demo they sent me. Only after I got a week into the project—the day vocals were to begin—did I get to know the truth: the singer had no sense of pitch!

His melodies were as complicated as opera, I kid you not—yet each note was not even in the same neighborhood as the ones he was intending to hit. I was so furious, because [it transpired that] the engineer had painfully and meticulously auto-tuned each note of the demo into place!

The same engineer was on this job too, and I swore at him and said "goddammit, if that's what you did on the demo, you are gonna do it on every song now, cos I have not the patience nor interest to fine-tweeze vocal notes! Fuck that!."

For a week, eight hours a day, I had to hear that singer singing every note off key, while I lectured his band in the control room about this nonsense, and blatantly looked at music gear on ebay to sooth my frazzled nerves.

Gordon Raphael

Everything I do is by total fluke, or I've just expanded further on a mishap.

Kev Oyston

We record in a friend's home studio so it's all very civilized, but we do have to halt proceedings whenever anyone uses the toilet, and wait for the cistern to fill, because otherwise the noise of that gets picked up on the recording.
Joanna Swan

Ditto the central heating. We recorded *CunningFolk* in January / February 2013—and that turned out to be a slight error of judgement, because it was a particularly cold winter, and we couldn't have the radiators on because of the noise from the pipes!
Tom Conway

It was worth it. If someone's recording you because they personally love your music, rather than because they're a company employee, you know they're going to do right by you.
Joanna Swan

I'm always pretty triumphant when I manage to double or triple my vocals successfully, and when I record multiple parts of harmonies. Getting everything tight and fitting together feels incredibly satisfying every time!
Ellie Coulson

I usually do my own recordings. Once I went to a studio, smoked pot and drank with the guys, made some takes and then sent them to screw themselves up because their work was shit and I really hate wasting my time with pretentious wankers.

Now I'm pot free and mostly sober.
Francois Sky

Recording a Mellotron through a fuzz pedal, and the pedal breaking as a result
Aaron Hemington

I had a band up until 2003, and we usually recorded stuff in studios around here [Tuscany]. But I never had fun (only once during our nine years story) recording in these studios, where you have to work with sound engineers and producers who refuse to practice / do what you ask 'em about the sound you want; and who don't have a various and valid musical background beyond musical taste.

So, they cannot satisfy the simplest request: "Can you put this guitar phrase on the left speaker, editing it with a resonant delay?."

It sounds stupid but it has happened to me. Sound engineers in the nineties here in Tuscany were terrible… because most of 'em came from the indie-punk scene.
Lorenzo Bracaloni

When I was about twenty-one, the band I was playing with went to a studio in Reading to record a demo. We needed an intro for a song and found an old piano. I couldn't play very well, but I knew where the notes were, so I suggested to my bandmates that it might sound a bit like the intro to "Melody Lee" by the Damned.

It did, sort of—I was quite pleased with how it came out, as were most of the others. Only trouble was, when we went back a couple of weeks later to mix it, the studio gave us a different engineer who thought it was shit, wheeled out an electronic keyboard and overdubbed the thing with his own take on it, featuring ghastly lush strings like he was making a Whitney Houston record or something.

Rather than tell him to fuck off, we gave him a credit on the tape!
Graeme Lockett

Not so much a mishap, more of an oops. Pink Floyd, I believe, had been recording at Sound Techniques before Fairport Convention had their turn.

We were recording "Portfolio," the little piano riff ending up in another free for all, and I was playing the piano.

Unfortunately, it hadn't been tuned since the Floyd finished their session, so the last few notes were horribly off key.
Judy Dyble

My favorite story was going to Phil Manzenera's uber-studio and entering the inner sanctum to try on his famous diamante bug-eye sunglasses.

I felt then that I had achieved everything I needed to.
Mikey Georgeson

We've never been into a proper studio. Starting off in the spare room in my tiny house, we moved from one warehouse / joinery workshop to the next, to record and practice. Nowadays we have a space in an old attic niteclub, which hopefully we'll keep for a few years.

The last place was a derelict workshop in an empty shopping mews. We put up some double doors in the corner, and shut ourselves in; there were no windows. Wallpapering the breeze blocks didn't make it much prettier; it was a damp, dark place, uninspiring, but okay for practicing.

One day I opened the doors and the ceiling had dropped over all our kit, dust and plaster everywhere. Apparently some homeless people had lit a fire outside, and the fire service had sprayed all over our roof. It was cheap rent, mind.

Sproatly Smith

I used to play in a psych-folk band called Betty Rats. While recording our second album, we brought along a can of Heinz Spotted Dick and, when the recording sessions were over, we celebrated by getting drunk and eating Spotted Dick. It was... hilarious.

Jeb Morris

Not really a studio story as such, but I once spent twelve hours 100 feet underground in an abandoned nuclear command bunker, and recorded an album influenced by the place.

Drew Mulholland

I particularly enjoyed making *The Spirit of Saint Mary*, which was a collection of field recordings around Saint Mary's Minster in Reading.

I recorded and slowed the sound of beer pouring at the local pub, until it revealed its separate musical notes. I looped a photocopier and a crashing market trolley to give a beat.

But all of this was played back by the church itself; the Lusum Magnetite in the stones reacting to the damp October night played back sounds from the past and present, while an audience watched an impressive light show in the drizzle.

Chris Lambert

When the Striped Bananas were still based in New Jersey, we lived in a tiny cottage in the middle of nowhere.

The road we lived on is actually a local attraction, due to rumors of a wandering child's ghost. We set up the basement as our recording studio—it had all the typical psych-music mood setting items, such as gnomes, candles, paintings, guitars and even a disco ball.

We were in the middle of a take on our first album, and a shadow caught the corner of our eyes. It looked like a ten foot spider was crawling up the wall. We immediately stopped playing and stared at the wall in fear.

What actually happened wasn't a recreation of 1958's *Earth vs. the Spiders*, but just a spider no bigger than a coin, standing behind one of the candles. The spider was silhouetting on the wall. It ruined our take, but inspired me to write a song about a slug who is a sleuth, and investigates spiders who appear at the most inopportune moments.

Duncan Shepard

I remember well a great episode with my previous band, Hipnótica; we were invited by a multinational record label to record a song for a compilation, and for that they booked us a twelve hour session in a great studio.

What happened was that we recorded that song in a couple of hours, and afterwards we convinced the sound engineer to embark in an delirious adventure.

We brought some food and, especially, wine; and recorded a jam session for about ten hours non-stop. The result was so amazing that we decided to release some extracts of it as an EP; we called it A Circle so Blue.

João Branco Kyron

The recording was made in a semi-clandestine way. It was in our rehearsal room. We used the equipment of the other band with which we shared the room, hey, but their amps and cabinets were used to build a wall in order to isolate our different instruments.

We were caught red-handed, and they decided to expel us and not share again the rehearsing room.

Narsis Passolas

When Scarlet Rivera sent over her violin part for my song "You're An Island," it was like a teenage dream. As a Dylan fan and, in particular, his *Desire* album where she plays violin throughout, it was just an amazing moment to hear that sound on one of my tracks.

I used to dream of recording "proper" music when I was a kid, so having my first CD released and people actually buying it was just something else too. I feel lucky to have a job where I can be thrilled by it every day.

Chris Wade

We have always recorded our songs in our rehearsal room and sometimes things work good, and sometimes not.

Of course, some mishaps happen to us in our "studio" now and then, but I don't remember any case that would be interesting enough to mention.

Except I once ruined one mic when I tried to record some instruments through water, but I wasn't careful enough this time and the mic got wet. After that it was an ex-mic.

Jaire Pätäri

Well, one time Chris deleted the master take...(yada yada)

Pete Meriwether

I remember the first rehearsal session I did with a drummer from Cardiacs, Dominic Luckman. I was positioned next to him.

We get through the first song and I said, "Bloody hell, that was loud!" Dominic had the perfect repost: "Loud? That was polite!"

Mordecai Smyth

We record nearly everything at home, so if anything goes wrong we could restore it. When you are in an expensive studio, it's more likely that anything goes wrong and you don't have the time to do anything about it, until it's too late.

But one thing on the negative side was when we had finished the recording of the song "Julia Dream of all the Pretty Little Horses."

We send it to Fruits de Mer and were rather satisfied with the result. Then came the answer from Fruits de Mer: The song is fine, but it's a couple of minutes too long for an EP.

Then we had some frustrating evenings trying to cut out parts of the song. We thought the song had an epic feeling that was necessary for the song to work.

But the story finally got a happy ending. Fruits de Mer found another record plant that could press EPs with a longer playing time, and we just faded the song a bit at the end.

Anders Håkanson

I would say nearly everything I have recorded is forged from mishap, and then rescued with varying degrees of acceptable listenability—depending upon the ear of the listener.

Stephen Stannard

The craziest session I did is, without a doubt, the one for "Hermetic Spell" on 12 Visions album with my friend's musicians.

I wanted to know if ambiance, lights, concept... could have influence on the way we record a song. We played by night, only with candlelight and all dressed in capes.

I brought to the studio a tape with a basic track (mainly with synthesizer drones and effects recorded at home in the same condition) and a sheet full of lyrics for Alice Artaud, the guest singer.

We made a soundcheck on one chord and, at this early moment, I already knew this session would be amazing. After one minute of silence, we recorded Hermetic Spell in one take, a perfect black musical Mass exploring unknown and terrifying landscapes.

Will Z

The best jams a band ever has are frequently accompanied by nobody pressing "record."

Sneaking instruments into the cabin on a ferry ride from Denmark to England was time well spent, as was carting instruments up a boggy mountain to record the sound of horns echoing across the valley.

Following that up with a session inside a 5,000 year old tomb on top of the mountain sealed the deal.

The magical moments for me are in these kinds of scenarios, rather than in the studio, which is usually just someone's bedroom anyway.

David Colohan

Last August, we recorded a new album in Barcelona with the Britpop guru producer Owen Morris (Oasis, the Verve, the View) and it was exciting. We really enjoyed the recording with passion, but sometimes it was very hard.

The studio was very nice and it was really a dream, but we got into a bit of pressure because we wanted to have a perfect recording, and control everything, and maybe it was a mistake because we were shocked with Owen and his way of working, more calm and relaxed.

But it all (studio, production, accommodation) was very expensive and we had only one month to make the album!

Finally all went fine, and we found the correct balance to work, the right vodka, wine, drugs, valiums and everything flowed properly, especially in the highest moments. Hope someday people understand our music and the feelings of that recording.

Jordi Bel

My friend Joe Giddings, a phenomenal guitarist, played with us for a few years and wailed on some of Ormythology before he moved, eventually to L.A.

He was back in Atlanta for a brief visit in October of 2014, and we got to hang out for an afternoon. I was finishing up the record and he agreed to lay down some solos for "Teli Teli" and "Yedikule."

We were in the back of my record store, and there was a frame shop next door. Joe did a take or two for "Teli Teli," and then there was a loud banging on the wall.

I went next door and the framers were very unhappy about the noise, so I went back and hooked up my Vox Tonelab (direct box) and Joe finished the "Teli" solo and cut "Yedikule" almost silently.

I said he could probably turn up the monitors a little but we were both pretty terrified, and he said that's how he does it at home. If you listen to "Teli Teli," you can hear where the solo switches from amped to direct.

Ted Selke

Recently, I recorded Beck Sian's third solo album at my studio. We made a deal where I would record and co-produce her album for free, if she sang the songs on the Mooch album *Stations Of The Sun*.

She has a stunning voice, and we worked well together. One day, however, we'd had a number of failures, and nothing seemed to be working out right. At the very end of the day, while she was making a cup of tea in my kitchen, I put together a brief track using a couple of string orchestra parts.

When she walked back into the studio, I pulled the curtains shut to dim the light, then told her to step up to the microphone and imagine that she was walking towards "Ye Olde Silent Inn" that was the heart of her album. Then I hit the record button, and told her to sing.

She had no time to think about it. At the end of the recording, I told her to add a second track; I gave her no time to think about that either, or to consider what she'd just sung. It turned into a wonderful track, and she was thrilled with it. The power of improvisation!

Steve Palmer

I record at home on a home set up. I've had quite a few moments I'd call personal little triumphs. I remember the thrill of hearing Trees singer Celia Humphris' vocal that she did for one of my songs.

When I got the file through, and played it along to my music, it was an amazing moment for me. It doesn't get much better than that feeling. In music that is….

Chris Wade

I was waiting at the mic to do a vocal take for "Piccadilly," on our first album… and waiting… and waiting! It eventually transpired that someone had just erased some really important stuff, involving the orchestra(!), who had just left! Good news was, while I was sitting outside in the recording room, waiting, I wrote "So Freely," which appeared on the next album… time management!

Leo O'Kelly

Brouhaha were prone to mishaps. We once borrowed a friend's car to drive out to a studio in Kent, laden with all our gear and drum kit stuffed into the boot.

One of our number had just lit a big spliff and filled the car with smoke when we were pulled over by a police car. He stuffed the offending bag of bad stuff down his trousers and we all held our breath, expecting the worst.

The cop was puzzled by the fact that none of us knew whose car it was, and got us all to get out. We were seriously freaked by this point.

Anyhow, him and his pal insisted we get all of the gear out of the car, and they meticulously searched all the bits of drum kit, to no avail.

Eventually they decided the only thing they could do us for was a bald back tyre which they made us change for the spare.

King Penguin

Octopus Syng

So… we breathed a massive sigh of relief and drove off to the studio, where we had quite a successful day's recording. Apart from the lead singer passing out in the cafe next door and ending up face-down in his fry-up. But that's another story….

Anyhow, on our drive back, guess what? We were stopped by another cop car, who also searched us. And they decided our back tyre was bald, and told us to put back on the spare we'd taken off earlier!
Stephen Bradbury

I remember being a session musician for a band who were recording at John Mitchell's (singer / guitarist with It Bites etc, etc) studio. I was the guitarist for the session.

I was shitting myself having to play in front of him, so I couldn't get this slide guitar part right and the chap whose session it was was getting a bit stressed and started to try to show me how to play it (he was the singer!)

Anyway, John Mitchell tells him to go and make us all some tea. With just the two of us in the studio, he started making me laugh, with various music anecdotes and then says, "Right, let's give it another go!"

Having put me at my ease and got rid of the stress merchant, I played it right first time—before the tea had arrived! It just goes to show that good producers are also good psychologists.
Mordecai Smyth

This was back in the 2005, and the Bordellos was coming to the end of its time as a six piece although at the time we didn't realize this. But there was a lot of friction between myself and our then-lead guitarist ,who also was the producer of the band in his own barn studios.

We had just recorded a song called "Arthur Lee" (which turned up on our *Songs for Swinging Stalkers* LP), but I hated the effects they had put on my voice, making it sound more polished and airbrushed than my taste allowed; you cannot have airbrushed garage rock!

So after much sulking from both parties, he reluctantly agreed to rerecord, myself being at the time quite difficult and annoying, especially to our U2 loving guitarist / producer (but actually a nice guy).

I would not acknowledge him unless he called me Baron Bordello; I also, for this recording session, insisted on talking in a World War Two fighter pilot way, including accent and phraseology and holding my trousers just above the knee to make them more Biggles-like.

Whilst taking this approach and stance, I rerecorded the vocal in one take, still in Biggles character, and it can be heard on the finished version. Still one of my best ever vocals—check it out on YouTube.
Brian Bordello

I did backing vocals for a song written by Terry Dempsey for Tina Turner in Johannesburg in 1980. I didn't meet her. I had to get up at about seven AM, as Terry wanted a scratchy vocal effect, and did the track around nine with a few session singers.

It was fulfilling doing something so professional ,and totally different from a lot of other work I had done in the past. Wish I had a copy. Can't remember the title of the song even.
Alison O'Donnell

I had started working on a new song and sent the track over to Meurig, our drummer, to add some ideas. He messaged me back straight away and said "you know those drum tracks that I did for 'I Feel Love' that we didn't use? Just drop them onto this new track"

I thought "what a bizarre idea," but I did it and they fitted perfectly. They even had a drum roll and an ending in perfect sync with my guitar track. So that was a triumph.
Pete Bingham

We've never let anything stop us in the studio, including having no access to one for the first two albums.

We broke into *Uncut*, *Q* and *Mojo* with the first two albums, and they were recorded with a laptop and a boombox. Paul Johnson from *Uncut* gave our second album *Diamond* 4.5 / 5 stars and finished the review with the one word sentence "Extraordinary." His editor cut half a star and the "Extraordinary."

Paul Johnson was the first journo to discover us. He gave us 3.5 / 5 in *Uncut* for our first album, which was really lo fi. I wonder if *Uncut* has ever reviewed anything that lo-fi since. Mr. Johnson has some stones to him for giving us attention. We were completely unknown, had never played a gig and had not one piece of press. It seems like that could never happen these days.
Jet Wintzer

I have seen master tapes disintergrating and flying around in the air... twice! All these disasters were fixed, though.

Another memory of searching in our producer Bill Leader's waste paper basket through miles of tapes during our final mastering, searching for a two inch length of tape from "Boat Song," which had been mistakenly cut out (we used razor blades then!) We found it!
Leo O'Kelly

I mainly record at home, on my own, and that's so absolutely boring. The only thing I can say is that I mostly work in underwear, and I swear a lot. Loudly.
Paolo Sala

I leave studios to musicians and other people who know what they're doing. I should probably do the same with record labels
Keith Jones

Live on-air guitar twanging on Dutch radio, realizing, too late, that the guitar was hopelessly out of tune. I believe someone recorded it (and thus regularly wake up feverish at the thought of its unbidden return).
Sand Snowman

In 2009 I went to Scotland with my girlfriend to meet Daniel Wylie (Cosmic Rough Riders) for a vocal collaboration on the song "Someday," from our third LP *Passport to Freedom*.

It was amazing. He really did a masterclass and was really special. I was listening for years to that superb psychedelic Byrdsy jingle jangle "Enjoy the melodic sunshine," and I couldn't believe what I was seeing. Daniel Wylie is really a pop genius!.
Jordi Bel

A disaster occurred during the early recording stages of the *Anima Mundi* album. We were jamming this blinding track, and when we finished were all smiles in the live room, but they quickly disappeared when the engineer said it hadn't recorded.

We tried playing it again, several times, but sadly never achieved the same soaring heights.
Pete Bingham

One sort of mishap that readily springs to mind (although we didn't actually know it until much later) happened when the Thanes were recording our very first record, the *Hey Girl + 3* 7" EP for DDT early in 1987.

The recording all went off fine, and we duly sent off the master tapes, but when we got the test pressings back, there was a note saying there was a serious drop-out on one of the tracks—our cover of "What Can I Do" by US sixties group the Jackson Investment Co—and that we should consider re-recording the track ... which is exactly what we had to do, cos when we listened to the test press, it was glaringly obvious that there was a serious drop out / loss of sound for a second or so ...
Lenny Helsing

The most memorable triumph from the studio must be when we received the files from Tony Swettenham for the *Summerisle* EP.

Tony is a Mellotron wizard from England who we had never met. He had released some records with his alter ego the Frobisher Neck on Fruits De Mer, and Keith Jones thought we could collaborate well.

We sent the four songs from the *Summerisle* EP to Tony, and a few weeks, he uploaded a couple of files for us. We were a bit nervous—would this fit into our music or not ? When we placed Tony's files into our songs, we were shocked about the result. The most beautiful and otherworldly sound of Mellotron and hammered dulcimer came out of the speakers. We were speechless. It was so sensitive, and fitted so perfectly into the music.

Anders Håkanson

[I collect microphones, so when we recorded *Reverberating Garden #7*] we were using mostly old, quite lo-fi dynamic mics. The older ones were from the thirties, and the newer ones were from seventies. Then we used some quite unusual recording techniques, searching for personal psychedelic sounds, not just "normal" sounds.

But thinking about the result, I can describe it as a many-sided psychedelic album, including electric rock, delicate pop and beautiful folk songs. With a couple of more sinister and dark songs too.

Jaire Patari

As Pete and Leah mentioned, I accidentally deleted a master take, or at least what we thought was going to become the master take.

You see, for the last record, we decided we would record nearly every take of every song until we got it perfect, and then do one more pass just to see if it could possibly be topped, as the pressure was now off to produce a master take.

With "Lady Juniper," we did in fact top the previously thought-to- be-best version, only I never re-labeled it as not being "best" any longer.

In a daze after spending three days in the studio, and needing to do some hard drive cleanup, I went through and deleted all of the non-best labeled versions, which of course, wiped the song away forever.

All I can say is, thankfully, not only did I miss getting rid of a previously thought-to-be inferior version, but it turned out to likely be stronger that what we had lost. It all worked out in the end, but the feeling of losing a master is devastating.

Chris Sherman

One time a bulldog came running into a jam session and peed on my tenor banjo, right in front of me.

Jefferson Hamer

"Sorry.....I wasn't actually recording... could you just do that again?"
Tom Woodger

Angeline Morrison

CHAPTER EIGHT

Fruits de Mer's 2014 release "Postcards from the Deep" represents one of the most adventurous, eye-catching, and utterly bat-cookies crazy, packages released this century. So how did its contributors react when a record label called them up and said, "hey, we're putting out a box set of psychedelia covers, and pressing it onto postcards like those old Polish singles. Do you want to be on it?"

"Back to the DIY ethic."
    That's what I thought when Keith Jones [Fruits de Mer] told me about *Postcards From the Deep*. Pressing into paper, totally mad, but to me that's what Fruits de Mer originally started out as, something different. Wrap-around covers, strange free gifts, basement recordings, that was the pull for me, back to the late seventies punk DIY ethic.
Ken Halsey

Ten bands? Yeah!
    Ten songs? Cool!
    Ten postcards (and poster!) with art by Mick Dillingham? Yes!!
    A box to contain it all? Great!!
Tom Woodger

As the project grew, it was found that the original postcards idea wasn't going to work, so flexidiscs were suggested. That was really back to the early eighties. I couldn't recall the last time I got one of those. It was probably stuck to the cover of an early eighties magazine. And that's how the idea went forward.
Ken Halsey

I've never had much affection for flexidiscs, to be honest. I mean, who does? They always sound pretty ropey, and are easily damaged, and most times wind up getting lost or misfiled somewhere in your collection
Mike Stax

I collected a few Flexipop discs… "Looking For Footprints" by XTC! I really didn't care about sound quality at the time, just wanted to hear the song. The only drag was, if the punch holes weren't large enough, the discs would get caught up on the record player spindle and couldn't spin.
Gregory Curvey

Flexidiscs? Brillia…..hang on!
   What?
   Flexidiscs? That's mad!
   Totally mad!
   Insane!
   Totally insane.
   That's brilliant!
   Sign us up!
Tom Woodger

[I remember] reading about illicit flexidisc-type releases circulating in the Eastern bloc countries in the sixties—forbidden or, at the very least, restricted Beatles, Dylan and jazz recordings, some of them pressed on X-Ray film.

   They must have sounded dreadful, but at the same time unimaginably liberating for those who didn't otherwise have access to these subversive sounds
Mike Stax

They don't rank high in sonic audiophile quality.
Marc Swordfish

National Geographic's flexi of Neil Armstrong talking on the moon was the first one I remember seeing.
Gregory Curvey

The Puppies were very pleased (to put it mildly!) to be invited to take part. As a long time fan of sixties freakbeat, to be given the chance to contribute to a modern version of the kind of compilation I have come to know and love was too good to miss
Tom Woodger

As a bit of a vinyl maniac, I love flexidiscs. The Swedish Bildjournalen varieties, with groups like the Mascots, Lee Kings and Namelosers, are rather tasty, as well as some punk-era and early indie specimens.
Lenny Helsing

The idea of having a release on such an obsolete and inherently dodgy format appealed to me on a perverse level.

I like to think we're doing something in the same spirit [as the old Communist Bloc postcards and flexis] with this release—getting our way-outside-the-mainstream sounds into the hands of that small coterie of non-conformist music fans who actually "get" our kind of music.
Mike Stax

All the bands gave a resounding thumbs up, so away we all went to record our tracks.
Ken Halsey

I only recently came upon [Dana Gillespie's "You Just Gotta Know My Mind"] on the radio. At once I told Icarus to source and start work on it. I loved the words.
Crystal Jacqueline

Do you remember the film *Drugstore Cowboy*? That was where I first heard "Psychotic Reaction." I bought the film soundtrack and played it to death the summer of its release, and I really like the manic part of the song. It jumps off the cliff and speeds you toward the ground, only to be saved at the last minute. We had fun recording that part….
Gregory Curvey

The Thanes had already been part of the double vinyl set, *Not Pretty*, issued over a decade ago on Australia's Corduroy outlet; we do a very raw and basic take of "Honey I Need."

We were also both honored and privileged to play out live with the Pretties a couple of years ago in Glasgow, and had a great time swapping tales of vintage instruments with Dick Taylor and Phil May, and chatting to them before and after the show.

[So] when I saw "LSD" was on the list [of possible songs for the box set], I thought, "yeah we could do a pretty good instrumental take on that for sure."

And, funnily enough, Angus McPake [Thanes' organist / guitarist] and I, independent of each other, both thought it would be a great idea to include sitar… which is what we've done.

Sitar and fuzz to give it that early psychsploitation feel that was going down on some LPs Stateside back at the time.
Lenny Helsing

"Soul Fiction" by the Hippies stood out for us. As an instrumental, there aren't any vocals to get in the way, so you can tend to go a bit more crazy with instrumentals.

The idea was to really garage / fuzz the track up, but with the fact the release was originally going to be pressed into paper, we tried to get a happy medium by not going to over the top on distorting the recording, as the pressing on card would have done that for us.

Now that it's flexidiscs, our track and probably others aren't as fuzzed up as perhaps they should have been, but at least they are listenable.
Ken Halsey

We got the opportunity to record... Dragonfly's "Celestial Empire."

Dragonfly were this amazing psychedelic band from the Netherlands, who only released a couple of singles, both of them fantastic.

They had a striking image, with wild face paint, not unlike Arthur Brown or a trippier forerunner of Kiss. [The song has been in and out of the Loons' live repertoire for many years] and Keith's flexidisc concept seemed like a good excuse to actually record it.
Mike Stax

I always loved *The Avengers*. I think the theme tune is fabulous. The Honey Pot drummer, Wayne Fraquet, always does these fast, tight little beats to warm up, so he was a natural choice to join in, and after that it was just having fun with as many guitars as I could squeeze on.
Icarus Peel

[The Sorrows' "Take A Heart" was] my first falling in love with freakbeat, seeing them [perform it] live in what looks like some kind of auditorium; you can see it in old black and white YouTube.

It's just a wonderful snapshot that captures the zeitgeist of the era. Keith [Jones] gave instant approval, and we set out recording it on half-inch 8 track reel to reel in our studio lair above the funeral home in New Jersey.
Jet Wintzer

"Flexidiscs may not be the highest sound quality, but as the medium for a 304-Holloway-Road-in-yer-face-"You're-Holding-Me-Down"-compression-on-the-compression-gimme-more-coffee-and-diet-pills-Crawdaddy-Simone style sound, I have to say it works for us!
Tom Woodger

It was an honor to be involved with this. I just hope Keith doesn't decide to do wax cylinders next. They sound even worse.
Marc Swordfish

[Eschatone Records] put out my track "Yuppie Exodus From Dumbo" on cylinder because the song is in part about antiquarian fetishes.

The format becomes part of the story. Plus it happens to be a gorgeous package. Michael Doret did the design, and signed and numbered the lot. Odd formats are fun, and even if you don't have the means to play them, they can still deepen the meaning of a release.
Jed Davis

Blue Giant Zeta Puppies

The Bordellos

CHAPTER NINE

Wax rhapsodically, please, about any unusual musical instrument that (a) you can play; (b) that you wish you could play; (c) that someone else in your band can play; or (d) that you simply like listening to.

I would like to be able to play the harp. There's a ceremonious and baroque feeling that appeals to me. Then Us and Them could sound like Bert Jansch's version of "January Man" (which is a fantastic duet between guitar and harp) as often as we wish.
Anders Håkanson

I think the only real contender (as such Zeta Puppies staples as toy train whistles, kazoos, stylophones and spinning round a length of rubber hose are not that unusual these days...) has to be the mighty Suzuki Omnichord.

It is simply the weirdest, maddest instrument I think I have ever seen. For those of you not familiar with this device, it is a sort of electronic autoharp, with a built in rhythm unit, made in the early eighties.

You hold down a chord button with one hand and "strum" or "finger pick" a touch sensitive strip with the other... it has this weird, but, in its own way, rather beautiful sound.

We recorded a session with a friend of ours who plays one, and produced a version of "Better Off Without Me" with just the Omnichord, no other instruments. We are still saving that one... maybe for a Christmas single.
Tom Woodger

I can't play anything apart from the recorder and the odd percussion instrument, and even then I struggle.

A few months ago, I did a bit of research to try and see if there was anything at all I might be able to pick up in order to accompany my own singing, when Tom isn't available.

I looked at the Appalachian dulcimer, the bowed psaltery and the autoharp, all very wonderful simple stringed instruments that produce shiveringly beautiful sounds.

I managed to borrow an autoharp, too, but I haven't made any progress with it, sadly. I lack the fine motor skills required.

Even singing and banging a drum simultaneously can trip me up. So I'll just keep working on my vocals and hang onto the "my voice is my instrument" line.

Sorry, that wasn't especially rhapsodic, was it?
Joanna Swan

I'm constantly jealous of anyone who can play the violin. I have owned one for years, but have never allowed myself the time to properly learn.
Richard Thompson

The bowed saw is quite a thing. I first noticed it being rather beautiful on the Mercury Rev album, *Deserters Songs*. It's lovely, like how an acoustic Theremin might sound.

I know a chap, Adam Bushell who plays it as well as another interesting instrument, the phonofiddle which is like a violin with a trumpet horn poking out of it. Now there's a thing too.
Chris Anderson

The Moog Theremin is such a cool instrument. Wish I could figure it out. My bandmate Patrick Schizo owns and plays it like he's dancing to a trance song at a rave. It's incredible.
Jayne Gabriel

I think my favorite strange instrument we've used is the kid's toy: the Xyclomatic, a "programmable" eight noted automated xylophone. I used it to mimic a peel of eight church bells on "Shadows In The Water" on Thomas Traherne. Also on that track I play a Mickey Mouse bontempi reed organ.
Sproatly Smith

It's not an unusual instrument particularly, but I've recently found myself getting a little obsessed with the sound of a hurdy gurdy, and am dying to have a go on one.
Graeme Lockett

I think it would be awesome to play the baglama or the oud. The baglama is a type of Turkish saz, a stringed instrument. There are a few varieties, but I love the long-necked one.

I was turned onto it by my friend, the great Namik Ciblak. It is difficult to play because there are extra frets. We have twelve notes in an octave, but there are fifteen on a saz. And for better or worse, the oud doesn't have any frets, so there would definitely be a learning curve for me.
Ted Selke

Ukeleles are 'hip' now, so I had to record some "uke" on a recent track. This is the only time I've turned up at a recording session and Googled chords prior to recording; what an amateur!

I wish I could play the piano properly, I've not really progressed far from my Grandma's piano shenanigans. Listening to a full orchestra and choir live is marvelous, hard to beat, really. The bass saxophone is bonkers! One listens and watches in disbelief…
Mark Reuter

I am very fortunate to have a friend, Ken Lund, who likes to make unusual instruments. He has made me a strange guitar.

It is like a cigar box guitar, except he made the box too! It is tuned G / D / G, but has six strings instead of the usual three for this type of instrument.

They are, in fact, three pairs of two strings—so like half a twelve-string guitar! I used this on "Out in the Stars" and have just written an entire song with it, which will be on my next album, plug, plug….
Mordecai Smyth

Any instrument is unusual if I'm playing it. I wish I could play
Dan Bordello

Well, I have an autoharp on my website. I have two good vintage autoharps. I often write my songs on them with "near as dammit" chords, usually.

It's fairly idiot proof in terms of the actual playing, but to play one well, like everything, requires practice, time and energy which I don't have enough of.

That's reserved for writing, recording, performing and maintaining my voice, which is my best instrument. I am dreading the day I have to do anything technical like changing strings or pads. Argh. It will be "call a friend" time.
Alison O'Donnell

I really enjoy listening to the Sea Organ in Zadar, Croatia—it's a series of funnels going underground, exiting further up the beach, that behaves like a monumental pipe organ when the sea forces air, randomly, through the tubes.

I've only heard recordings of this, and to my ears it is the most hypnotic sound I've ever heard. I would love to experience it in the flesh. as I could quite happily pass away whilst it makes random melodic connections.
Alan Murphy

I'm a sucker for flutes of various kinds, since I've been playing one for so long, and I really do love Japanese flutes.

The shakuhachi sounds incredible, and is not easy to play at all. Made from bamboo, tuned to the minor pentatonic scale, they just sound incredibly beautiful and haunting.

It's the sound of something you'd happily follow into a dark forest to some ruined, ivy covered temple. The sound of ghosts of ghosts.
Amanda Votta

I try to use toy instruments as far as possible, or bits and pieces that I find in charity shops. "I am Peter the Hermit (Part 1)," for instance, features a Stylophone which I picked up in a Dr Barnado's shop.

It was one of the Rolf Harris special editions, still in its original box, so it may be worth a bit of money now, you never know.

Another fortuitous charity shop find was a bliptronic sequencer, which has since become central to the Palace of Swords sound palette, having been employed on "The Castle Spectre," and a number of other songs. One of its buttons is missing, but it's still in good working order.
Peter Lyon

We love the Mellotron. Especially how it sounds on *Odessey and Oracle* by the Zombies, and the early Moody Blues stuff.
Aaron Hemington

I love the sound of sweeping orchestral arrangements. French horns, cornets, strings, flutes, cellos, kettle drums and stuff. I don't have access to any such instruments, so I'm grateful that it's now the future, and I can just press buttons and keys.
Simon Berry

This doesn't really count as an unusual instrument, but there's an intense love and understanding between my black double bass, whose name is Dilip, and myself. Dilip and I play off each other. He understands me. The lower notes are always the most emotional ones for me.
Angeline Morrison

We love to use the Omnichord; it has an interface where you can play the chords at the same time as you produce magical, harpish sounds in a slide. We use it a lot.
João Branco Kyron

Duncan plays the sitar and the Theremin. He has been trying to create a Theremin controlled by sitar strings. Chantelle plays the ocarina. Try playing an ocarina through an amplifier with delay, echo, pitch shift and tremolo. It sounds like aliens are trying to contact you.
Duncan Shepard

I collect ethnic musical instruments, and have done for all twenty-three years of Mooch's history. I own about a hundred and twenty of them now.

I have quite a few favorites: my red and white Balinese flute, which plays and records beautifully; my Turkish saz, which, with its very light strings, is a joy to play; and a bendir drum that I particularly like.

At the moment, I am waiting to take delivery of a Greek laouto that Stelios Petrakis is making for me on the island of Crete. It's costing me an arm and a leg, so I hope I like it!
Steve Palmer

I picked up a duduk in Istanbul recently, and really hope I can get to grips with it as it is one of the most haunting sounds I've ever heard.

My friend John Cavanagh let me play his VCS3 and a Farfisa that Rick Wright and Brian Eno once owned, so that has been my biggest joy in recent times.

I've entered the world of modular synthesizers now, which means I will always be broke, but I am loving the adventuring involved in that.
David Colohan

I play a mean kazoo, and my hand clapping is only slightly off-time.
Joel Slevin

Mizmar, an Arabic wind instrument. Exotic, cutting and entrancing. Best listened to by a camp in the open, under the desert stars. Definitely would not want to play one myself, but I love that sound.
Crystal Jacqueline

I used to play the cornet. Not really unusual, but quite appropriate given that I hail from "up north." Can't really wax rhapsodically about it—I realized my vocal talents far superseded my brass playing ability, so I quietly consigned my cornet to the loft. On the plus side, it does mean I can read music!
Ellie Coulson

I'd love to play the sitar, I find the sound very interesting and mystic, a glider side. Otherwise, play perfectly the harpsichord.
Maxine Schwartz

As a "laptop-musician," I'd just like to be able to play keyboards properly! But I really wish I could play the vibraphone.

I love the purity of sound of all those tuned percussion instruments—xylophone, marimba, glockenspiel. I love them all, but hearing the vibraphone played well in a Jazz solo is wonderful.
Chris Bond

I really love a split toy whistle we have; the sound cannot be overstated. It can only be described as White Light White Heat, but in a whistle form. I would use it on all our tracks, and… in fact, thinking about it, I may record an LP based around the feedback sound it emits.
Brian Bordello

I see the orchestral harp as the ultimate instrument. The harp, with its multitude of open strings, offers so many harmonic possibilities both beautiful and dissonant. We make do with a bodged folk harp which goes just luvvly with a bodged alto flute.
Stephen Stannard

I'd quite like an ondioline.
Nick Salomon

I will give rhapsodic waxing a try! Presenting the Mongolian horse fiddle! This is a two-stringed, horse-necked instrument with a deep voice that speaks like the empty, barren spaces of the Mongolian steppe. Trying to tune it is akin to taming a wild stallion.
Tom Conway

I really like the sound of a banjo. I did two lovely CDs with a USA based banjo player named Joelle Premo .She goes under the name of "All In The Merry Month Of May." She plays so nicely, with a rustic feel. I am so envious.
Roger Linney

The glass harmonica, invented by Ben Franklin in the year-of-our-Lord 1761: it's basically a series of spinning glass bowls that sit inside each other, and are arranged horizontally in a row running from largest-to-smallest.

One simply presses one's fingertips against the edges of the bowls to emit different tones. It's a slightly deranged, dreamy sound, like going to heaven in an ice-cream truck.
Jeb Morris

I love the musical saw. I think it is the manual equivalent of the theremin, and two fine exponents are Kaspar Kronk of the Skiff Skats, and the delightful singer Lucy Farrell.
Diana Collier

I think it's fair to say I don't really use any conventional instruments. At the moment my favorite toys are the EigenHarp Pico which is one of the most sensitive midi controllers out there, with 3D controllable buttons, a breath pipe, and touch sensitive pad that mimics bowing, which I use to control the soft synth Omisphere which is just a powerhouse for the sound tinkerer.

I also use the Foltek Luminist Garden, which is basically a box with varying length wires poking out of it, which can be poked , scraped and waggled about to produce all manner of interesting soundscapes.

One of the fun / scary things about Chonyid is having Ben in the band, as he's something of tinkerer to say the least; so you never know what random breadboard with seemingly random wires and dials he will produce.

Andy Hokano

A while back, a friend challenged me to make an entirely acoustic album, and I have just about finished it.

During the opening stages, it occurred to me that I could try to use every single one of my instruments during recording. I wasn't sure at first if it would be possible... but it has worked out. This album has been immense fun to make, and it's taught me a lot about how to use various unusual instruments in unfamiliar structures and settings.

Steve Palmer

I performed and recorded with a little Russian balalaika given to me as present by my cousin's uncle, after an holiday in Russia during the eighties.

It has a nice intimate sound, and sometimes I used it as a soft "percussion," just tapping the guitar plectrum on its back.

I also have a great seventies Austrian zither bought on ebay some years ago. I love it, it sounds magnificent, and I use it on most of my records. And I love listening to the mountain dulcimer... one day I'll surely buy one. And, obviously, I'd love to have a real modular synthesizer.

Lorenzo Bracaloni

I bought an Irish bouzouki five years ago, a mandolin with four strings (each one double), and though I don't really spend much time in playing it, I recorded a few songs with it.

I used it in Instant Flight for "The Land is the Same" and "Endless Journey"; and in Mark and The Clouds for "Spirits in the Wind," "Darkened River" and "I'll Follow the Sound."

It's very nice on folk songs I think, but I'm a bit of a lazybones in trying new instruments, apart from knowing I play guitar and bass. Keyboards are something I wished I played a bit more, as I lived for seven years with a keyboardist, but you can't always get what you want.

Marco Magnani

Lost Harbours

Paolo Sala

I love recording with Rob Jones (the Voluntary Butler), and he is an inspiration in terms of trying your hand at any instrument that comes to hand.

He is now in demand as a horn arranger, precisely because of this non-purist make-it-up-as-you-go-along attitude.

I got to record violin on some tracks with him, which would have infuriated my violin teacher, Mrs Saunderson, as she always hated my long finger nails, and never encouraged me a jot.
Mikey Georgeson

Not so much an instrument, but I just love choral music. I wish that I could have a chorus of singers at my disposal to make beautiful, ethereal sounds together. Never gonna happen of course…
Kev Oyston

Our drummer owns a typical German-Argentinian instrument called a bandoneon, but he can't play a note… well, maybe two or three.
Narsis Passolas

When I was a child, I started to play violin. It was a short "career" and I quit; it was too difficult and the fingers were aching. Now, when I am an adult, I regret it of course. It would have been nice to put some violins in our music. I also think it would have been very cool to play Theremin.
Britt Rönnholm

Unusual instrument has to be the ondes martenot. I thought Coil used one when they remixed a track of mine ("Hobgoblins"), but it turned out that it was Jhonn Balance singing.
Drew Mulholland

I've got loads of weird little instruments I play on my albums. I do my partner Linzi's head in with this annoying little wooden flute I have. I dance and prance about playing it, very badly, although it makes my daughter laugh.

I also have a twelve string harp I love to play. I can just sit there for hours on end with a prattish grin on my face, plucking it like a fool.

I wish I could play the sitar though; I need to buy one and really have a crack at that. The chap who plays sitar on Dodson & Fogg albums is Ricky Romain, a brilliant player well and truly, and I love getting those recordings through and giving them a good listen.

I don't know what it is about the sitar. Psychedelic clichés aside, it has a lovely sound to it. I love a lot of world instruments actually.
Chris Wade

I have one of those Yamaha windsynth things—actually a MIDI controller, rather than a synth in its own right, with a fake reed thing, that plays a bit like an oboe. I used to do some wild stuff on that, despite not being able to play the bloody thing at all!

I did a gig with a band from Milton Keynes called the Irritants, who did completely improvised stuff, and included a bloke called Stray who was a DJ and mixed the whole shebang.

I got a bit drunk… well, a lot drunk actually… and was playing so wildly, leaning back, leaning back, blowing the thing up to the sky and… I fell over backwards. Very embarrassing, and Stray nearly punched me for messing up the gig. Can't say I blame him in retrospect!

I've also got a flute that I'd love to learn to play. Gotta find the time and get a lesson or two, sometime. I've also had a yearning to play a sax—maybe a soprano sax? That's one of the few instruments I don't already have in my collection!
Stephen Bradbury

I love the drums and find that, in rock music, it's the instrument that excites me the most.
Sand Snowman

Ken has built me an incredible fretless upright bass guitar. This is played like a traditional upright bass, only it is made and tuned the same as an electric bass guitar.

The reason for this being that I can't play a normal bass guitar with my fingers—my wrist will not twist around to do that, but turn the instrument through 90 degrees and I can.

It really is a monster and I love it to bits, as it has opened up the world of "proper" bass playing to me, rather than just using a plectrum!
Mordecai Smyth

I love to play world percussions (tablas, cuica, darbuka...). I use them a lot on my albums but my favorite "unusual" instrument is the sitar. I always love that sound which is, for me, the essence of acid folk and psychedelic music.

It was a long quest to buy one but suddenly, following the explosion of electronic commerce, I had the chance to find a webstore selling Indian instruments.
Will Z

Really, really, love using my loop pedal. I use it to layer sounds and try to recreate some of my studio (small study)-bound work live, using it with varying degrees of success. I find a loop pedal is a good alternative for friends or bandmates. It never lets you down.

I have created zombie groan loops created by the audience to sing over. I have combined home-made drone from my laptop, with spoken word extracts and then looped whistles and chants to pleasing effect. I love it!

(Since starting on my loop odyssey, I have been introduced to the wonders of Peter Broderick who is a looping genius—I think his pedal is a bit higher spec than mine...)
Chris Lambert

One instrument I like to listen to is the sitar. I have a small one from India, but I need to learn how to play it. Jose (our sitarist and tambourine man) can play it very well, and knows how to tune it. It's outstanding, and fits properly with classic rock and pop songs. It gives a very special atmosphere.

The other instrument that I liked a lot is an old Hammond organ through a Leslie or a Twin Amp. Both instruments are therapeutic and relaxing.
Jordi Bel

Well, Lord Sealand plays Theremin...... does it get any stranger than that? An instrument you don't actually touch!
Pete Bingham

I'd like to learn the Chapman Stick as well.
Tom Conway

I am oddly adept at guitar, bass, piano, singing and drums. But I'm horribly stunted at all wind instruments. I hate playing guitar, hate singing, kinda like bass, and really hate practicing piano, so I play drums. I love playing guitar alone, but hate playing drums alone...
Pete Meriwether

I really like the dulcimer, zither and autoharp; not particularly unusual, but lovely instruments, and we have used them on lots of songs.

The zither gives the perfect Orson Welles *Third Man* spooky vibe. The Mellotron has a special place in our hearts and songs, particularly the less used settings, like the choir and the trumpets ("We Love You").

Paul has an electric mandolin that sounds great; we used it on our cover of "Live and Let Live" by Love. We also use a real sitar, like not a loop or sample. Bit of a bugger to mic up, mind.
Dave McLean

With music videos, you can involve two of the senses at once, sight and sound. It would be great if, one day, smell could be added to music as well. You could put in a lovely lilac smell on a particularly delicate tune, or the smell of a roast dinner (which is, let's face it, one of the best smells in the world) on a bombastic brass section.

I do get the impression though, that most of Kanye West's songs would end up drenched in the smell of sixteen-year-old-boy aftershave… you know, the Lynx effect, when your little brother walks into the room on the way out to meet his friends (when there might be a Girl there), and the rest of the family is simultaneously choking on the vapor and stifling giggles.

Notice I don't suggest involving the sense of touch in music videos. This is because of Miley Cyrus.
Emily Jones

Oh yes, I can play the wonderful charango! I fell in love with that instrument when I was a kid, and listened to Andean folk records. I always wanted to play a charango, as I still think it sounds the best, but I had to wait until I was thirty-four to have one, when it was given me as a birthday present by my family.

So I started to study some tutorial on the Internet, learnt the chord fingering and eventually practiced on old Inti-Illimani songs that I love.

The charango is a cross between a ukulele and a mandolin, with ten nylon strings and a convex bottomed body. The modern charangos, like mine, are entirely made of wood, but the traditional ones were made out of armadillo shells!
Paolo Sala

Buffy Sainte-Marie… performed a haunting rendition of ["Sir Patrick Spens"] on an instrument that I had never heard of, called the mouth bow. A twangy, single-note drone instrument that resonated similarly to a jaw harp (which at the time I hadn't heard of either).

I was intrigued and interested in this instrument that looked like a hunting bow, but seemed both very easy to play and make.

As an artist working in ceramics and photography at the time, instrument-making was something completely different, that I had no experience in (but a mild interest) so I though I would experiment with this simple instrument to see what I could come up with.

I made a few mouth bows out of sticks and guitar strings that failed, but through trial and error I was able to come up with a decent bow and began to learn how to play it. After a few months of practice (and looking kind of like a crazy person holding a stick up to their face), I had it down, and began singing.
Ellie Bryan

I play the sitar—or, I suppose more accurately, I can find my way around a sitar and play some scales or figure out western music melodies and give them a different spin.

I had initially become fascinated with the sound of the sitar at the start of college, during a world music course; it was soothing and exotic, and unlike anything I had heard before.

Then of course, upon discovering that George Harrison played as well, I knew I had to buy one and learn immediately.
Chris Sherman

Love the sitar and tabla drums… Ravi Shankar… you get the picture.
Marrs Bonfire

I own and play a few instruments. I've got to improve on sitar; and I bought a drum kit last year, to have one at my studio, and I would really like to learn to play it.

So far, I'm terrible at it, but I have high hopes that I'll learn. I'm self taught / autodidactic in music. So I can play whatever I decide to play.

"Learning by doing," I was told one day at someone's studio; this is indeed a great way to get on.
Francois Sky

Once when I was eighteen, I took LSD and plugged headphones into my ARP Odyssey synthesizer after a late show in Pullman, Washington (WSU).

The rest of my band was asleep in a dark hotel room, and I was having this lightning storm behind my eyes, turning the knobs and flicking the switches of the Odyssey aimlessly—unable to see anything except internal light shows.

Well, after ten minutes, the synth started talking to me, and I kid you not, in a voice that sounded like a cross between wind and birds chirping. It told me quite clearly how it worked, and how to always get the best sounds out of it. I wrote my first song that night (and forgot it by noon the next day, when I awoke!)

However, I can make the most incredible and infinite sounds on that instrument, and I have always felt it was my best musical gift.
Gordon Raphael

I have two violins, one which I hardly used, and against all advice from friends, I put viola strings on it… and it now sounds rather more virile.

I've just recorded "The Dark Dance," title track from new Tír na nÓg album, with it and it's... dark!
Leo O'Kelly

Well, I play guitar and sing, and I play drums too—in a group called the Wildebeests—and a bit of harmonica now and again.

The Thanes' organist / guitarist Angus McPake has a real knack for playing all these and other instruments too, including sitar, which I would love to be able to play properly, beyond getting a guitar-based one-string tune out of it... yeah that would be pretty cool.

As I've mentioned before, I love stuff like the Incredible String Band and all those sitar psychers from the mid to late sixties and beyond.
Lenny Helsing

I would like to get my hands on a hurdy gurdy. No electricity needed. Droning psychedelic bliss at the turn of a crank.

Okay, I'm off to Andy's Music shop!
Gregory Curvey

I made a guitar from an ice cream tub and rubber bands when I was really little, and boasted that I had written 100 songs on it (it was really only ninety)
Chris Wade

The sitar—even played badly, it makes a sixties cover sound good to me
Keith Jones

I rescued a balalaika from Oxfam. It was a mess. The base of the body was split open, top nut hanging off, one rusty string, flaking marquetry and battered varnish.

Ken sorted out the main repairs and I dealt with the finish. When I looked in the sound hole, I found a blue sticker. It gave the maker's name and address in Moscow and was stamped 1973. So, I decided to make some stickers, depicting the Soviet side of the "Space Race."

I now have a Soviet balalaika, complete with Mega Dodo sticker. I can't play it for toffee, but have recently bought a book (published c.1964) on how to play it. I don't understand that either!
Mordecai Smyth

On "Goldfish Bowl," from *Sunflower Army*, the rhythm was supplied by me stamping on a loose floorboard, and the guitar was an electric one not plugged in.

On one of the songs from Crystal Jacqueline's Sun Arise album, I forget which, Brian Rushbrooke, drummer extraordinaire, forgot his sticks and had to play with two wooden kitchen spoons.

And on the next Honey Pot album, *Inside The Whale*, John plays melodica, loads of reverb and phasing, which I loved playing around with, very Augustus Pablo....
Icarus Peel

I did at one time have an enormous autoharp, a parlor grand with shifters with a total of thirty-eight chords to mess about with. I never quite managed to get the hang of it. It now resides in my sister's attic. I might see if she will let me borrow it
Judy Dyble

I have an interesting collection of instruments that I like the sound or look of, but have no time or proper inclination to learn how to play. Dulcimers, autoharps, bouzoukis, mandolins, electro-thingies. I can make a sound on all of them, but not a technically proficient sound; maybe this is best.

I have no need to be a virtuoso dulcimer player; I'd rather use it to get the sounds I have in my head, and create some atmosphere.
Grey Malkin

I played oboe in middle school and High School band. I was usually the only oboe, so I suppose I was technically "first chair" by default, but I never practiced, outside of the occasional half hearted attempt to learn Swan Lake, and I wasn't very good.

During marching band season, my freshman year in High School, I also played xylophone, which I think I was pretty good at—I even got learn a (very short) four mallet vibraphone solo, which I consider impressive.
Leah Cinnamon

I love the sound of the ulliean pipes, well played. It doesn't get any more rock and roll. You have to wrestle this sheep's bladder like a python while simultaneously fingering a chanter in the most delicate way. Set the drones, accompany yourself with the regulators. It's a one-person orchestra, a call-to-arms, a celebration, and a lament. I'll never be able to play a set of those things.
Jefferson Hamer

I play the Roland SH 101 monophonic analog synth, but I usually don't play it like a normal keyboard. I play one note and it has a function that keeps that note going... then I jam the sliders—LFO / resonance / frequency / oscillation etc—usually linked through massive effects, but sometimes just raw.

You could put me on stage with that thing alone at Wembley, and it could shake the rafters. It is an amazing piece of architecture in the right hands.
Jet Wintzer

There are few things finer in this world than the sound of a banjo ukulele. I decided to buy a good one a few years ago, because I wanted to learn to play in the George Formby style.

There's quite a bit of technique to playing the different strokes that produce the distinctive syncopated rhythmic style. It's not as easy as it looks. But even a beginner can get a half decent sound on the instrument, and be playing a simple tune in minutes. It does take a bit longer to play the flashier solos.

They are also really loud and produce a nice "snap" when you hit the strings really hard. Above all, they are fun, and really piss off ukulele snobs who don't consider them 'real' instruments and think Formby's novelty songs puerile.

John Blaney

Rowan Amber Mill

David from The Chemistry Set

Dodson & Fogg

CHAPTER TEN

Can You Say "I Love You" with a mix tape MP3? Adventures in modern sound marketing.

I never really made mix tapes for other people. I just made them for myself. I got a very early cassette player in the late sixties, and made loads of mix tapes for my own pleasure.

They just had all the stuff I was into then on them... like Country Joe, Blue Cheer, Steve Miller Band, Ultimate Spinach, Mad River, Savage Resurrection, Clear Light, Spirit, Taste, Blossom Toes, Caravan, Electric Prunes, Hendrix, all that kind of music
Nick Salomon

Everyone knows that some records can be played backwards to reveal hidden messages from Satan, but did you know that if you reverse the turntable in a microwave oven, it actually makes things colder? This is almost certainly how they make frozen peas.
Emily Jones

Remember when they said vinyl was dead? Remember when they said painting was dead? I suppose a certain online retailer would have us believe that the printed book is dead.

Well, vinyl is going to be around for a long time, for the simple reason that people like to hold things, touch things, smell and taste things. You can't do that with a MP3, jpeg or ebook.

A record is a tangible connection with the artiste that made it. You connect with the artiste on so many levels with a physical artifact, that you don't get with a digital release.

I've no doubt that the market for vinyl will ebb and flow. At the moment it seems to be flowing. Who knows how long that will last? But even when it starts to ebb, there will always be the old and bold who'll prefer a hard copy to play, and a new generation to discover records and the thrill of tracking down that elusive Mega Dodo rarity from 2011.
John Blaney

Vinyl never went away—it was the record companies that deserted it, believing they could make better margins out of CDs.
Keith Jones

I can only speak for myself, but I welcome any way of getting your music out there—Bandcamp and Soundcloud are two of the best, and they can really be used to positive effect.

Bandcamp is particularly useful for me. Setting up your own mail order site for CDs and vinyl was easy as soon as we had PayPal, but offering downloads was much harder. Bandcamp offers a full digital

solution for artists and labels, allowing them to manage their own content and set their own prices, and it's a much nicer interface than many other regular digital music stores. I'm extremely thankful for its existence.
Steven Collins

Artists are so mercurial—which makes them a terrible investment! You have to love the music so much, want it to exist so badly, that no amount of navel-gazing bullshit can faze you.

We've had bands break up within weeks of their record coming out, or change direction and disown music we'd dumped thousands into. That's thousands of dollars that we went to work every day to earn, with the only results an immovable record and an artist blaming us for not making them famous.

You need thick skin, and an appreciation for small victories. Helping make something happen that you think is great is always a win, regardless of what comes after.

I've also developed empathy for the labels, managers and collaborators who've had to put up with my "artistic" nonsense—or refused to do so—over the years. I can totally appreciate their perspective now!
Jed Davis

I'm really pleased to see the resurgence of interest in vinyl. Bevis began just before CDs started taking off, and to my mind, though they were kind of useful, they were always an inferior product.

The packaging was shit, and at first they sounded really tinny. Now they sound great, but the packaging is still crap. So, yeah, vinyl is great and the album sleeves are the right size. It's music and art winning through.
Nick Salomon

I don't see much of a commercial future for bland, sterile CDs, and even less for paid-for downloads.

The only future for paid-for recorded music that I can see is to create something that looks and sounds great, has lasting value, means something to the buyer, makes them feel good about spending hard-earned cash on it, makes them want to repeat the dosage.
Keith Jones

We've always put a lot of time and effort into our artwork and concepts. The visual identity of the Ghost Box label wears its references on its sleeve (even if they are a little obscure sometimes), so I guess that helps drag in the right audience.
Jim Jupp

I love immersive listening experiences, with packaging that provides complementary visual and tactile elements to accompany the music. I just got the Led Zeppelin III reissue the other day, and I spun that crazy cardboard wheel for the entire duration of the album. It never stopped being awesome!
Jed Davis

A release on vinyl sounds better, looks better and means more. Music on vinyl gets listened to. Maybe by relatively few people, but it does get heard—and by people who care about the music
Keith Jones

We tried to make CDs that were products that you'd want to own for themselves, in addition to the music.
Joel Slevin

I'd been self-releasing my own music since 1993, with stints on a couple of indie labels, and some work as a sideman for various acts. I had a reasonable understanding of what it took to get an album produced, pressed and released.
A few friends of mine got major label deals in the early 2000s, and I was surprised to learn how little money actually changed hands in those situations—more than we could match, sure, but we realized that if we pooled our income and kept our roster small, we could provide a pretty nice opportunity for a couple of artists a year
Jed Davis

We did a little advertising, and were very lucky to find some friendly and helpful radio presenters and online bloggers.
The bands have also worked very hard to promote their records and the label. It's been a team effort and I like to think of Mega Dodo as a workers' cooperative.
We're all working together, and the label wouldn't have got this far if there had been any ego wars.
John Blaney

Our artists don't do much live performance, and are happy to remain fairly anonymous. So the label acts as a kind of identity for everyone—getting equal billing to the performer name.
Effectively, we're a small collective of very like-minded artists that work on solo projects and often collaborate, [although] we also have occasional guests like the Soundcarriers and the Pattern Forms who are more like regular bands.
The main thing is that everyone understands and fits into the Ghost Box aesthetic.
Jim Jupp

I would love for Mega Dodo to eventually be a vinyl-only label, but there is still a market for CDs. Not everybody has a record player, so for the time being, the label will be releasing CDs alongside vinyl.

But vinyl is what everybody associated with the label loves. We did dabble with downloads—the Mordecai Smyth album is still available at your favorite digital retailer.

But while digital formats have a place, I've stopped making Mega Dodo releases available as downloads. Downloads are boring, and our audience much prefer a well crafted physical artifact.

John Blaney

The piracy thing is part of the landscape, and we all have to get used to it, unfortunately. There's a few tools to mitigate it, but it's not going to go away. The pitiful income from the streaming services is also a little depressing.

But I think you either have to take a stance and face not making any money from music, or embrace the whole damned lot and see all these things as marketing opportunities.

Jim Jupp

I'd like to see the return of the quality album sleeve, with a laminated front and a matt back, and flipover tops and bottoms.

Nick Salomon

I've always been able to see the positives of file sharing. Not in the Napster / Limewire way, where everything is out there on websites available to anybody who wants to grab it for free, but I grew up taping music from the radio, and from friends' records, and in some ways, file sharing is no different.

There's small communities out there who use file sharing to discover what's new, and these are people who then go out and buy the records, or the t-shirts, or go to the shows.

Steven Collins

Sadly, disposable music and a disposable medium go together. If music doesn't mean as much to people as it used to, asking them to shell out for it becomes more and more of a challenge.

Thank god there are still plenty of music junkies out there, and plenty of scope for artists and specialist record labels to feed their habits.

It's possible to do something interesting and creative with the CD format—but there's a lot more scope with vinyl formats.

Keith Jones

Our first experiment with vinyl was a 7″ co-release with JAXART in 2007. It was JAXART's first-ever project—a single by the Valley Arena.

Not an auspicious beginning; we didn't do enough homework and went with the first "manufacturer" we found.

They turned out to be more of a print broker, with no real control over the output, and we blew our street date by over a month. We learned that if we were going to try vinyl again, we had to better understand the process and options.

Jed Davis

I'd like help a few established acts get their music out on vinyl. Too many established acts who release their own albums ignore vinyl, because it looks expensive and time consuming to produce.

Mega Dodo can change all that and get more musicians releasing their music on vinyl… the way it should be heard.

John Blaney

There's a lot of people who use Bandcamp to discover new music. Our fanbase is absolutely tiny in the grand scheme of things, so it's a very good way to help the music find a wider audience.

Since making the whole Owl Service discography available on a "pay what you want" basis, the amount of downloads we've had has gone through the roof.

I've no doubt only a fraction of those people would have ever checked us out if we'd been charging for downloads, and if just a few of them return to buy the next physical Owls release, then I'm happy.

Steven Collins

When it was time to do our first vinyl full-length, in 2008, I did tons of research and discovered that we were operating in a sort of Wild West.

One reputable printer manufactured jackets, but couldn't do inner sleeves, because their folding machinery had been out of use so long it no longer worked properly.

Nobody could make center labels, except a handful of printers who did nothing but center labels.

There was also the matter of mastering. Michael Bassett's Soft Verges was recorded live to two-track at Electrical Audio, sequenced and spliced into master reels in Brooklyn, and mastered by Kevin Gray in LA. No backup copies, just irreplaceable tapes zigzagging across the country. It was so nerve-wracking.

The process has, mercifully, evolved a lot since then—many more manufacturing options at every step.

Jed Davis

There are plenty of bands now enjoying successful careers whose star initially began ascending after their records were initially enjoyed by thousands of people for free via file sharing networks.

In a nutshell, I believe that getting your music onto a lot of hard drives is a very good way of spreading the word, and when you're a tiny little cottage industry like us, you have to give your content away for free to begin with.

As someone who loves physical formats, I can't help but find no real value in digital formats, and so I don't see it as a big deal to give files away purely as listening matter.

Steven Collins

There are so many great new acts out there who deserve to be heard. We hope to continue giving our favorites that opportunity. 10″ records are perfect for that.

We love the 10″ format. We don't see the 10″ as a mini LP, but rather as a big brother to the 7″—specifically, the split 7″.

Doing 10″ splits means we can allow one artist per side an EP's worth of material. It's cost-effective and the package is unique and striking.

Jed Davis

David from United Bible Studies

CHAPTER ELEVEN

What is your favorite among all the recordings you have made, and why?

I love all recording, simply because to do so is to enter an empire outside of the absurd… which is not to say that those of us involved aren't sometimes absurd.

With recording, I prefer to let things happen once you roughly know what you're doing. Rob Jones is very much like this, so the album I recorded with him as Mr. Solo called Wonders Never Cease is my favorite.

We seem to share a joy of melodic exhilaration.
Mikey Georgeson

Well, it's always hard to make a sensible judgement about one's own albums. As I've been in the fortunate position of releasing my own stuff, I only ever put out records that I'm really happy with.

Having said all that, I suppose after a certain amount of time you're able to have a more detached view.

I guess my favorite Bevis albums would be *New River Head*, *Valedictory Songs* and the most recent two, *The Leaving Of London* and *White Numbers*. I think they all have a very solid mixture of good songs, good playing, and they can occasionally catch you a bit off guard too.
Nick Salomon

Mine is "Martyred Heart," the title track of our 2014 release of all-original work. I love it for its sweet harmonies, reminding me of when I was a child. It is simple, based on real-world events, and in the protest tradition.
Tom Conway

Hard to say, sorry! So many… I'm gonna cop out and say: the Absinthee albums; *Soviet Kitsch* [Regina Spektor]; *Is This It* and *Room On Fire* [the Strokes]; the Satellites' *Our Very Bright Darkness*; my own album *I Lick the Moog*.

These all come rushing into my mind! One more… a "Queen Bitch" cover with Sarah Maguire.
Gordon Raphael

My song "Little Ghost," recorded in 2005. I wrote it sometime in the nineties, and it was inspired by the death of a lovely little dog I knew called Tiny, who belonged to a very unique, but very messed up gentleman that I had been involved with.

After his dog died, he started using heroine full time and there was nothing I could do. There was a lot of secret heartbreak in that song—so much that I didn't record it for years, not until the pain had faded into wistfulness and sorrow.

When I did, my own lovely long-lost dog, Daisy, was pattering around the room and you can hear her collar jingling on the very end of the song, when she came up to me at the end of the best take and gave me a loving lick on the hand.

So there are two special ghost dogs in that song, which makes it very special indeed.
Emily Jones

The Volume—*Timelines* (recorded Summer 1994). I've never played better, alas, in my life. I have no idea what went so right that day.
Pete Meriwether

The Wood Beyond the World is easily my favorite of the albums I've made. I had such a definite idea for it, and everything I did in making it was done with only that in mind.

It's probably the most cohesive of my albums sound- and theme-wise, and it's also the nearest I've yet come to making music that really does capture that liminal state I love so much. Silvery, rainy, full of ghosts.
Amanda Votta

["Song to Comus"] …was based on the story of Comus from the *Masque of Comus* by John Milton. Actually I wrote the whole song in one afternoon on an acid trip.

The whole concept of riffs, lyrics and ideas all came together in one intense LSD buzz. I remember it vividly.

I was back at Eynsford (the family home) after leaving Perth Road (Comus' communal house). My mum was downstairs and I secretly dropped a tab out of sheer boredom really and "Song to Comus" just started.
Roger Wooton

[*Wake the Vaulted Echo*] is the sound of me cramming as many of my influences into twenty minutes as possible, and if you listen closely, you'll hear that at that time I was obsessed with Boris, Alice Coltrane, Six Organs of Admittance, Bohren Und Der Club of Gore, Funkadelic, and the British folk revival of the 1960s / seventies.
Steven Collins

The first album *Hymns & Ghosts* is my favorite of all our releases. It flowed very naturally from conception through to the recording process.

During that period, I picked up a band mate, played the songs hundreds of times and became a lot better musician.

The reviews we received from its release really bolstered my confidence, and made me think that it was worth carrying on making music.

Richard Thompson

I'm very proud of "Forgive Me I Love Her."

The goal is a song that speaks of myself and reminds some people that I'm in love with a charming girl, so you have to accept it, even if it bothers you. But given that I am a pacifist, I try to smooth the path. "Try trying to love and soothe the burning flames"

The instrumental is quite comprehensive and coherent, even if the main theme is repeated throughout the song. I find that the balance is not too bad.

Maxime Schwartz

I have a soft spot for "Spencer The Rover" by the Magickal Folk of the Faraway Tree.

We sang harmonies together in the kitchen into a single mic and it felt beautiful. That kind of thing was new to me, and I couldn't get enough of it.

Alas, that band never played live, but I doubt we could have topped whatever came out in that moment anyway.

David Colohan

I have to say my favorites on Reverb Worship have to be Sproatly Smith and the Hare And The Moon. Both are really wonderful artists, and I am very pleased to think that I have been associated with both via Reverb Worship

Roger Linney

As many people say—my favorite recording is the one I'm working on at the moment, the one that's still full of unexplored possibilities and that still might turn out to be the best track I've ever made.

All the pieces I've ever recorded mean something to me, and have memories and stories attached, so it's difficult to choose a favorite. However, some of my favorite recordings are ones that I've made of performances by musicians or poets at parties, just capturing the moment with a hand-held recorder.

After a bit of processing, I've given CDs back to the performers as a memento of the event. I've been thanked several times by people who were really pleased to get a recording as they'd been too

occupied (in the case of a wedding) or too drunk (in the case of a party) to have much of a memory of the event themselves afterwards!
Chris Bond

"Compound Eyes" off of our second album, *Praying Mantis*. I really like the composition, and I feel it's one of my least embarrassing performances.
Jeb Morris

My last album, *The Carmelite Divine* (Original Soundtrack), is in fact the original soundtrack to my actual life. From beginning to end, all the songs are about my relationship to my perfect wife Hannah and my family, and it contains lots of privately coded, heartfelt, personal references.

Also, "Gemini From Golden Grove" means a lot to me, because it is about my twin sister, who died a few years ago.
Simon Berry

So far it's the original theme from *Tales from the Black Meadow*. I'm proud of that piece, as it grew out of one of my many flukes when I was experimenting.

Basically, it was really unlike anything I'd done before, and it led me down a road to a new type of genre or sound to play with, and I've never looked back.
Kev Oyston

I love "Wildflower"—I find it a joy to sing, and love its ethereal otherworldly feel. It is really atmospheric.
Ellie Coulson

I think I'm pleased with Mark and The Clouds' "The Grudge," considering there were so many musicians in it, as I had to push volumes up or down to create dynamic space in the song.

When you have, for instance, a guitar soloing at the same time as an organ, it can sound a bit too much, so I had to move the faders down to let others be heard. But I like the result.
Marco Magnani

My favourite Chonyid recordings would be "3," as it has such a different atmosphere to our other pieces, and the *Live at Unearthing Forgotten Horrors*, which makes me smile at the accidental mayhem we caused with eight pint glasses shattering, and one person spontaneously throwing up... much to the annoyance of Constance Humphries, who had joined us as dancer for the event; and another person complaining that not even Sunn O))) had vibrated his earplugs loose.

Andy Hokano

It's our last album, *Reverberating Garden Number 7*, that came out last summer through Mega Dodo. It's the first real band album by Octopus Syng (the two earlier albums were my one man's band albums) and it's the first album that I recorded and mixed by myself.

But the biggest reason why it's my favorite recording is simple; they are the best songs and the best sound. I hope the next album will be even better. It will be out next autumn on Mega Dodo, and it will be titled *Hollow Ghost / Rochelle Salt*.

It will be quite a different album; it'll be interesting to hear what people will think. I like the new stuff that we have made, but do other listeners? That is the question.

Jaire Pätäri

It's the first song Jayne and I ever recorded, "Neo Theme." It has made its way onto all of our proper albums (*Imperial Quasar* is a compilation, and it isn't on that) in one form or another, and always will.

Jayne and I recorded the vocals with a hand held micro cassette in the shower of a bathroom in a motel in Taunton, England. It is my favorite song I've ever written, or ever will write.

Jet Wintzer

The favorite tune I've recorded is "Song For Annie Needham," on *Minstrel's Grave*. Annie was one of the ladies I looked after in the day centre for people with learning disabilities that I worked in. She was fun to be around, and we all had a soft spot for her.

I heard she'd died peacefully in her sleep after a party, at a ripe old age. I was notified about her death by text at a service station on the way back from a gig. I went home, wrote the song, and had it recorded and mixed before her funeral. It's based on John Denver's "Annie's Song."

Later on, I transcribed it for a music box, and it is usually in our live set. It's a tricky one to play, I have to concentrate, which isn't easy as I'm thinking about Ann's cheeky laugh.

Sproatly Smith

"Rise and Fall" and "Trip in D," both instrumental tracks off my album *The Fall and Rise of...*, because they just worked. I learned that there's a fine line between something still being not quite there, and it

being absolutely (subjectively) perfect. Both tracks allow improvisation within their structures, and another bonus is that they haven't got me warbling all over them.
Chris Anderson

"Dark Peace" was a culmination of each band member's best traits. Andrew has very steady and primal drumming during it.

Chantelle has very smooth backing vocals that add an airy atmosphere to the recording. Duncan flexes his sitar playing, and arranged a trippy harmony for Andrew and Chantelle to sing.
Duncan Shepard

I can just imagine [Roger Wooton's] poor mother (a very nice lady by the way!) sitting downstairs, reading the paper, or cooking dinner, and hearing this frenzied, manic, rasping voice, screaming about rape and taking of virginity, emanating from the bedroom....
Bobbie Watson

Usually whatever I am working on now! But probably "Martians Don't Surf!"

It has been a very lucky song for us; it was our first play on BBC national radio, and our first original release on Fruits de Mer Records. It was the first song I wrote after the Zeta Puppies actually existed... pretty well all the songs on *Burying The Bones* were written before I had any idea of actually recording them.

Also, "Martians Don't Surf!" sort of defined the elements of the Zeta Puppies style... the low, twangy guitar riff, prominent bass, weird electronic noises and fifties movie influenced lyrics.

Also! I recorded the keyboard part with my arm in a sling.

It was going to be an instrumental called "When Martians Attack!", but then I came up with the line "Martians Don't Surf!" and the lyric wrote itself in about five minutes.
Tom Woodger

Our favorite recording is our song "Checking the Weather," because it's upbeat, has a positive vibe, and has sunny harmonies.
Aaron Hemington

The title song on the *Execution of Frederick Baker* album with Alison [O'Donnell]. It just feels like an enormous clash between the nineteenth and twenty-first centuries to me.

Putting it together was like a really difficult puzzle. I had a version that was pretty much finished, but neither of us thought it was good enough, so I started completely from scratch, apart from Alison's vocal and Tony Swettenham's keyboard parts.

The end result was "yes, this is what I've wanted to do for years."

I particularly like the bit where Alison sings "he mounts the scaffold and the drop is falling" and the music stops dead. I didn't notice the relevance until after I did that. A happy accident.

Graeme Lockett

'A Smashing Day Out pts 1-3' from my album *The Midwich Youth Club and Hobby Centre*, as it encapsulates all the lovely daytrips / holidays spent with my Grandad in the 1970s.

I loved him very much, and he was always made the most tedious, banal experience the best fun you could ever have, and it's sort of my tribute to him.

Alan Murphy

"The Pleasures of the Long Thin Garden" is a great recording. Guest vocals, and guest violins. There is quite a lot going on but everything seems to come together into a great little upbeat "alt-pop" song.

Mark Reuter

I like everything Mega Dodo has released. The reason I released the first record was because I wanted a copy of the Mordecai Smyth album on LP, and the only way to get one was to release it myself.

If I had to pick one, it would be Ivan Ivanovich's version of "Mull Of Kintyre." It's the best version of the Wings "classic" ever recorded, and the worst selling record Mega Dodo has released thus far.

John Blaney

Another recording I'm particularly pleased with is "Drifting into Wonderland," by Instant Flight, as there were lots of backwards noises I had to take care of.

Funnily enough, I was using a Roland digital 8 track machine which had all the options except the one to reverse the sound, so I had to mix the track first, and add the backwards guitars on top of it using an old program called Cooled Edit Pro.

Now, using Cubase, I don't have those kind of problems anymore.

Marco Magnani

Mine is... "52 Hz Whale." It's the only song I've written that dares to express something very personal about myself.

I was diagnosed with Asperger's syndrome—a form of autism— just under two years ago, at the age of thirty-seven, and the song isn't just about a lonely whale, it is about my condition and the feeling I often get that I am not communicating on the "right" frequency.

An astute listener described it as a cri de coeur. That can be sad and frightening, but what balances it is the fact that the song's very existence as a thing of my creation also declares, "look! See what a gift

my condition has given me, that I could make this lovely expressive thing!" Tom's spare playing on the track really gives the feeling of depth and remoteness I wanted.
Joanna Swan

Easy. "Sinister Cyclist" Why? Well, the best songs, in my opinion, are usually the ones that write themselves, and this one did exactly that.

Originally, it was called "Serious Cyclist," and was about a girl I used to see each morning on my way to work. She had all the latest gear; top of the range bike, cycling clothes, ray bands, flashing lights, the lot.

Anyway, my imagination took over and I thought, "what if she was a witch on her way to a ritual?"

Once that thought had taken control, it wrote itself. Recording was easy and fun too. I love the way the drummer and bass player gave it a swing / reggae groove in places, which is unusual for this type of song.

Also, the chord progression is easy (good for lazy guitarists like me), so this all went towards creating a lovely vibe in the studio. I think it is a fun, catchy character sketch and I still like it to this day.
Mordecai Smyth

At the moment we are working on an album, so it would probably be one of those songs that would be the favorite at the moment. But, if we choose among the songs that are available on one of our records now, I choose two: "Do I Know You?"—the rather epic song from our *By the Time it gets Dark* EP on Fruits de Mer which has an otherworldly feel which I like. When I haven't listened to it for a while, I think, did we do this ?

"Julia Dream of All the Pretty Horses," from our first record, was in some ways the song that started what Us and Them is today, so that song has got a special place in my heart.

When Andy Bracken at Fruits de Mer suggested that we should add one more song and make the single an EP, this idea came up. I have always liked "Julia Dream" by Pink Floyd, and Andy said that the song was loosely based on an old American folksong called "All the Pretty Little Horses."

So we brought these two songs together with some of our own songs. Then we got a song that showed a darker side of Us and Them, and also a more untraditional way of arranging songs.
Anders Håkanson

My favorite of my recordings is the Greanvine album *Mark You That and Noat You Wel*. It is the album that is most mine that I have done (apart from my solo album), but it has been so finely rendered by Steven Collins, who it has been my greatest blessing to know and to work with.
Diana Collier

This is another tricky one. If I had to single out one particular track, however, it would probably be "Echoes from a Distant Star," which first appeared on my second EP.

I've always seen myself as working towards a minimalist ideal in the studio, and the first version of "Echoes from a Distant Star," with its single bliptronic sequence, could perhaps be seen as a culmination of this approach.

More recently, the track has been remixed by the wonderful Joe Foster. "The sound of star light, mixed with deep space desolation." Available now at all good record shops.
Peter Lyon

"Temperature Drop" from *Ronco Revival Sound*, even after Ant said it reminded him of "Biko" by Peter Gabriel, which was quite distressing.

I like it, because it has moved several people to tears, and it's usually me being moved to tears by other people's music; the first time I heard "Fire of The Mind" by Coil, to quote Chris Morris, I damn near cried all the water out of my body.

There's also the fact that when we recorded it, as I was getting to a particularly emotional crescendo of the words "Will I awake and will I scream?," Ant awoke from his booze induced slumber on the settee and screamed "what're you fucking cunts doing here?."

A less disturbing comparison comes from B.B. (Brian Bordello, not Brigitte Bardot) repeatedly calling it "Great Dominions" by mistake.
Dan Bordello

My favorite album so far is *And When the Light Ran Out*, the album I released this January. I am really pleased with it as a whole. It sounds like I was really singing about things that were bothering me, and I think it was all quite cathartic to record it, because it definitely made me feel better.
Chris Wade

"Bergerac," because it's the type of song I enjoyed listening to with my headphones when I was a teenager, smoking and tripping in my room.
Narsis Passolas

My favorite recording is a song called "Running Back to You," which can be found on our *Extra Smooth* EP on Small Bear Records. I love it so much because I am a huge Walker Brothers / Scott Walker fan, and this song catches the feel perfectly.

I actually have nothing to do with the track; it was written by Dan, who plays all the instruments on it, and it was sang by Ant and Dan as a duet.

Ant is not the greatest singer in the world, but he has a frailty I like in the verses which he sings, but then when Dan comes in it, is like God has entered the room for a moment; a stunning vocal which sends shivers down my back and has made more than a couple of people cry.
Brian Bordello

Last summer, during the recording of our last LP (not released yet) with Owen Morris, he had the idea of recording a very psych outro for the song "Pinkman," with a Spanish guitar and an acoustic guitar at the same time (Martin HD28) as a battle of guitars.

Jose (our sitarist) played the Spanish guitar, as he is very good playing flamenco style as well. It was a very exciting moment, and the final result was very cool. We made only four or five takes and the flow and the atmosphere we got was really nice . Hope you like.
Jordi Bel

Always the one to come. I get fed up rather quickly with things when they're done.
Francois Sky

I love Crystal Jacqueline's version of "Remember A Day." It was always my favorite Floyd tune and I think we really nailed it.

Most people do not do Floyd vocals well, but Crystal can match that pure Englishness and the slightly strange harmonies. The drumming from Mr Rushbrooke was perfect too.

I also love "Let's Go Fly A Kite" from *Sun Arise*. Actually persuading the drummer that I wasn't joking when I said we were going to plunder Mary Poppins's back catalog was quite a task. I was very pleased with the guitars, too, on that one, and I think we soared at the right moment.

From the next Crystal Jacqueline album, *Rainflower*, I particularly enjoy "Water Hyacinth." The acoustic guitar is in a different tuning for a change, and is a real pleasure to play. The idea was to make a musical version of [Sir John Everett] Millais's painting *Ophelia*, and I think Crystal brings the scene to shimmering life.
Icarus Peel

I rarely listen to my own music, but there are a few of the Mooch albums that I do return to. I suppose—if I had to choose—my favorite would be "A Samhain Mask" from *Stations Of The Sun*. It's one of my best melodies, I think, and Beck sang it beautifully.
Steve Palmer

My favorite tracks so far are the ones I've done for Fruits de Mer Records. I've gotten to pay tribute to bands and songs I love, and have the tracks included on cool vinyl compilations, so I've given it my all every time.

"All The World is Love" is special to me because it was the first time I played and sang everything on a track.

My friend Chris Griffin and I gave it a psychedelic mix and it got played on the BBC a few times! I would love for Graham Nash to hear it!
Ted Selke

Ahhh… a hard question to answer. Maybe my favorite is my third record as the Child of A Creek, *Find A Shelter along the Path*, because I think I could say it's a very complete record, warm, cozy like a friend and very intimate.

It's a diary of a surreal day I spent across the mountains near home during the wintertime in 2009.

Once back home, I picked up the guitar, trying to summarize in the most harmonious and natural way what that day has meant to me.
Lorenzo Bracaloni

I don't really have a favorite. Once it's recorded, it's gone.
Drew Mulholland

The best recording I have done is with the Green Question Mark and is a cover of the Sonics's "Santa Claus," because it was easy, effective, and fun.
Marrs Bonfire

I'm Not Here from 2006; my second album, but the first that I found satisfactory in that it contained so many elements I had been dreaming of for a long time, such as the marriage of song structures to strange sound worlds; the acoustic guitar layered in an approximation of a sort of Scraibinesque piano style; haunting female vocals evoking an ancient world that lies within and beyond nature; a faun's dream, a musical equivalent to the art of Claude Lorraine, Gustav Moreau and Austin Osman Spare. Or so I'd like to think; the listener may feel otherwise.
Sand Snowman

That's a really tough one. We are very prolific and had lots of highs, and we love recording as much as playing live. However, last year we did our first gig ever in Germany, and it may have been the excitement of playing in the birthplace of all our seventies musical heroes, Neu, Kraftwerk, Can, etc, as

Sandman Snow

Sendelica

we ended up playing a really long show with a monstrous forty-six minute version of "Master Benjamin Warned Young Albert Not to Step on the Uninsulated Air."

Luckily the gig was recorded on a multi track recorder, and is being released later this year as a two LP / two CD set on Sunhair Music. I'm very pleased about this recording.
Pete Bingham

Usually the songs that record themselves end up sounding best. I would say "Blood and Bones" is probably my favorite thing I have written and recorded.

It was one of the first things I recorded solo after previously being in a band, where every single note recorded got argued over (endlessly).

That lack of stress and the sense of freedom made the recording of "Blood and Bones" a pleasure, and it was one of the rare occasions that the song ended up sounding like what I had actually envisaged.
Stephen Stannard

My favorite of all recordings is always the last one that I have just made. It cannot be otherwise, because it is the only one to be still extremely exciting. I can listen to a new recording up to a hundred times in a couple of days.

After that initial excitement, the magic fades a bit, and I start finding flaws and imperfections everywhere. Of course there are recordings that I like more than others, but I don't have a top favorite, nor some top three or top five lists to talk about.
Paolo Sala

The first Tír na nÓg album… a bit like first girlfriends. Freshness and optimism of youth, and a whole lot of magic!
Leo O'Kelly

I have a soft spot for the stuff we did for Pete Jackson's show on Dandelion Radio, both the 2011 and 2014 sessions; the chance to just let rip a little and blast through some old tunes we haven't played for a while, and then throw in a cover version or two.

Some of the sessions would end up with our kids playing tambourines and cow bells and things, while I played kazoo. It was fun!
Tom Woodger

The last single, "Elapsed Memories." It has all the elements we strive for; harmony, melody, a varied sonic landscape and lots of interesting production techniques to keep the listener interested for multiple plays.
Dave McLean

The Book of AM because it was my dream to meet great artists I love so much, and who influenced me. And it was a bigger dream to make music with them in the legendary Deià place, and to collaborate with Daevid Allen and Gilli Smyth from Gong.
Will Z

Head Music—a double LP of Krautrock / kosmische covers. I've loved German progressive / kosmische music since I "discovered" Grobschnitt in a Virgin record shop in Birmingham in the early seventies; *Head Music* was the first Fruits de Mer album I was let loose on to compile from scratch and even design, and Grobschnitt's Eroc recorded a mad intro especially for it.
Keith Jones

I suspect that I'm like most other musicians in that it is the thing that I'm currently working on which always seems like the best! The latest is called "Darkness Into Light," and is due to come out as the cover disc on the great *Optical Sounds* zine sometime soon.

It is a bit heavier than some of the other recent Black Tempest recordings and features more guitars and basses. It's a kind of doom / raga / synth / noise thing.

Apart from that, I'd say it's a toss up between an early Black Tempest release, *Proxima*, which was put out by Apollolaan Recordings, and the collaboration we did with Dead Sea Apes, *The Sun Behind the Sun*, on Cardinal Fuzz.

I love Dead Sea Apes, and it was a stone privilege to work with them. I hope that at some point in the future, we'll get a chance to work on another collaboration with them.
Stephen Bradbury

I quite like our recording of Bob Dylan's "It's All Over Now, Baby Blue" which we did at London's Toerag Studio for our Screaming Apple issued album *Downbeat And Folked Up* back in the early 00s.

We'd been doing it live for a while, and had been getting a pretty good feel going, so when it really came together for the recording, that was a great bonus.

Same goes for our cover of the Sandy Coast song "I'm A Fool," that we cut at the same session. It's another of those sixties Dutch beat treats—we've done quite a few—and I just feel that we did it some justice.

Aside from that, I'm really encouraged by the recordings we've been doing at Angus' Ravencraig studio set up, including our recent cover of the Pretties' "LSD" on the Fruits de Mer flexi box set project, and also those that have come out on singles in the past year on the labels Dirty Water (London) and State (Folkestone).

We've another couple that have yet to make it out, including "What You Can't Mend" and "Don't Change Your Mind," which I'm inclined to think are among our very best efforts too, with a pretty solid sound and some gnarly fuzztone that really brings out the best in the songs.

Lenny Helsing

[On our cover of Moby Grape's "I Am Not Willing"], one of the special unique ingredients we've used is probably slidey things; and there are a lot of slidey things on "I Am Not Willing.'"

Which is great, because flip the single over to "Sitting by the Window," and there's lots of bugs as well, crickets and cicadas to be precise. Insects and slidey things.

Tom Hughes

Having to choose from a back catalogue is tough. I can only remember smatterings of the Mellow Candle demos and album recording, as the air was thick with mind-altering smoke, not to mention joss sticks.

The way I record currently is a lot different due to budget constraints. Swaddling Songs was recorded daily until it was done. Albums recorded now are spread out over months, a bit here, a bit there so there is much less of a sense of continuity.

I love recording for United Bible Studies. Some of it is downright bonkers and not a choice cup of tea for many, but it is so creative, and at turns serious and lighthearted.

"Rosary Bleeds," not yet released, is a particular favorite because it stretched my songwriting and recording abilities. I love all the work I have done with all the collectives I am involved with.

I can't really pick one favorite recording. "The Wooden Coat," on its own, with The Owl Service stands out. I am completely at one with it. It is meaningful, but also satisfies the dark psych folk side of my nature.

Alison O'Donnell

"June Sunshine" which, for me, is the entire essence of Sky Picnic, wrapped into four minutes. It grooves, it's got melody, a bouncy bass line and bursts of fuzz guitar. It's the song I would play for someone who has never heard us before.

Chris Sherman

I am very proud of *Songs from the Black Meadow*. It is a project I was mulling over for some time after *Tales from the Black Meadow* was first published.

I particularly enjoyed the notion that the original Tales album and book influenced each other, and wanted to see if something could be created by other artists that would add to the world.

What I love about it is the eclectic mix of artists, genres (Folk, Drone, Classical, Spoken Word and Soundscape) and the fact that they come from so far afield (Greece, USA, Newcastle, Cornwall, Scotland, Ireland and Reading!).

The Internet is a great bridge builder. This, in turn, influenced a little book of the same name. With this whole experience we can see pop chowing down on itself with great enthusiasm.

Chris Lambert

I guess I will say "Sister Strange And The Stuffed Furry Things." I worked on that song for years, mainly rewriting the lyrics over and over again. I had the chorus worked out, but couldn't find a theme / story for the verses, and I really loved the melody so I refused to let it die.

We played earlier versions of the song in our live set in the nineties, but it never included the string parts I was hearing in my head, thus never quite fulfilling my vision for the song.

When we recorded a demo of one of the early versions with a cellist, it didn't quite work either. It was actually the Mellotron that really made the final version come together. I suppose that it had the sound I was always hearing in my head, instead of cello.

The lyric came to me one day after watching a Queen reunion video, with Paul Rodgers filling Freddie Mercury's shoes. I think Paul influenced my voice that day too. I'm still really happy with how the final mix came together.

Gregory Curvey

From the first album, *Sun Arise*, the song "By The Way." Simple baroque style over gorgeous intricate guitar. I was also very pleased with how the vocals sounded.

Crystal Jacqueline

"Little Joe was blowing on the slide trombone." What was big Joe doing? Is there a non-slide trombone that only Big Joe knows about?

Tom Hughes

My favourite recording of mine is our new album *Wood Witch*. It feels like the pinnacle of the Hare And The Moon, all that we are.

In terms of length it would be, in ye olde parlance, a double album; it has drones, heavy guitars, strings, harp, experimental moments, instrumentals, twisted folk music… everything that I ever wanted to be a part of the music that we make.

If we are talking about a non-the Hare And The Moon album, then it would be *The Floating World's We Hunted*; I'm incredibly fond of that album, and proud of my part in making it.
Grey Malkin

Each one has my heart, but my favorite is "Atom Spark Hotel.' It makes me believe in dreams.
Jayne Gabriel

I personally liked the intro of our song "The World is in Our Hands," from the album *Passport to Freedom* (2010). We had the idea of matching a Martin Luther King speech with the music.

It was magic, because when we imported the audio in the pro tools session, we blew our minds with the result. It seems that Martin Luther King is singing in some moments.

His speech fits perfectly with the intro, and we didn't need to edit it at all. It was very funny.
Jordi Bel

I love the *Lost In The West* record I co-produced with Reed Foehl and John Raham. All the sounds are really great on that record, drums through Neve's, bass through a Telefunken V72, Reed's singing is very strong and emotional. I also like how my electric guitar parts came out. I played almost all Stratocaster through a Roland Space Echo.
Jefferson Hamer

My favorite is always the next album I make, because I never know what it will turn out like, or what will be on it or indeed who will be on it. It's the next adventure. I am proud of all that I have done.
Judy Dyble

We had to have cicadas.
Marco Rossi

CHAPTER TWELVE

What is the most bizarre thing that has ever happened to you, or that you have witnessed, in relation to being in a band?

Probably this!!!...
Tom Woodger

I was playing in Mr. Crowe's Garden, and I booked us a date opening for the Mercy Seat at Einstein-a-Go-Go in Jacksonville Beach, FL.

I was checking out the little adjoining shop and was looking at a calendar or something. A few months later, Jefferson Holt booked us a show in New York City (our first), at a club called Drums.

I hit up my childhood friends about the date, and Josh Braun (Circus Mort, Del Byzanteens, Lizzy Descloux, Deep Six) showed up with a girl on his arm.

He said "this is Faye, she plays in a band called Let's Active." Then Zena Von Heppinstall showed up, and she had brought me the calendar from Florida. She invited me to go out on the town but I told her I had to help with the band's stuff, then the band called me a wuss when I told them about it later.

That was also the night that George Drakoulias came out to see us, and talked to us after the set about his idea for a Stones sound-alike band.
Ted Selke

Drinking hard liquor and talking Stravinsky, whilst having a midnight sauna in a Swedish forest with supermodels and members of a popular death metal band.
Chris Anderson

That gig at Cromer Pier was quite bizarre!
Tom Conway

We had been booked to play at an outdoor café on the far end of the pier during the summer holidays and we were doing it as a favor to a friend.

We were performing songs from *CunningFolk*, which all have quite a strong pagan flavor, but there was an Evangelical Christian outdoor service going on simultaneously only a few yards away, so that made us feel… rather uncomfortable!
Joanna Swan

Even without that, I think we were a hard sell for the kiss-me-quick-hat and ice-cream brigade.
Tom Conway

Nobody knew what to make of us and it didn't help that we were playing un-amplified, and the sea breeze just whipped our voices out to sea! We were completely ignored.

Of course, it's expected at gigs that not everyone will like you, and might chat while you're performing, but I am not exaggerating when I say not one single denizen of Cromer Pier took a blind bit of notice. It was our nadir!
Joanna Swan

It was a complete contrast to our rehearsal the day before, which was actually far more successful. My extended family were camping at Whitlingham Broad, just outside Norwich, so I thought it would be nice for us to combine our practice with a bit of camp-fire entertainment.

We sat on cushions, there were babies crawling around, there was bunting, wildflowers, rapt attention…
Tom Conway

Just like a hippy commune in the acid-folk heyday! It was—dare I say it, Tom?—magical!
Joanna Swan

And then the Pier the next day—Shudder!
Tom Conway

No more end-of-the-pier shows for us.
Joanna Swan

I was hanging out in the Casbah in Hillbrow, Johannesburg, in the early eighties with musician Colin Shamley, who I used to work with quite a bit at the time.

I was having a double thick malt milkshake and there was a small TV high up on the opposite wall which caught his eye.

Suddenly he said, "Isn't that you up there?"

"Yeah," I replied. For a brief spell, I was fooled. It looked and sounded like me, but I certainly wasn't prancing around to "Love Connection" by Plastik Mak, and couldn't recall having done so.

I had left Terry Dempsey's band some months before, with the result that a lookalike had been hired in my place to do a television appearance to promote the single. It was a surreal moment and I had a bit

of trouble convincing Colin it wasn't me. The thing is, it could so easily have been me in my own head. I could sing and dance.
Alison O'Donnell

Performing as part of a Victorian insane asylum (immersive theatre) can be pretty good. There was a half-naked bloke chained to the wall behind me.
Mark Reuter

My bandmate drinking too much honey beer. No further explanation of that situation will be forthcoming.
Richard Thompson

Being invited to play in a small town, arriving there and discovering the concert was part of a political party campaign, with the stage being the huge trunk of a truck.

But the straw that broke the camel´s back was when the guy asked us to play with a T-shirt with his face on, asking for votes. We told him to f*** o** and left.
João Branco Kyron

The most bizarre incident was discovering that, while gigging with Stereolab in a theatre in London, we had been given Larry Grayson's old dressing room.
Drew Mulholland

Gotta agree with Mark [Reuter] on this one—immersive theatre Victorian insane asylum was pretty out there!
Ellie Coulson

During the recording of our first album *The Thanes Of Cawdor*, in the summer of 1987, we had noticed a really intrusive humming noise coming from one of the amps—an old semi-triangular Farfisa—and so our studio engineer told us to disconnect the earth wire.

We did and the noise disappeared. Later that evening, while trying to get mine and organist / occasional guitarist Bruce Lyall's guitar in tune, I was sitting near him on a stool and was reaching over to tune one of his strings when I think the loose ends of string poking out from the guitar head-stock must've touched and out of nowhere—boom! A small ball of fire rushed up the neck, singed the strings and my arms were flung involuntarily up and onto the wall behind me. I'd just been electrocuted!

Fortunately, I wasn't wearing my guitar strap, and so was able to let go of the guitar! Unfortunately, we had forgotten to reconnect the earth wire to the amplifier.

Of course, it was pretty scary, as I seemed to be unable to move or speak for some minutes after.

Once I came to and got my bearings again, I declined the offer of going to hospital to get checked out. Thankfully, no damage was done, and I actually felt quite invigorated, and very much had a real sense of being glad to be alive, which lasted for the rest of the night!

Lenny Helsing

A friend of mine used to work for a record company (Phonogram). He was selling his wife's car in the local newspaper. This guy came round to look at it and said to him, whilst looking at his CD collection, "oh I see you like music."

"Yeah" said Brian.

"I'm in music management" said the guy. "I manage a guitar player called Stevie Ray Vaughan, and we are off to the USA for some gigs next week."

That following week Stevie Ray Vaughan was tragically killed in a helicopter crash….

Roger Linney

I guess that would be the occasions when I've ended up playing with people whose records I bought as a kid. I mean, standing on stage with Country Joe and most of The Fish, being Barry Melton, was bizarre. Playing guitar for Arthur Lee, that was unreal!

Randy Hammon of the Savage Resurrection got up with the Frond and we did two Sav Res songs with him. Brilliant!

I've even given Randy California a lift across London to Waterloo Station!

Nick Salomon

The fact that I'm not rich and famous, and Ed Sheeran and his like are.

Simon Berry

Music has always been a strange, synchronous, bizarre journey, full of weird, wonderful, and sometimes horrible, experiences. So, in short, the entire thing is a bizarre thing.

Amanda Votta

What I find bizarre at present in my performances of Black Meadow stories and folk songs is the fine line I tread when speaking to audience members afterwards.

Should they write to their MP about the disappearances on the North York Moors? (Of course!) Why has nothing been done about this? (Well, only a few have known up until now, but it has been my mission to spread the word further).

I find myself continuing the world building even in conversation, and willing the Black Meadow into existence with my utterly serious answers.
Chris Lambert

Getting off the plane at Geneva airport with Fairport Convention on our way to Montreux, and finding a brass band serenading us.

Only it wasn't for us, sadly.

It was for the Sherlock Holmes Appreciation Society, on their way to re-enact the death of Sherlock Holmes and Moriarty at the Reichenbach Falls. At least, I think that was it.
Judy Dyble

Playing a gig in a farmyard.
Aaron Hemington

United Bible Studies played in the Tunnels in Aberdeen and we couldn't find our fiddle player, who had fallen asleep behind an amp. After this gig, we were told that a ghost had hovered above us while we played. I didn't witness it, but I often think of that ghost. It was probably our fiddler astrally projecting.
David Colohan

To set the scene—I was playing keyboards for a friend's band at a private party in a barn, at a farm, in the middle of nowhere in the Norfolk countryside a few months before the first Gulf War.

We went outside for a breath of fresh air, and looked up to see a group of red, green and white lights pass silently directly over the top of the barn, over the adjoining field and then come to a halt over a road junction a hundred yards or so away.

Suddenly a spotlight shone down from between the lights and swept up and down the road, before switching off and gliding away. All the time in complete silence.

We just stood there with our mouths open in astonishment. I'm convinced it was some sort of stealth aircraft from the local American airbase at Lakenheath being tested before being shipped out for use in operation Desert Storm, but it was almost exactly like that scene in *Close Encounters of the Third Kind*, just after the UFO flies over Roy Neary's truck.
Chris Bond

Playing a squat gig in Manchester, and the room was getting a bit full, so it was decided a bigger venue was needed. Next thing we know, two guys with sledgehammers turn up and knock down the back wall of the room. Hey presto! Bigger venue.
Andy Hokano

We once smoked crack on a national radio interview in Spain in the late 1980s. We thought the DJ was handing us a joint, but we only found out after that it was crack.

Anyway, after the radio interview we all went for a beer and a game of pool. By then, we were in a state of absolute hysterics.

The DJ had a bad case of facial acne (you will see why I mention this in a minute) and he started moving some of the pool balls with his hands into more favorable positions.

With no inhibitions whatsoever, I shouted "Hey! That skag head is cheating," and he was like "what did you say?"

Our sides were hurting so much with laughter; we got out sharpish and spent the rest of the night totally off our nut, wandering around Madrid laughing at everything.

Dave McLean

It was actually as an audience member rather than a band member. A couple of friends and I went to a gig at a very odd location—a pub on a housing estate in Swindon, if memory serves me correctly.

We arrived before the band did, and the people at the pub thought we were the band, and wouldn't believe us when we explained that we weren't.

We then found ourselves getting involved with moving furniture around to make room for us to move in the gear that we didn't have.

Then, when the real band finally turned up, they found themselves being supported by a bloke spinning around upside down on the floor with his head in a bucket, being chased by a terrified three-legged greyhound. A magical night!

Graeme Lockett

I write "music" (or try to, at least), and I work on having a melody line or something tuneful.

However, last year I was asked to play an event that, to be fair, I'd never really took the time to research. Turns out, it was an evening of nothing but deep dronal noise. I mean, it was the loudest electronic drone you'd ever heard. It sounded like a tank factory on overtime. Talk about being the odd one out!

There was about three acts on before me. One of the acts kicked the decibels up to such a level that it literally smashed glasses on the bar area. I was actually scared of the noise / drone and the artists performing the pieces!

Then on comes little old me with my synths and laptops, feeling so out of my depth, worrying half to death about being out of place—which I was.

I completed the set, thankfully without hitch, and for the rest of the night, I listened to more drone acts smashing bottles and glasses with their noise.

But it was the amount of people (who had no doubt turned up for the drone acts) that came up to me the rest of the night to thank me for giving their ears a rest and for playing nice music. I thought it was just a weird old night.

Kev Oyston

A massive fight starting during the last song of a gig I played with Avvoltoi somewhere in south of Italy, circa 1989.

Lots of people outside this big venue decided they should get in for free, so they pushed their way in and I remember that as we were grabbing our equipment to try to get to the van outside, this big wave of people pushing each other with punches was storming towards our corner of the room.

I remember putting my amp back down where it was, waiting for the madness to calm down. I also remember our drummer Tiberio Ventura briefly laughing, while saying "merda!" and leaving pieces of his drums where they were.

I was later told that during our performance, a guy on LSD was about to grab me to get my electric guitar off me to play it, but I didn't see him as he was arriving from behind me, when one of the security guys grabbed him before it happened.

Thanks security guy!

Marco Magnani

Accidentally pulling up for a beer at a redneck bar outside Nashville with our band, and suffering some serious attention for our relatively androgynous look. Surrounded by a pack of wolves, we were.

"Hey, this one's got titties," one said about our (male) drummer as they closed in on us. Made the mistake of watching *Deliverance* the day before....

Chris Anderson

Since I didn't talk back then, when I sat down with Ian Brown, we wrote back and forth (no talking) at our Tis Was Don Hills gig with Death of Fashion and the Soft Explosions.

He wouldn't take my record, because it was too big, and he wanted me to mail it and I was pretty miffed and wanted my way or the highway. He won.

Looking back now, it's pretty funny. I can be pretty stubborn. Afterwards he danced a little, and left.

Jayne Gabriel

If you consider stage / backstage fights as bizarre, then I think that would be this. You know when it's going to happen, and even push a bit to it; you know you'll feel shit afterwards, but you go for it, head or whatever first. Although I've really calmed down and don't do that anymore. Not only is it not worth it, but I wouldn't want to break some pricey pieces of my gear.
Francois Sky

A crippled midget in a wheelchair in the audience of a Sky Cries Mary show in Vancouver, Canada. He was drinking tons of Vodka, just wasted out of his brain, sitting directly in front of the stage, yelling at the top of his lungs that our singer was a poser, and swearing at him! It was tragic, nerve-wracking and completely freaky.
Gordon Raphael

A gig went well once. Seriously, that's a strange event in itself, considering my two main collaborators, one of whom I'm related to and one of whom is one of my best friends, are both fucking nuts.
Dan Bordello

I can remember that guy Chris Farlowe eating a sandwich during a performance with Atomic Rooster. Or Albert King filing his nails in the middle of Stevie Ray Vaughan's solo.
Narsis Passolas

We were driving from Huntsville to Nashville after a very late show; I was nodding and, as it turns out, so was the person driving. Very dangerous, both lulling to sleep.

Suddenly a giant green fireball swooshes right over the top of our car and crashes into the road to the side of us. We were wide awake at that moment.

I kept saying "Did you see that?? What was that? What was it?!?!?!"

The person driving, eyes bugging, just kept saying "It was green! It was green!" over and over… and, sure enough, next day the news reported that an asteroid had crashed. I'm not sure what would've become of us had that asteroid not woken us up at that moment.
Pete Meriwether

When I was in Joybang!, we got to open for Miracle Legion at T.T. the Bear's in Cambridge, MA. This, in itself, was weird for me, because I had opened for them there a decade earlier, when I was in Arms Akimbo.

After soundcheck, we went to get the van, but it was gone. It had been towed and Roe and I went to retrieve it, but it took a long time to get there and get through the processing.

We high-tailed it back to the venue and made it back a few minutes after 10pm. Our stuff was set up, and our drummer Steve was standing by the stage sweating bullets. We ran in and jumped on the stage and started wailing; we only lost a few minutes of our set time!
Ted Selke

I did an album called *In A Strange Slumber* last year, and wrote two stories to go in between the songs. I somehow got the actor Nigel Planer to narrate them.

On the day of recording, I went to Leeds coach station at 5.30 in the morning to get to London. I got there and hung about for a bit, all knackered out; met Nigel at a studio in Shepherd's Bush, had a chat about comedy, films and music over milkless tea, then we recorded the voiceover.

Nigel went home, so I walked from Shepherd's Bush and ended up at the British Museum eventually, after what felt like years of walking, on what was one of the hottest days of the year and one of the busiest days in London (as a taxi driver told me).

I got to the museum, had a look at all the dinosaurs and got back to the station at 6 PM, to get the coach back up, getting home to Leeds just before midnight. I was knackered.

Also, it was the same studio where I did an audiobook with Rik Mayall, where the voice booth was really just a cupboard and I had to cram him in and shut the door behind him, just hearing his muffled voice through the door. I suppose that's all quite bizarre.
Chris Wade

Or, traveling on the tube with Ashley [Hutchings], and Simon [Nicol] and Richard [Thompson], and an enormous white Perspex banjo shaped bass (which lit up), which we had persuaded Ashley he had to buy from one of the music shops in Tottenham Court Road. It was a hoot getting it up and down the escalators.
Judy Dyble

Most bizarre thing… hmmm. My early childhood was very strange. I had very strong hallucinations in my childhood, because of my strong imagination. I was playing in the woods and saw many very strange things there that I have later realized didn't exist, not in this physical world anyway.

It's quite fun that these hallucinations are still part of my childhood memories, although I know they were just hallucinations, but were they?

Maybe they were real things in another dimension and I was able to see there. Who knows? I think these experiences have affected strongly the way I see the world around me nowadays.
Jaire Pätäri

The most unbelievable musical thing that happened to me was not hearing my own band on my favorite radio station. This bizarre chapter goes way back before that, to junior high school and Levittown. To Lanny and me as members of the Ravens.

My deep appreciation for rock music was almost certainly instilled at Levittown Memorial High School, where I attended seventh and eighth grades. It was strange that junior high school kids could walk the halls with seniors too old to be juvenile delinquents. But there we were.

Maybe because it was close to the Grumman aerospace plant, LMHS had a diversified student group. There were many Europeans, with odd cars to match. One such import was Pete Taylor, the lead singer of the Lonely Roads, who changed to Strange Brew when Cream replaced the Rolling Stones in the building psychedelic scene. Taylor remained a pint-sized Mick Jagger who was actually English. He was outrageous on stage and wild in appearance. And he knew things.

We recognized Cream, and Hendrix, but Strange Brew were serving an unfamiliar mix that was conquering the school. The songs, as far as we could tell, were called "Substitute," "I Can't Explain" and "The Kids Are Alright." They even recorded their own version of that last song and it was played in the halls.

Yet, when we went to the expansive TSS record shop (the same one favored by famed songwriter Ellie Greenwich, we would learn later), there was no trace of those titles.

Then we found it. There on the cover of some collection was a listing for "The Kids Are Alright." It was not the original but the songwriting credit was for Pete Townshend. We knew he had written the U.S. hit "Happy Jack" and was in the Who. We became huge fans.

The Who were also the band that smashed their instruments and we had seen the Strange Brew sacrifice at least one scraggily six string. Meanwhile, we still had our own little band of Ravens and were trying to incorporate the newer exciting sounds emanating from our town.

When summer came around, our whole family would go "upstate," really just to the Bear Mountain area. Now of a certain age, I hated the isolation and wanted to be back where the action was. I soon got my wish.

Our house in Levittown was broken into not once but twice. They left the TV on the lawn but took some items, among them my unbearably cheap guitar. I didn't think much of the incident. My father's solution was to leave me at the house alone, at 14. That was fine with me.

Then the news broke that a rock band of Levittown locals had been nabbed for breaking into houses, stealing instruments and sacrificing them on stage. It was in The Times, the New York Times. The Who was mentioned as likely role models. There were no names, but Lanny and I didn't need any.

My father took me to the police station to look over guitars. There were a lot of them. I imagined them being smashed on stage by our hometown heroes, and hoped mine had already met that fate. Despite my father's protestations, I refused to "just pick one." He would have to get me something decent, and eventually did.

Soon we would see the Who at Westbury. Lanny and I and my younger brother Bob. Fifth row, Townshend's side. Unbelievably loud, constant motion, windmill arms, a twirling microphone that just about encircled the stage, a one-man barrage of sticks and drums and cymbals. They did destroy their instruments. It was the first concert I attended and will always be the best. And yes, the Strange Brew was there. The kids were alright.
Bill Sweeney

With David Devant and His Spirit Wife, our norm was the bizarre, but being fired out of a canon at the end of a show has to be up the top of strange experiences. It was at the Duke of York's cinema where we had arranged a gig with the film *Dr. Phibes Rises Again*.

The film's star, Vincent Price, died the week of the gig, which consequently sold out, and the event became a celebration of his twisted penchant for the macabre.

At the start of the show, we were all petrified under sheets as the audience slowly filtered into the cinema. After what felt like hours, my sheet was lifted up to reveal me lying atop a tomb upon which I was duly cut in two, and the lower half of my corpse held aloft to thunderous cheering.
Mikey Georgeson

There's been so many bizarre incidents and weird gigs; when you wear red trousers and a sombrero and get plied with tequila, strange things happen. Most of which I can't remember!

One of the most unsettling was playing with a jazz band at a Halloween gig. It was a party in a recently abandoned psychiatric hospital. We were playing in the morgue, which still had the cold chamber drawers and paraphernalia and implements. It was a truly scary night, maybe I should have kept clear of the mushrooms that night.
Sproatly Smith

Human competition, ego battles. I hate these stupid things and they're the reasons why I left my previous band.
Lorenzo Bracaloni

I think being in a band is a very bizarre situation to be in—especially when it gets "serious." You end up living together, traveling together, eating together, everything.

Anyone that has said it is like being married to three or four other people at once got it spot on. It can be heavenly when rehearsing new material and getting into that "telepathic zone" which I think all good bands do—because you know each other so well.

And then it can be hell, because you end up getting easily irritated during the humdrum of daily life. It is no surprise to me that many bands who were once best friends end up hating each other.
Mordecai Smyth

One time, we were heading to St Louis to play a gig, and made a wrong turn into East St Louis. East St Louis is a run down city located across the river from St Louis. Thankfully our manager at the time, a suit wearing Irishman named Sean Duffy, was with us when the battalion of squad cars bore down upon us.

At least ten police cars. Officers jumped out, swinging flashlights and guns, while Sean calmly murmured that he'd do all the talking. Four long haired guys in a van always seems arouse the law, but Sean calmly explained that we were headed to St Louis and showed the officers our map and directions (this was the 1990s, no GPS).

In the end they were very nice and showed us the way out of East St Louis. I suppose loads of cops coming down onto the innocent probably seems like an every day occurrence to those who watch the news, but it was bizarre to me.
Gregory Curvey

I went to see Dave Edmunds at the Hammersmith Palais and stood next to Doctor Who.
John Blaney

Onelovestory. Google that with the Stone Roses, and see what happens.
Jet Wintzer

One of the most bizarre (and pleasing) things is that people still assume that, because there are two of us, one is called "Hare," one is "Moon," and that I am "Hare."

I'm quite happy to answer to this; it just tickles me to think that there might be someone imaging a six foot lupine in britches emailing them back. Which, of course, there is, and this is exactly what happens.
Grey Malkin

A group of punters asking if they could jam on our instruments after our set, and being nonplussed at my asking if they were a band (they weren't and the idea had apparently never occurred to them)
Sand Snowman

Whilst working in Oman, we were asked to be on an Indian game show. So in the hot, steamy night air, we faced 5,000 excited Indian fans of the national quiz show in an outdoor arena.

We mimed, a Beatles song I think, and Crystal Jacqueline graciously intoned the answer to a mass of howls of joy and despair. Got very nicely paid for it though….

Icarus Peel

I was stood outside a venue in London when suddenly a red bus came around a corner and decapitated an unwary pigeon.

Quick as a flash, a woman rushed across the road and quickly stuffed the still-twitching pigeon into her shopping bag. Guess it was pigeon pie night. Next up would be seeing P.J. Proby throwing up into a grand piano... but that's a story for another day.

Pete Bingham

The development of a sixth sense, an almost telepathic sensation, created by playing with the same musicians for an extended period of time.

Before it even happens, you know what they are going to play next, and that in turn influences how and where you will go with your part. It's a bond that, when everyone is operating on the same wavelength, is one of my favorite feelings.

Chris Sherman

Mmmh, isn't being in a band already bizarre enough? Especially if you are in your thirties or even in your forties. Seriously... I am forty-five, and if I look around, I see most of my peers can't even figure out what's wrong with me.

As for me, I can perfectly figure out what's wrong with them, but I cannot tell them because... they are average persons, they are normality. The weird one is actually me. Haha, I'm afraid I probably answered another question... but this is what I wanted to say, really.

Paolo Sala

The most bizarre thing is, in fact, the fact of being in a band. Totally.

Jordi Bel

The most bizarre thing that has happened to me is getting an e-mail out of the blue from Dickie Harrell, the original drummer from Gene Vincent's Blue Caps, saying he had heard us on WFMU and how much he loved our *Songs for Swinging Stalkers* LP.

It was bizarre because, not only is Gene Vincent one of my musical heroes, but also because somebody not only liked our *Songs for Swinging Stalkers* LP, but actually bought it.

Brian Bordello

I once spent a whole evening recording a fiddle player who could not pick up the cue to play his fiddle solos.

We tried absolutely everything, from playing the whole song, to just a few beats before his solo, to making hand gestures, to miming playing of a fiddle right in front of him. Nothing worked, and whatever we tried, he just continued to play on the wrong bits.

After four hours odd, we ended with absolutely nothing. It was really like a four hour piece of performance art, which could not have been more perfectly written or acted. It was truly bizarre and it was spellbinding to witness it unfold—I just wish we'd had a video camera running.

Stephen Stannard

I was doing a week of solo gigs in Kerry, at the Rose Of Tralee Festival. Someone asked me to play an afternoon gig at a bar, which sounded better than just hanging around all day, trying to stay sober for the night's gig.

Playing time was 5-7pm, but about twenty to seven, the young barman asked if I could finish. The gig was going well, so I asked why?

He politely explained that someone had just ordered a hot whiskey, and that the cable I was using for my sound system was the one they used for their electric kettle!

Has this ever happened to Bruce?

Leo O'Kelly

Back in 2006 I was in a band that was touring and partying really hard. We were in Louisville, KY, driving back to the hotel after a gig and our drummer hit me over the head with a beer bottle. He felt bad about it and decided to hitchhike home to Colorado. The cops picked him up a few miles down the interstate, sleeping under an overpass. They brought him back to the hotel and we found him in the morning out in the parking lot, sleeping underneath the van. Nobody spoke a word the whole way to Chicago.

Jefferson Hamer

The most bizarre thing that has ever happened to me was to have been in so many bands since I was a teenager, before understanding it was better for me to act as a solo artist. I understood this evidence after 12 Visions was released, because I was just fed up with what being in a band meant.

Will Z

The most bizarre thing that has happened to Mooch is probably the sight of people actually dancing to the music.

Steve Palmer

On another Middle Eastern occasion, Icarus and I were playing as a duo. We had to play by the pool at a private party for some very VIPs, including ambassadors and minor royalty. The surprise came when they all started playing bingo half way through the evening for cars, TV sets etc....
Crystal Jacqueline

Crystal Jacqueline

Diana Collier

Gordon Raphael

Head South

CHAPTER THIRTEEN

You have a time machine, which you can pilot to any time and place you like, for the purpose of making music. Where, and when, would you go, and why?

I should stay here, as evidently this is where I'm needed most
Sand Snowman

Woodstock 1969, with Mellow Candle. It's got everything including the legacy.
Alison O'Donnell

No hesitation. Late 1966, when in Britain, and also in America, the terrain of pop music was being turned into art music—mostly by the Beatles, but also by many other outstanding bands, such as the Byrds.

I sometimes wish I'd been born ten years earlier, so I could have experienced that wonderful, alas too-brief, moment of sonic magic.
Steve Palmer

I'd set the controls for Radiophonic Workshop in the BBC's Maida Vale Studios in Delaware Road, London, 1964, and ask Delia Derbyshire to interpret our music using the Radiophonic equipment.

Delia had already recorded the original Doctor Who theme, which is surely one of the most influential and perfect pieces of electronic music ever made.

Apparently Delia wasn't too big a fan of synthsizers when they eventually arrived in the Workshop, regarding them as something that actually reduced the creative possibilities of sound making. So there probably wouldn't be any point in introducing her to a laptop full of soft-synths!

It would be better to take the opportunity to ask her to interpret some of our songs from a score, and to see what she came up with. To watch her work on all those tape loops and sync-ed tape machines would be truly amazing.
Chris Bond

Sound Techniques in 1970 with John Wood at the controls. What right-thinking folkie wouldn't?
Graeme Lockett

Into the future, where I can do recordings and play instruments without any wires or cables! I truly think that this would be liberating, as it's like I've been surrounded by rubber coated wire snakes almost all my life, and they are always breaking down, falling out and begging for attention when I'd rather be getting on with the creative business of playing music.
Gordon Raphael

The future, on another planet—where else?
Emily Jones

I think I would like to trip out of the time machine somewhere on the West Coast of America around 1966, or in time to go to Monterey, at least. So many of my fave bands.

We play a game here at Peel Farm where we are given the choice of turn left to see the Doors, turn right to see Jefferson Airplane, or carry straight on to see Love. And all those other bands, It's A Beautiful Day, H.P. Lovecraft and all. Sure I could get a gig there somewhere....
Icarus Peel

I'm with Icarus on this one. There's no way he's leaving me behind....
Crystal Jacqueline

To a mythical time when rents were cheaper, and crowds for shows were bigger.
Richard Thompson

Germany, early to mid 1970s. I would love to been part of the Krautrock scene, especially the bands using Synths / sounds in a forward thinking way eg Cluster / Harmonia / Neu etc—just making sounds / songs, to play live when possible, that nobody had heard before, to receptive audiences.
Alan Murphy

This is the bad question. There are so many places where I wanted to go if I had a time machine. I could travel to Abbey Road studio to watch and learn how the Beatles made *Sergeant Pepper* or Pink Floyd made *Piper at the Gates of Dawn*, or go to Olympic to watch the Rolling Stones make *Satanic Majesties*.

Or maybe I could visit Phil Spector's very secret "wall of sound room." I have always been very interested how he created the "wall of sound," but only Phil Spector really knows.

Or I could go to Edith Piaf's legendary concert at the Olympia in Paris, or to watch Syd's Pink Floyd or... or... or... the list would be so long...

Psychedelic vibes and open minded visions for all the people!
Jaire Pätäri

I think I would have liked to have gone to Woodstock. That must have been pretty amazing.
Roger Linney

Edo-era Japan. The shakuhachi had come back in style, the poetry was amazingly lovely, mono no aware—a concept that describes the sense of transience, the impermanence of things, the constant passing away and the quiet sadness that brings, as well as heightened appreciation for their thus ephemeral beauty—was all the rage.

My kind of place.
Amanda Votta

This is difficult, but we would like to have been in both London and LA in 1966 and 1967. Such an amazing time for music. A period that has never been surpassed.
Aaron Hemington

I'm tempted to say that I'd go and stop Jhonn Balance from dying. While I was there, I'd say that since I was an angel who had saved his life, maybe I could join Coil. Of course Coil made an album called *Time Machines*, too, so maybe it's meant to happen.
Dan Bordello

Always had a hankering to hang out with early seventies Gong in their commune in France; in fact just generally following Daevid Allen around through the sixties and seventies would have been a highly enjoyable education in itself.

Although maybe it would be better use of a time machine to go further in distance and time, so maybe Athens in the 5th century BC.

Whatever was in the water there, at that time, which produced the first great dramatists and sculptors? If I was there, I'd invent the piano and change the course of music history.
Chris Anderson

I don't think I'd be too bothered about making music, really. I'd like to visit the sixties again, and see some the bands I missed.

Maybe take a few photos of buildings that have been demolished, see a few old departed acquaintances, and buy a load of psychedelic singles that I never bought at the time.
Nick Salomon

I think that I will conduct myself to the sixties. It was an extremely rich and varied musical period. A time when music was music, not a commercial product like today. They made music because they had the talent and something to sell.

Maxime Schwartz

London, 1975 till 1982, being part of the Punk / Post-Punk / Industrial scenes for the same reasons as mentioned above—when gigs were the equivalent to test-tubes, trialling potentially combustable musical material to potentially combustable audiences, as gigs today are usually old bands playing their back catalogs to pay the mortgage / next holiday etc; or bands following the same old paths that have been well laid, then claiming the discoveries on these paths to be their own.

Alan Murphy

I would start by transporting to the '68 / 69 London folk and psychedelic scene, UFO Club, Technicolor Dream, *International Time*s, *OZ* Magazine.

Then I would take Ash Ra Tempel's spaceship and go to Germany; Cologne and Dusseldorf were indeed places to be at the end of the sixties / early seventies. I also wouldn't mind to be in Manchester at the end of the seventies.

João Branco Kyron

February 10 1967, at Abbey Road Studios, for the recording of the orchestral glissando on "A Day in the Life" by the Beatles.

I recently stated in a Facebook comment that, if an alien came to me asking to give them one song from Earth, illustrating what our music is like, I'd probably say that one.

The first time I heard that song I was eleven years old, which meant it was 1979 (I was born a year after Sgt.Pepper's came out) when my brother had been given the record by a friend.

That whole sequence of "Sgt.Pepper's (reprise)" leading to "A Day in the Life," blew me away instantly and when the glissando bit came up, I thought "is there something wrong with this record?"

Then the "woke up!" part came on, and it was like entering a new room. But my favorite bit of the tune is really John Lennon's echoing voice doing "ahh ahh ahh ahhh!" after the "somebody spoke and I went into a dream" part.

I like to think it's the voice of an angel trying to come out of apocalyptic dark clouds, all wrapped up in them, struggling to be heard, and finally getting rid of the clouds to sing the last verse: "I read the news today oh boy…."

Marco Magnani

I'd have to head to Grantchester Meadows in '65 / 66 to meet up with Syd and the others before Roger Waters arrived, so I could play bass with them. Or maybe Roger could just sing. I liked his voice and he did write some good songs early on.
Sproatly Smith

The idea of time travel has always fascinated me, and has featured prominently in the music I've made as Palace of Swords.

Almost all Palace of Swords songs are set in a specific time and place.

"Live at the Aberdeen Witch Trials 1597" is perhaps the most obvious example of this—although "The Castle Spectre" and "Vicus Lemurum" also relate to particular locations or events in Aberdeen's past. (Vicus Lemurum, which roughly translates as "the street of ghosts or spirits," is the name of a long forgotten street in the city).

"The Black Lodge Will Rise Again," meanwhile, is set in Fin de Siecle Paris; "(We Are) The New Hyperboreans" is set in the counter culture of the 1960s; while "The White Goddess (Part 2)" takes place in a mythical pre-Roman Britain.
Peter Lyon

Liverpool in the early sixties was a hotbed of talent. I'd set up a recording studio, label and music publishers, and sign as many bands as I could, which would, of course, include the Beatles, Gerry and the Pacemakers, the Big Three, Cilla Black, etc.

Having established the label as the hottest in the country, I'd then sign all the best beat groups and R&B bands, folkies and finger snapping popsters, and buy a big house in the country.
John Blaney

On the Moon to play a gig to welcome Apollo 11 in July '69.
Francois Sky

Tough question, but I guess it would either have to be Cologne in the early seventies for the chance to jam with Amon Düül II, or Wumme same period for the chance to jam with Faust.
Andy Hokano

I'd go to Steve Albini's studio. I would go now. I would have him engineer an album for me. Why?

Well, as an artist, there is no time more important than now, and he is a man I have the utmost respect and admiration for. A man who is happy to experiment, who likes to be unorthodox and gets the most fantastic sounds you could wish for. He also has a healthy love of vinyl—in his words, the only way music should be listened to.

Mordecai Smyth

Marrakesh, '63. Davy Graham and I would go jamming in the souks with the North Africans. I'd take my friend Sefo Kanuteh, a traditional Kora player, with me.

Tom Conway

I would go to South Shields now, so I could work in the real world (not the virtual) with Kev Oyston of the Soulless Party.

There isn't enough time to get together, so a time machine would be very handy.

Chris Lambert

1967… wait, never mind. I'd have nothing to offer during such an exciting era of musical experimentation. I'll just stay right here, present-day, where I can rip-off all the great psychedelic music that's come before, and tell myself I thought of it.

Jeb Morris

I think the four of us would like to travel to the 1963-1973 period, who knows for what reason.

Narsis Passolas

If I had a time machine, I would use it to stay in the present. I really think we have so many treasures to mine from, that give me so much joy, that to go into the past would preclude us from so many things.

Also, I am able to work with brilliant people such as the Owl Service, Lost Harbours, Crafting For Foes and Melodie Gruppe, and I can watch so many amazing performers that I know unfurl their bounty of sound. I don't want it to end.

Diana Collier

I would, without doubt, go back to around 1962, and go to 304 Holloway Road—Joe Meek's studio. He was at his peak at the time, and was coming out with amazing productions.

I am a huge fan; we do all our recordings on a tiny 8 track in Ant's living room, and we tried to get the Joe Meek sound on our *Ronco Revival Sound* LP, but never quite managed it. We managed the madness and the strangeness, but not the sound.

I would have loved Joe Meek to have produced the Bordellos—the perfect match.
Brian Bordello

I have to be clichéd and say London in the sixties. Go and spy on the Beatles making music; maybe have a bit of a freak out at the UFO club. It's my favorite era in music.

Back then, people could make three albums a year and seem normal. I do it now, and people think I'm some kind of a freakazoid!
Chris Wade

1920s Weimar Germany, to enjoy the decadence and creativity of the theatre / cabaret scene.
Ellie Coulson

It would have been interesting to have been born into a time before pop / rock / jazz or big band music existed. I wonder if, without the access to radio and its perpetuation of ear worms, I would even have had the desire to create music?

I'm a visual artist as well, and have been able to draw since I was a kid, but it's music that inspires me to create. I only draw / paint when it's for a job, or album artwork and posters.
Gregory Curvey

Oh, time machine take me back to Laurel Canyon, Los Angeles, in the summer of 1967. Me and Arthur Lee hanging out, spiking Jim Morrison's lemonade, heading down to Sunset Strip in the evening, and I would play the Mellotron for Love at the Whiskey A Go Go.

That way, we could recreate the strings from *Forever Changes* live.
Dave McLean

Monterey Pop Festival 1967… cool and far out
Marrs Bonfire

London, spring of 1967. This would place me square in what I consider one of the most exciting times for music (all of which was, no doubt, fueled by the ideals, thoughts, substances, art and fashion that were prevalent).

I can't even begin to think about the amount of creativity and inspiration that would pour out of me there. Where is old Doc Brown when you need him?
Chris Sherman

I've lived a life that has included madness, poverty, bereavement, violence, incarceration, separation, homelessness and deep, deep love, joy and happiness.

If I had a time machine, I'd keep it hidden in a cupboard until the end, then I'd go back to the start and do exactly the same things over again.

Alternatively, I'd pop back to the early sixties and take full songwriting credit for everything that Lennon and McCartney did, then come back and be precisely who I am now, but much, much, much richer.
Simon Berry

Probably very predictable, but Abbey Road in 1967, when the technology and the technical know-how had not outstripped the curiosity and playful invention of artists.

With *Piper at the Gates of Dawn* down one end of the corridor and *Sergeant Pepper* at the other, it must have been rather exhilarating.

I think having technicians in lab coats and lots of cups of tea, bracketed by chemically fuelled nights out at the Flamingo, sounds like great fun too.
Mikey Georgeson

Swinging London, 1966-67. No doubt about it. Is it really necessary to explain why? It seems quite obvious to me.

Apart from the fact that many of the best songs ever were written in Britain in those very years, I think that the creative energy that pervaded every aspect of people's lives was unique at that time.

The best description of what I'm trying to say is in Ian MacDonald's *Revolution In The Head* book. Highly recommended!
Paolo Sala

I think I would have loved to be a part of Woodstock. So much raw energy, talented musicians and love. Doing a collaboration with the greats of that era would be mind-blowing. Things today are either so sterile, or over the top disgusting.
Jayne Gabriel

Here and now! I've done all the past stuff, and the future is coming plenty soon!
Leo O'Kelly

Ohhhh.. very nice question. No doubt: from middle sixties to late seventies.
Lorenzo Bracaloni

Liverpool, not Abbey Road (the title of the most overrated album in history, by the way), defines the Beatles. It's like they never left, and it many ways they have not.

There was something going on the day we visited that northern town, not directly related to the Fab Four, but so intrinsically local, you'd have to see some sort of connection.

Liverpool, the Football Club, was playing its legendary, nearby rivals Manchester United. Not just playing, hosting. Every waitress, ticket taker, barman, had an ear to the radio, and maybe an eye to the customer (by the way, everyone there does sound like Paul, and most look like him.)

We take our Magical Mystery Tour, we drop in on the raucous Cavern, we see sad Strawberry Fields. Soon it's over and we have to head back to the car park.

But then, coming the other way, marching, singing, swarming is the crowd from the game. It's over. Liverpool has won. Big bad Man U is defeated. And there is something in the joy, in the voices of the fans, in the spirit, that is Absolutely Fab.

For the purposes of this question, though, Liverpool would have to be just part of the answer. The ultimate place to be in the history of rock would be England itself in 1967.

That was when *Sgt. Pepper* came out, and everything got even more interesting. The Who could be Seen for Miles, the Stones signaled a Satanic detour, Cream was in the mix.

Of course, by this time Dylan had electrified New York and the Velvet Underground began to surface.

However, one has to have been "over there" to realize how intrinsic the big beat is to the UK. Rock 'n roll stars are just that in England, still. A guest on a chat show is just as likely to be a midlevel lead singer as a big screen bore.

Players play and then, instead of being shuffled off, are invited to sit and chat. Imagine that. There are rock documentaries on seemingly every night and some of the bands thus honored seem only vaguely familiar.

It's a place that embraces every form of celebrity, even musicians. After all, they gave us the Beatles. Beat that.

My most recent trip over there was to informally represent King Penguin at a Fruits de Mer all day festival. With the label's lineup plus London's legendary Pretty Things, it was a great day in a wonderful weekend.

Chelsea is a whimsical musical area, similar to what was Music Row in New York, but better, even though I once saw John Entwistle (and his Boris the Spider pendant) picking out amps on 48th St.

Everything about London rejoices in rock. On another trip, we stopped in a Hyde Park tea shop, only to find the place buzzing about Ray Davies having just left the premises. People at the next table were talking about having known the Davies family—sort of local to the area—back before the well respected days.

Us and Them

In 1967, I lived in New York. Things were happening. I want to go back to that time, but to London, with King Penguin. And with Mary Jo. She grew up there, in those mod, mod days. She speaks the language.
Bill Sweeney

As much as I'd love to travel back in time physically, musically I like where I am now and where I've been. It might sound cheesy and clichéd, but the experience I've gained over the years and the "being in the moment" moments have shaped me into what I've become now as an artist. It's taken a long time, but all those years and influences have certainly paid off, and I'm enjoying every minute.
Kev Oyston

I'd aim the DeLorean at Chicago, 1952. Leo Fender had just released the renamed Telecaster guitar, and Les Paul's Gibson would be along the following year, two instruments that are hard to beat, even today.

The Chicago Blues scene was getting established. The shape of modern pop / rock music was being moulded.
Mark Reuter

Difficult to answer: how can I possibly choose one thing out of an infinite range of possibilities? To say 1969 at the house in Farley Chamberlayne, where Fairport Convention recorded *Liege and Lief*, is probably a massive cliché!

But I do genuinely like the idea of that, to go away to an idyllic setting and just work intensively in that environment, far from the madding crowd.

Or that cottage in Devon where Heron recorded *Twice as Nice at Half the Price* in 1971 would be gorgeous. I love how you can hear the birdsong on at least three of the tracks.
Joanna Swan

Indian music tickles my fancy. South Indian flute and tabla music is dreamy. Okay, that's where I would like to go. Back to India when the Moguls introduces the sitar.

There I would be, me and my sitar living in a cow dung hut with banana leaf roof, woven grass mats, chai and mangoes. The problem with a cow dung sculpted veranda is that when the wind blows, it's not dirt that gets into your food. The dung flakes look like pepper in your rice, and chocolate in your chai. Subcontinental bliss.
Gregory Curvey

I might go back to the Zodiak Free Arts Lab in late sixties Berlin, and try to worm my way into joining Tangerine Dream or Kluster, just to hear a new music being born.
David Colohan

If I was to time travel, I'd go back to the seventies, to the era of browns, yellows and oranges. Why? Because it was grim and creepy, and I like things like that.

Plus, cinema and children's TV was the best back then—*The Wicker Man, Children Of The Stones, The Owl Service*; what's not to like?

It influences our music more than any other decade, so I think I'd feel quite at home there. Although this would also mean living with the constant threat of nuclear Armageddon and Rod Stewart being everywhere.
Grey Malkin

1967, EMI Studios. Check out some Beatles sessions, Pink Floyd, the Zombies, the Hollies, the Pretty Things.

Swinging London outside would be inspiring. I'd order up some ADT and the EMT plate. Maybe see if Jimmy Page is available to wail on some guitar.
Ted Selke

Denmark Street, London 66 / 67—the most creative period I can imagine in terms of bands, music, studios, labels.

Now they are bulldozing the place down.
Keith Jones

1965, NYC and California. This gets you near Burt Bacharach, Brian Wilson, Sergio Mendes and Jobim. And this gets you recording in those same studios with the old school boards, tubes, mics, serious musicians, no computers, and even though I do not smoke... I like being around folks who do.
Jet Wintzer

Abbey Road Studios, 1967.
Pete Meriwether

Maybe I would lead the machine to 2010, directly to the studios where the Coral and Dawes recorded their respective albums *Butterfly House* and *Nothing is Wrong*, in the UK and USA.

These are two masterpieces regarding the sound, songs, tunes and the production, one by John Leckie, and the other by Jonathan Wilson. I would bring a big, big notebook to make notes for everything, to catch every moment and learn.

Also, I'd like to travel thirty-five years before, into the wood-made studio that appears in the film *Heathworn Highways*, about Austin's neo-country scene in the seventies, and where Larry Jon Wilson is recording the song "Ohoopee River Bottomland."

Fully analog studio with perfect sound. Amazing. I'd like as well to go to the live recording of Supersession by Mike Bloomfield, Al Kooper and Steven Stills, and take the advantage of the session, mics and all the musicians and engineers involved to record some new stuff.
Jordi Bel

I would like to return to those few years of 1966-1970 with a proper camera and a big notebook, and while I was there, collect a copy of the recordings I made for Bryan Morrison of "Loneliest Person" and "The River."

Oh, and take a picture of DC and the MBs on stage (and record a bit of a gig.)
Judy Dyble

Back to late 1966 or early 1967, at the UFO club in Tottenham Court Road, London.

Because this is where I'd find the likes of the Pretty Things, the Pink Floyd, the Soft Machine and Tomorrow freaking out, and making some of the most trippy sounds they would ever make.
Lenny Helsing

Someone asked me a very similar question last year; they asked if I could play any gig in time, where would it be? So I'm going for the same answer.

I would love to have taken to the stage with Sendelica at the UFO club in 1966 London, at one of the all night shows. That would be just so incredible, playing to that audience….
Pete Bingham

I'd love to go back to the Pavillion du Hay in Voisines, France, and jam with Gong during the making of *Angel's Egg*. That looks like such an amazing scene, at such an incredible time. An historic moment in psychedelic music.

If I went back there, I'd love to take all my new-style synths and blow their minds with the new technologies!
Stephen Bradbury

That's an easy one. Pink Floyd at the ICI Fibres Club, February 16, 1968.
Drew Mulholland

The easiest question so far. Of course, the time machine would take me to 49 Greek Street in Soho, London, and the cellar called Les Cousins.

Al Stewart, Nick Drake, Bert Jansch, Sandy Denny are all there, and after Les Cousins closed, we all go to Roy Harper's apartment, where Paul Simon is staying. Paul is a bit nervous, but after some persuasion, 78 he plays a new song he just wrote that he maybe will call "I Am a Rock."

Us and Them would not play anything in this company.
Anders Håkanson

I would go to an alternative universe, in an indeterminate future / past, for a relaxed musical party on the grassy banks of a Swedish lake, during a pleasantly balmy, never-ending, Scandinavian Summer's day.

The party would be populated with a handful of characters from Bergman's romantic films, Gerrard Winstanley, Tony Hancock, Bill Hicks, Liz from *Billy Liar*, "Budgie" Bird from Budgie, family, friends, and all the good eggs you could muster.

Throw in a few members from each of the following bands—the Beatles, the Kinks, the Duke of Stratosphear, Espers and the Lilac Time—and that would be my idea of heaven. Realistically though, this would be a real bugger to organize.
Stephen Stannard

Now, most people will expect me to say that I would go to 1962 and play on the original "Telstar" session, or 1959 and play a comb or some other improvised instrument on the *I Hear A New World* sessions… and it would be pretty tempting to do either.

But the moment I think I would really choose would be to join Roky Erickson and The Explosives on the tour that produced the *Halloween Live* live album.

It's one of my favorite albums; Roky is just on fantastic form and the band are stunning. I'll stand at the back and shake a tambourine… I'd be fine with that.
Tom Woodger

1995. The internet was changing the live music scene for the better, but hadn't totally destroyed the record industry yet. People were making money, and you could still afford to buy a pre-war Martin 000-28. Either that or 1971, to see Zappa with Flo and Eddie at the Fillmore East.
Jefferson Hamer

I'll enter February 27, 1970 as a target date, and my machine will appear in a flash of colors in front of Abbey Road studios.

All I'll ask is to be there when Syd Barrett begins his second session for the Barrett album; to meet him, see when he will record fifteen takes of "Gigolo Aunt" with David Gilmour, Jerry Shirley and Richard Wright, and, alone, "Bob Dylan Blues," "Wolfpack," the unreleased "Living Alone" and "Waving My Arms In The Air / I Never Lied to You."

A very cool set list, great musicians, a true genius and a crazy production work by Gilmour.
Will Z

How did you know about my time machine? I don't normally tell people about it; they keep wanting to borrow it and it gets messy.

I'm due back in 1962 in a minute, actually. I'm booked in to record some backing vocals in Joe Meek's studio. I'm not being funny but he gets very stroppy if you're late, so I can't stop. Sorry x
Angeline Morrison

The Honey Pot

Tir na nOg photograph by Barry Burtonwood

BIOGRAPHIES

Most, if not all, of the artists here maintain a presence on the Internet, most notably Facebook and/or Bandcamp (with the Active Listener hard behind). Please check your friendly, neighborhood search engine for further details.

Army of Mice

"Army of Mice make music combining traditional song writing with electronic textures and found sounds. Mixing vintage analogue and modern digital synths, dirty guitars, and gorgeous vocals, AoM enjoys exploring a variety of styles, from down-beat trip-hop to bouncy electro-pop."

Lining up as Ellie Coulson (vocals), Mark Reuter (guitar) and Chris Bond (syntheizers - and ex-Stealing the Fire, whose 1999 album Hot Ice and Wondrous Strange Snow should be sought out pronto), the Army's debut EP *Wildflower* appeared in 2009.

Astralasia

Electro-heroes since time immemorial (or at least the mid-1990s), with a string of often majestic albums to show for it, Astralasia's Marc Swordfish was also instrumental in relaunching Judy Dyble's career in the early 2000's, overseeing her first three solo albums. Plus, *Wind on Water*, the band's 2014 album for Fruits de Mer, is simply one of their best.

Beaulieu Porch

Simon Berry's Beaulieu Porch launched in 2010 with the single "The Colour 55." Shindig! called it "the sort of thing we live for here at Shindig! Towers," while BP was named "psychedelic band of the year" in the Bamboo Sticks Internet Radio Awards. Two albums, beaulieu porch and we are beautiful, and The Carmelite Drive (Original Soundtrack) followed through on that promise.

Beautify Junkyards

Formed in 2012, and purveyors of one of the following year's most spellbinding debut albums, Portugal's Beautify Junkyards were responsible, also, for one of the most haunting singles in the Fruits de Mer discography, coupling Nick Drake's "From The Morning" with Os Mutantes' "Fuga No.2." Exquisitely influenced by what frontman João Branco describes as "British autumnal folk," their latest album is imminent from Mega Dodo.

Belbury Poly

Ghost Box founder Jim Jupp's haunting, haunted, recreation of the music that you remember the TV scaring you with in the seventies, whether it did or not. A brittle discography includes The Willows (2004), The Owl's Map (2006), From An Ancient Star (2009) and The Belbury Tales (2012).

Bevis Frond

When the authoritative history of all the noise in this book is finally written, Bevis Frond will probably be the first name included.

Since the mid-1980s, Nick Salomon has either heralded or inspired more or less every psychedelic reaction there has been, with a teetering heap of discs that represents both the genesis and revelation of the genre.

And with his catalog currently undergoing a massive CD and vinyl reissue program via Cherry Red, there's no excuse for missing a moment of it.

Black Psychiatric Orchestra

Hailing from Strrasbourg, France, Black Psychiatric Orchestra was launched from Maxime Schwartz's fascination with the Brian Jonestown Massacre, Black Rebel Motorcycle Club and the Doors—a delirious combination that sounds exactly as great as it ought to.

Black Tempest

The one man brainchild of prog monster Stephen Bradbury, Black Tempest's catalog abounds with multi disc extravaganzas, including the glorious triple *Secret Astronomies*; a split LP with Dead Sea Apes; contributions to Fruits de Mer's Head/Shrunken *Head Music* and *Strange Fish 3* collections; and a magnificent rendering of Spirit's "Twelve Dreams of Dr. Sardonicus" included within the *7 & 7 Is* box set.

the Blue Giant Zeta Puppies

Cross Joe Meek, Roky Erikson and even the Flaming Lips, and you are in roughly the same territory as the Puppies, another of those bands whose onstage identities… which include BG, Joey Zeta and Flossy Zeta… probably don't reveal the names their parents gave them. Probably because there is just one full-time Puppy, Tom Woodger, abetted by friends as required.

The Puppies' Active Listener debut album *12 Theories of Time Travel* compiled past self-released cuts; current releases include the EPs *The Devil is in The Detail* and *The Return of The Blue Giant Zeta Puppies*. They can also be encountered via sundry Fruits de Mer collections.

Marrs Bonfire
No relation to the slightly-similarly named "Born to be Wild" songsmith, DJ Bonfire is one of the leading agent provocateurs on the current psych-garage scene; but the ex-Land Registry and Inept frontman also now leads the Green Question Mark, backed up on the Pegasus EP by Icarus Peel, Crystal Jacqueline and Mordecai Smyth.

the Bordellos
Originally a six piece, in which form the Merseysiders released 2006's "Arthur Lee" and the albums *Songs For Swinging Stalkers* and *Meet the Bordellos*, the Bordellos are now a trio of Brian Bordello (guitar / bass / vocals) and Ant Bordello (percussion / harmonica / vocals), plus Brian's son Dan Bordello (keyboards / bass / guitar / drums / percussion / vocals).

Comparisons to the Dolls, the Velvets and sundry other low-fi favorites abound, with their version of "I'm A Man" (for the 2011 Fruits de Mer Annual) one of old Bo's diddliest covers. Recent releases include the Art Whore EP, the albums *Ronco Revival Sound* and *It's Low-Fi Folk Volume 2*, and a split single with Schizo Fun Addict.

Ellie Bryan—see Crow Call

the Chemistry Set
Formed back in 1987, veterans of the late eighties neo-psychedelic boom, regularly aired by the legendary John Peel (who even sent them a hand-written fan letter), the Chemistry Set released their first album, a cassette of bedroom demos, on the Acid Tapes label.

This was followed by a flurry of flexi discs, and the group's official biog laughs, "for a period from 1988—1990, it seemed that every other fanzine was including a Chemistry Set flexi disc."

They maintain a prodigious rate of releases today, including the first ever release on Fruits de Mer's Regal Crabomophone subsidiary with the stunning *The Impossible Love* EP. A second 7-inch matched their own "Come Kiss Me Vibrate And Smile" and "Time To Breathe" with a stupendous cover of Tomorrow's "Hallucinations."

the Child of a Creek
Tuscany-based Lorenzo Bracaloni is a singer / songwriter with his roots firmly planted in folky fields.

Seven albums have appeared over the past decade, among them the wonderfully titled *Unicorns Still Make Me Feel Fine, Find A Shelter Along the Path, Under an Emerald Sun, The Earth Cries Blood, Quiet Swamps* and *Hidden Tales*.

A new LP, *Secrets of the Moon*, appeared in 2015 under the alter-ego of Fallen; promised for the next Child of a Creek LP is an appearance by Alison O'Donnell.

Chonyid

"Featuring members of the Psychogeographical Commission, BONG, and Joseph Curwen. Chonyid explore liberation through hearing during the intermediate state."

The Newcastle-based band has released no less than six self-titled/numbered albums, plus the live albums Live at Unearthing Forgotten Horrors 15.11.2014 and Live at The Northumberland Arms 25.02.2015.

Diana Collier

First coming to general attention as one of the voices of the Owl Service, and the voice of Greanvine, Leigh-on-Sea based singer Collier also was responsible for one of the loveliest albums of recent years, All Mortals at Rest, utterly unputdownable since its release in 2013.

Comus

Formed in 1969 by Roger Wootton, Glenn Goring, Colin Pearson, Andy Hellaby, Bobbie Watson and Rob Young, Comus are best remembered for the legendary *First Utterance* debut album in 1971 (and the less-fondly recalled *To Keep From Crying* three years later). Having broken up piecemeal during the early-mid seventies, Comus reformed in 2008 for the Swedish Melloboat Festival (since released on DVD), surfing on growing critical and musical recognition for their early accomplishments (including a terrific Current 93 cover of "Diana"). The band have continued gigging since then, with an excellent new album, *Out of the Coma*, emerging in 2012 .

Country Parish Music—see the Owl Service

Crayola Lectern

Self-confessed "English psychedelic musician, composer and lovable weirdo freak," Worthing-based Chris Anderson's Crayola Lectern emerged with the 2013 album *The Fall and Rise of Crayola Lectern*.

Crow Call

Formed following the release of Minneapolis singer Ellie Bryan's so-haunting *Am I Born To Die* debut album (2012), Crow Call is a duo of Bryan (vocals, banjo) and Peter Ruddy (12 string guitar, Bajo Quinto). Their own debut album, *Crow Call*, was released in 2014.

Crystal Jacqueline

Denizens of the same west country household, and therefore regular guests on one another's records, Crystal Jacqueline and Icarus Peel met ("many, many years ago") in a covers band performing "everything from Lynryd Skynryd to Cole Porter, Abba to Gram Parsons," in hotels and aboard cruise ships.

Peel's *Tea at my Gaffe* in 2009 launched their recording career; since then, Jacqueline's "A Fairy Tale" and and the Honey Pot EPs (both Fruits de Mer), and albums *Sun Arise* and *Rainflower* (Mega Dodo) have set ears a-tremble worldwide. Peel, meanwhile, has also teamed up with Mordecai Smyth for a sensational split EP; that pair, plus Jacqueline, also accompany Marrs Bonfire as the Green Question Mark; while the Honey Pot—Peel, Jacqueline, Wayne Fraquet and Iain Crawford—are also actively recording.

Dodson & Fogg

Shindig called the eponymous debut "a godsend"; The Active Listener compared 2013's *Derring D*o to Donovan and Nick Drake… Chris Wade's Dodson & Fogg represents a glorious resurrection, and a fervent re-investigation, of the instincts that lie at the heart of so much of what is important about British music these days.

Eight albums released since their debut in 2012 include appearances from Alison O'Donnell, Nik Turner, Amanda Votta and Judy Dyble (among others); and the latest, 2015's *Warning Signs*, is as enthralling a brew as any that has rambled from the acid folk undergrowth in recent times.

Judy Dyble

The magnificent Ms Dyble is routinely described as ex-Fairport Convention, ex-Giles Giles and Fripp, ex-Trader Horn, ex-DC and the MBs.

Historically accurate, but musically, it is more rewarding to view her as creator of half-a-dozen albums reaching back to 2004's *Enchanted Garden* (one of three cut with Astralasia's Marc Swordfish) and forward through *Talking with Strangers* and *Flow and Change*, to a career spanning live set in 2014 and the 3CD anthology *Gathering The Threads-Fifty Years of Stuff* the following year.

She has also collaborated with Dodson & Fogg, Sand Snowman, the Conspirators, Electronic Voice Phenomenon, the Field Mouse Project and more.

Emily and Angeline—see Angeline Morrison, Emily Jones,

Eschatone Records

Eschatone has been in operation since 2006, releasing a stream of music in a variety of imaginative packages, from co-founder Jed Davis, Michael Bassett, the Visitors, Brian Dewan and seventies glam rock icon Jobriath, among many more.

Fallen—see the Child of a Creek

the Familiars
Fronted by actress Joanna Swan (vocals, percussion), with Tom Conway (acoustic guitar, vocals) and Vincent Maltby (violin), Norfolk's Familiars have released two albums (*CunningFolk* and *Martyred Hearts*) of dark and spooky folk. If Herne's Wild Hunt was led by Queen Boudicca, this is what it would sound like (catch the Familiars' take on the traditional "Cuckoo's Nest"), with arrangements as alluring as they are fresh.

the Floating World—see Amanda Votta

Fruits de Mer
Now firmly established among the UK's leading vinyl-only boutique labels, Fruits de Mer started out, says founder Keith Jones, "very much as a label that would hopefully appeal to people like me and a friend [Andy Bracken] who jointly launched it—vinyl junkies who love music rooted in the sixties and seventies, whatever their age."

An earlier Bracken label had already worked with Schizo Fun Addict; that band duly delivered Fruits de Mer's maiden release, to be swiftly followed by what—at the time of writing—has escalated to around 100 separate releases including much of the cream of world psych / electro / prog and more.

the Gathering Grey
Weymouth-based duo Gathering Grey are Marco Rossi (guitar, vocals) and Tom Hughes (keyboards), and reading the biography pasted to their Facebook page, it's unlikely that you'll want to believe anything they say.

Unless Marco really was raised by wolves and made his first guitar from the jawbone of an ass, and Tom truly does possess a head the size of a pistachio. Either way, they are Fruits de Mer regulars, with appearances aboard the Hollies and SF Sorrow tributes, and 7 & 7 Is.

Ghost Box
The haunted radiophonics of Belbury Poly epitomize the sound of Ghost Box Records—hardly surprisingly, as the Poly is Jim Jupp, one half of the label's founding team (the other is Julian House, aka the Focus Group).

Darkly electronic (for the most part), plunged into a land where all is half forgotten TV themes, sinister public information movies, and the rest of the societal detritus that marked out Britain in the early 1970s, Ghost Box is probably the project for which the term "hauntology" should have been coined.

Grandpa Egg
Range through the back catalog of Pittsburgh's Grandpa Egg—Jeb (guitar, vocals), Inga (bass, keyboards), Jordin (percussion) and Bart (ebow bass, resonator)— and you'll come across two albums… *Songs for my Cat* and *Praying Mantis*.

And, if you've ever enjoyed the Mighty Boosh, then we're all on the same page together. With added Donovan, Syd and a demented brother Gibb. There's certainly no place else you'll hear Comus playing reggae on a didgeridoo.

Greanvine—see the Owl Service

Green Question Mark—see Marrs Bonfire

Jefferson Hamer
New York based Coloradan Hamer is probably best known for his 2013 BBC Folk Award winning collaboration with Anaïs Mitchell, Child Ballads. He also pursues a remarkable career both solo and as a member of the Murphy Beds, acoustic collaboration with Dublin-born musician Eamon O'Leary.

the Hare and the Moon
The superbly enigmatic Hare and the Moon, led by the equally mysterious Grey Malkin, launched in a cloud of anonymity in 2009 and remains there today.

Responsible for a truly cinematic vein of folk-inflected darkness, as caught across an eponymous debut, the magnificent The Grey Malkin, and the absolutely spellbinding *Wood Witch* (Reverb Worship), the Hare and the Moon also collaborated with Alison O'Donnell on *Songs of the Black Meadow*.

The Hare has contributed, too, to such compilations as *We Bring You A King With A Head of Gold* and *Hail Be You Sovereigns, Lief And Dear*; it can also be heard alongside Amanda Votta in the Floating World and Spectral Light.

Head South By Weaving
Graeme Lockett was still a member of Kilter when he first formulated Head South By Weaving in 2006, a solo project that seeks a happy place between folk, psych and metal, but was first heard on "Harbour Boy," a co-write with Alison O'Donnell for her 2009 album *Hey Hey Hippy Witch*.

The pair conspired again for O'Donnell's Fruits de Mer single; and again on the joint album The Execution of Frederick Baker. HSBW can also be enjoyed on the Fruits de Mer compilations *Head Music* (with Frobisher Neck), *We Come Bearing Gifts, A Phase We've Been Through* and the Eddie Cochran Instrumentals EP

the Honey Pot—see Crystal Jacqueline

Emily Jones
Daughter of the late Al Jones, himself recently (re)discovered as one of the founding fathers of acid folk, Emily Jones was first heard by many as one half of *The Book of the Lost*, that so-scintillating soundtrack to the TV show that never was, cut with Rowan Amber Mill in 2013. Since that time her solo debut, *Autumn Eye*, has beguiled all who have encountered it, while she also serves in the duo Emily and Angeline with Angeline Morrison.

King Penguin
Reforming their old high school band Grey Matter, New Yorkers Bill Sweeney, Lanny Sichel and Gary Moran originally reunited to contribute to a Gene Clark Internet fan club project, the album Here Without You: A Tribute to Gene Clark. Since that time, they have become Fruits de Mer regulars, appearing on the *Keep Off The Grass* compilation; tributes to the Hollies and the Pretty Things; and 7 & 7 Is.

La Meccanica Sonora
Spain's La Meccanica Sonora formed in 2011 around ex-Danger Mouse bassist Narcis Passolas. Exploring improv and experimental music, playfully heavy on late sixties Floydian textures, Eno-esque agitations and some astonishingly soaring somethings, the line-up of Passolas (bass, vocals), Gil Roman (drums, vocals), Patricia Serrano (guitar) and Eric Valls (guitar, vocals) should immediately be heard on the albums *Mercury Mission* (2013) and *Tesseract* (2015).

Chris Lambert
Lambert is author and instigator of *Tales of the Black Meadow*, a gripping collection of short stories and verse comparable in scope, if not girth, to that Victorian era favorite The Ingoldsby Legends.

It has spun off a marvelous spoof BBC-style documentary and an accompanying soundtrack album by the Soulless Party, as well as a Songs from the Black Meadow tribute that includes contributions from Alison O'Donnell and the Hare and the Moon; Angeline Morrison and Rowan Amber Mill; and Emily Jones (whose late father, Al Jones, presciently referred to black meadows of his own on "Black Cat," a cut from his 1973 LP Jonesville).

The Loons
Fronted by Mike Stax, founding father of the ever-wonderful Ugly Things magazine, the Loons are the Pretty Things incarnate, shot through with a healthy dose of everything else that makes freakbeat so irresistible to all. Stax (vocals), Marc Schroeder (guitar), Chris Marsteller (guitar), Anja Stax (bass) and

Mike Kamoo (drums) released their incendiary debut album, *Love's Dead Leaves*, in 1999; *Paraphernailia, Red Dissolving Rays of Light* and *Inside Out Your Mind* have followed in similar high octane fashion.

Lost Harbours
Richard Thompson (no, not that one) and Emma Reed front Lost Harbours, a self-styled free folk duo from Southend-on-Sea. Since forming in 2007, Lost Harbours have by their own reckoning released "two full albums [*Into the Failing Light* and *Hymns and Ghosts]* and many EPs… disseminated in a variety of formats."

Lost In Rick's Wardrobe—see Me and My Kites

the Luck of Eden Hall
Not a medieval beaker (thank you, Google), but a psychy-proggy, Chicago-based Behemoth formed in the late 1980s and carving a livid swathe through several genres ever since.

Releases over the past few years include *When The Clock Starts To Wake Up We Go To Sleep* in 2009, two volumes of *Butterfly Revolutions*, the exquisitely named *Alligators Eat Gumdrops, Victoria Moon* and the forthcoming *The Acceleration of Time*. The Luck are also mainstays of the Fruits de Mer catalog.

Mark and the Clouds
Ex-Instant Flight singer / guitarist / songwriter Marco Magnani launched Mark & the Clouds in 2013, a shifting aggregation of musicians who came together for the Mega Dodo album *Blue Skies Opening*.

Me and My Kites
Sweden's Me and My Kites grew out of the earlier Lost In Rick's Wardrobe—who themselves earned a mighty reputation as one of the psych era's most painstaking modern-day mirrors.

Wardrobe specialized in period covers, although by the time the band finally came to cut its Fruits de Mer debut, the Wardrobe had closed and been renamed for a song on Fuchsia's classic (1971) acid-folk / prog album… and they borrowed their Fruits de Mer debut from that band too, teaming up with Fuchsia frontman Tony Durant for a spectacular version of his own "The Band."

Mega Dodo Records
Music writer and collector John Blaney launched Mega Dodo with a 45 and an album by the marvelous Mordecai Smyth.

Since that time, the catalog has expanded to include similarly stellar releases by Icarus Peel, Octopus Syng, the Green Question Mark, Strange Turn, the Honey Pot, Mark and the Clouds, Ivan Ivanovitch (a Ukrainian performer whose debut transforms Paul McCartney's "Mull of Kintyre" into a creature of impeccable wonder) and Crystal Jacqueline.

All catering, says Blaney, for an "audience [that] has a taste for well crafted songs, an eclectic taste in music and prefers to listen to music on vinyl."

Midwich Youth Club

Taking their name (in case you hadn't guessed) from the John Wyndham novel The Midwich Cuckoos, MYC is the brainchild of Alan R Murphy, and purveyors of a deliciously raw electro creepiness spread over such albums as *TV Themes from Nowhere* (2010), *We Swim in the Neon Sea* (2012), *The Midwich Youth Club and Hobby Centre* (2013), *Gamification* (2014), two volumes of *Orphans from the Electronic Landfill* (2015), and, most recently, a dazzling cover of the Fall's "What You Need."

Murphy is also responsible for the truly, and gloriously, mindbending Pages from Ceefax.

Mikey Georgeson

When you spent the 1990s (and beyond) fronting David Devant and His Spirit Wife—perhaps the ultimate trip for the pop-loving Hauntologist; when you are responsible, too, for two of the most atmospheric b-sides of the era, both concerning the spoken word adventures of Cookie the Ghost; coming up with a solo career… initially under the name of Mr Solo… cannot be an easy ask.

But with a background in art, painting and "the power of following passions to lead to instances of backwards causality," as well as a past partnership with Jyoti Mishra (of White Town), Georgeson has moved through a variety of themes and schemes, culminating most recently in the Civilized Scene (their debut album, *Blood and Brambles*, appeared in 2014) and still, the continuing saga of the Spirit Wife.

Mooch

Steve Palmer launched Mooch back in 1992, a largely (but by no means exclusively) space rock project that debuted with the cassette only *3001* and *Planetfall* before 1993 brought *Postvorta*.

Regular releases since then led up to Mooch's twentieth anniversary *Twenty Year Trip* DVD in 2012, while a collaboration with ex-Hawkwind singer Bridget Wishart (the *Beltane to Samhain* EP) prefaced the band's 25th album *Mrs Silbury's Delicious Mushroom Flavoured Biscuits*.

Angeline Morrison

Work with Frootful, Lack of Afro, the Ambassadors of Sorrow and more preceded the release of Morrison's *Are You Ready Cat?* debut, a spirited blend of folk, bossa nova, RandB and jazz rhythms.

More recently, Morrison has recorded with Rowan Amber Mill (the mid-winter chiller *Silent Night Songs for a Cold Winter's Evening*) and the *Mighty Sceptre*s, while she also performs alongside Emily Jones in the duo Emily and Angeline.

Drew Mulholland

Wikipedia says "Mulholland has been described as the 'godfather' of psychogeographic rock," and why not? Composer-in-residence at Glasgow University's geography department, Mulholland's music is weird, wonderful, darkly electronic and deeply ecstatic.

Recent(-ish) releases, as Mount Vernon Astral Temple, include *Musick That Destroys Itself* (2003) and *Bent Sinister By Sound* (2005), and follow exquisitely on from the earlier Mount Vernon Arts Lab's 2001 masterpiece *The Séance at Hob's Lane*—featuring Adrian Utley (Portishead), Isobel Campbell (Belle and Sebastian) and a wealth of Victorian skullduggery and quatermass-ive demons. It has since reissued by Ghost Box (where else?).

His most recent album, *The Norwood Variations*, arrived in 2014.

the Nomen

Scotland's Nomen—Allan, Brian, George and Jamie NoMan—take pride in the fact that, after ten years together, they have still only played one gig.

However, a packed discography is stuffed with sonic niceties, a space age psychedelic jamboree bag that includes the delightfully titled *Ways to Annoy the Devil*, the cult-hunting *Nine Men's Morris* and many more.

Alison O'Donnell

Fronting Irish folk rock band Mellow Candle from the age of fifteen, (the slow-burning acclaim meted out to their debut album Swaddling Songs was one of the greatest achievements of the 1990s); and moving onto the South Africa-based Flibbertigibbet (ditto Whistling Jigs to the Moon), O'Donnell returned to Ireland via a few years in London and began a solo career.

An influential touchstone for several successive generations of aspiring folk vocalists, recent years have produced a string of new releases that are at least the equal, and oft-times superior to, anything she recorded in her youth.

Solo recordings include a Fruits de Mer single coupling Nico and Nick Drake, and the startling *Hey Hey Hippy Witch*; she has also collaborated with the Owl Service, *Head South* by Weaving, Dodson & Fogg, Adam Bulewski, the Child of a Creek and United Bible Studies.

Octopus Syng
Finland's Octopus Syng have been flourishing since 1999, a one man outfit formed by Jaire Pätäri that only slowly metamorphosed into a full band.

Two early albums featuring Pätäri alone likewise have crystallized into the band's 2014 Mega Dodo album *Reverberating Garden Number 7*, and while lazy comparisons raise names as far apart as Syd Barrett and Pekka Streng, the octopus has plenty of tentacles of its own.

the Owl Service
Steven Collins launched the Owl Service in 2006, swiftly establishing the band in the very vanguard of the 21st century folk rock scene via both Collins's own dexterity and imagination, and an ear for some of the most remarkable female vocalists on the scene—Alison O'Donnell, Rebsie Fairholm, Rachel Davies, Nancy Wallace and Diana Collier—his collaborator, too, in the side project Greanvine.

Two Owl Service albums, *A Garland of Song* and *The View from a Hill* (a third is in preparation) have appeared alongside the compilation *The Pattern Beneath The Plough Parts 1 + 2* and a slew of EPs.

Collins also headed the Stone Tape Recordings label, home to Greanvine, Country Parish Music (Collins and Rosemary Lippard), You Are Wolf, Driftwood Manor, Alasdair Roberts and O'Donnell and Firefay's superb Anointed Queen.

Pages from Ceefax—see Midwich Youth Club

Palace of Swords
With sole member Peter Lyons culling influences from as far afield as Kenneth Anger soundtracks, Eric Satie and Nico, Aberdeen's Palace of Swords has released two essentially self-titled CDs via Reverb Worship. They feature, too, on compilations released via Fruits de Mer, Active Listener and Recycled Handmade.

the Past Tense
Currently completing their third album, Kingston trio the Past Tense are Fruits de Mer regulars, with a sharp eye for breakbeat riffery and a golden sense of what made the Who so special, once upon a time.

Ken Halsey, Warren Samuels and Andy Norrie-Rolfe's two past albums, *Take Three* and *Pick 'n' Mix*, are unimpeachably cool; the new one will doubtless be the same.

Icarus Peel—see Crystal Jacqueline

Gordon Raphael

Berlin based Seattle-ite Raphael was keyboardist for legendary 1990s psych experience Sky Cries Mary, before moving into production and helming the first two Strokes albums.

He has since worked with Regina Spektor, Skin, Ian Brown, Ian Astbury and many more, while also fronting his own Gordotronic project.

Regal Crabomophone—see Fruits de Mer

Reverb Worship

As label head Roger Linney puts it, the Reverb Worship label has been "purveyors of quality limited edition psychedelic folk drone wonderment since 2007," with a mission statement insisting on "the best and most interesting music from the current underground scene."

Furiously limited editions seldom exceed 100 copies, and have included releases by Sand Snowman, Wyrdstone, Sproatly Smith, the Hare and the Moon, Palace of Swords, United Bible Studies and Amanda Votta's Floating World and Spectral Light projects.

Rowan Amber Mill

Hard to believe we'd never heard of "Woodland Folkadelica" before, but it's been a major part of our lives for almost a decade now; ever since Stephen Stannard's Rowan Amber Mill emerged with 2008's Folk Devils and Moral Panics mini album.

The Book of the Lost, imagining the soundtrack to a lost supernatural TV series, saw the Mill link with Emily Jones for a slice of dark-dreamy lost and lovely psych, with Jones's marvelous voice a wraith-like presence that is both childlike and ageless.

A second Book of the Lost album is preparation; in the interim, the pair also alchemized a best-ever cover of Gary Numan's "Are Friends Electric"), while Stannard's partnership with Angeline Morrison most recently brought us *Silent Night Songs for a Cold Winter's Evening*.

Christmas will never sound the same.

Paolo Sala

Arch-Cardiacs maniac Sala's 2014 album *You Don't Know, Do You?* is so wryly titled that it seems almost churlish to spoil the fun and tell you anything.

But the Genova, Italy-based Paolo was also bassist for Emily Jones's peerless Autumn Eye; and one half of the Senpai, with Renzo Sala. A mighty catalog reaching back to the dawn of the century should be checked out immediately.

Sand Snowman

In 2013, the enigmatic Sand Snowman released Private Culture, a "best of" style compilation that drew in collaborations with Judy Dyble, Comus's Bobbie Watson, Steven Wilson, Moonswift and more; yet only scraped the surface of a discography whose own parameters reach from Krautrock to folk, and onto ambient chamber music.

A clutch of frighteningly limited edition Reverb Worship albums opened the Snowman's discography beginning 2007 (all have since been reissued); recent releases include *The Twilight Game, Nostalgia Ever After, Vanished Chapters* and *Otherness*.

Schizo Fun Addict

Responsible for the first release ever on Fruits de Mer, the New Jersey trio of Jet, Jayne and Patrick had already been around since 2000, when they unleashed the album Just a Dimension Away.

Subsequent releases included the *Diamond* EP (with real diamonds mixed into its hand-crafted artwork) and album, *Atom Spark Hotel, Imperial Quasar* and *The Sun Yard*, together with a flurry of further Fruits de Mer contributions. Frontman Jet Wintzer is also an acclaimed film maker.

Sendelica

In a world where Hawkwind and Ozric Tentacles represent Godhead, Sendelica are the Welsh Holy Spirit that goes as far, if not further, via more albums than most people can even keep up with.

All of which explore the multitudinous avenues of space rock from fresh and even frightening directions. 2015's *Anima Mundi* is the most recent… or maybe a split LP with Da Captain Trips… or maybe a searing live performance taped at Fruits de Mer's Crabstock festival. It doesn't really matter. Play one, play all.

Sendelica…Pete Bingham (guitars, electronics), Colin Consterdine (synths, rhythms etc), Glenda Pescado (bass), Lee Relfe (sax), Jack Jackson (drums) and all their fellow travelers… will never let you down.

the Seventh Ring of Saturn

A founding member of the Black Crowes, Ted Selke's TSROS debuted in 2007 with a still astonishing debut album, following through since then with magnificent appearances on such Fruits de Mer projects as *Sorrow's Children*, the White EP, *The Crabs Sell Out; The Crabs Freak Out, Re-Evolution: Fruits de Mer Sings The Hollies* and 7 & 7 Is.

Their second album, *Ormythology*, appeared in 2015.

Francois Sky
French born, Berlin based, Francois Sky had been gigging around in various permutations before taking a decade-long break in 1996; then resurfacing a decade later as the mastermind behind a steady stream of superb single downloads

Sky Picnic
With a combined vision that drifts from King Crimson to Donovan, the trio of Chris Sherman, Leah Cinnamon and Pete Meriwether were responsible for that version of "Bracelet of Fingers" which was one of the wildest highlights of Fruits de Mer's SF Sorrow tribute.

Sherman and Cinnamon had been playing around New York City with various guesting drummers before, in 2008, linking with Meriwether.

They released their debut album, *Farther In This Fairy Tale* three years later; *Paint Me A Dream* followed, while the band (now signed to Mega Dodo) were also among the highlights of the 2014 Crabstock festivals.

Soulless Party
The Soulless Party's long and fascination journey into the heart of eerie electronica commenced in 1998, with the first of the pieces since served up on the Archive Material 1998-2002 collection.

Other projects have included the 2011 EP *Exploring Radio Space*, while Kev Oyston also curated *Electronic Encounters*, a tribute to the movie *Close Encounters of the Third Kind*.

But truly, the Party's breakthrough arrived with the score for Chris Lambert's Tales from the Black Meadow project, a breathtaking creation that stands among this century's most timeless pieces of music.

the Spectral Light—see Amanda Votta

Sproatly Smith
Dark folk hero Smith has maintained a stream of near-perfect reflections on the English countryside's most disquieting elements, as reflected through the idyllic prism of rural calm that cloaks all but the blackest spinneys.

First sighted in 2009 with *Pixieled*; following through with the *Yew and the Hair*, the acclaimed *Minstrel's Grave* and *Times Is N' Times Was*, Smith was also responsible for the one festive season album that is possibly as chillingly lovely as the Rowan Amber Mill's Santa slayer, 2012's Carols from Herefordshire.

Mordecai Smyth
The first artist released on the Mega Dodo label… which in turn only formed so founder John Blaney could have some Mordecai Smyth wax in his collection… psych-pop superstar Smith debuted with 2011's "Georgina Jones" 45 (followed by "Dial M for Mordecai").

There's also a terrific album, *Sticky Tape and Rust* (recorded in his mum's garage), with CD copies packaged in exactly what it says on the tin. And it is impossible to say too many nice things about 2014's *Barnburner* EP, split down the middle with Icarus Peel.

Smyth is also part of Marrs Bonfire's Green Question Mark.

Stay
Formed in the early 2000s, Barcelona's Stay released their first single in 2005, although the previous year saw Matchbox Recordings release one of their demos.

Since then, four excellent albums have pursued Jordi Bel and co's alchemical blend of Madchester psych and indy stroll: *Starting to Lose Control*, *Things You Cannot See*, *Passport to Freedom* and *The Fourth Dimension*.

Stay were also among the earliest acts to appear on Fruits de Mer, with a three track single just the third release in the catalog.

Stone Tape Recordings—see the Owl Service

the Striped Bananas
Duncan, Chantelle and Lowden rocket across a brace of albums… a self titled debut and the 2015 Lady Sunshine… like the Beatles never buried "Carnival of Light," with controls indisputably set for the heart of 67, and the sonic battery sliding straight out of a teetering pile of psych compilations. Exquisite!

the Sunchymes
Two albums, *Shifting Sands* (2009) and *Let Your Free Flag Fly* (2011) capture the sheer summer sounds of the Sunchymes—described by popgeekheaven as a "unique synthesis of *Magical Mystery Tour* era Beatles and *Pet Sounds* era Beach Boys"; with Aaron Hemington, even more intriguingly, styled "Mycroft to Brian Wilson's Sherlock."

It's really hard to resist anything that sounds like that.

The Thanes
Stomping furiously since the late 1980s first saw the garage beat drive out of the garage, Edinburgh's Thanes are: Lenny Helsing (vocal, guitar), Angus McPake (keyboards, guitar), Mark Hunter (bass) and Mike Goodwin (drums), and are initially best experienced via the double album *One Night As I*

Wandered On The Moors, a Best Of that ranges throughout a voluminous catalog… and naturally, leaves you begging for more.

Tír na nÓg
Crusading folky proggers at the dawn of the 1970s, the Irish duo of Leo O'Kelly and Sonny Condell released three crucial albums between 1971-1973, then split the following year.

They reformed in 1985, but only on a very sporadic basis—the first decade of the 21st century brought two live albums from the duo, but 2014 saw the release of a a new EP on Fruits De Mer, presaging the 2015 album *The Dark Dance*.

United Bible Studies
Across some twenty exemplary albums (including 2015's spellbinding *So As To Preserve The Mystery*), Ireland's UBS have been compared, with some accuracy, to the Incredible String Band, Broadcast, Current 93 and Sweeney's Men.

David Colohan and James Rider first set up tent in Dublin in 2001, and proceeded to lure in a small army of fellow players, some passing through for just a song or two, others locking in for the long haul.

Right now, Alison O'Donnell, Richard Moult, Áine O'Dwyer (whose *Music for Church Cleaners* solo album, by the way, should also be sought out) and Michael Tanne are among those who are united in their studies.

Us and Them
The Swedish duo of Anders Håkanson and Britt Rönnholm launched in the mid-2000s with a beautiful, and so idiosyncratic version of Roy Harper's "Another Day."

Still working towards their debut album, they have released a string of acclaimed EPs, including the *Summerisle* collection of songs from *The Wicker Man*.

Amanda Votta
Beginning with 2005's *We Hunted*, four albums by her Floating World project readily established Detroit's Amanda Votta's darkly, starkly atmospheric credentials, drawing in contributions from Grey Malkin and Neddal Ayad.

A decade later, the spin-off Spectral Light allowed her to explore harsher territory, whilst retaining the shimmering purity of her earlier releases.

A skilled flautist, Votta has also collaborated with Dodson & Fogg.

Will Z

Ex-Cosmic Trip Machine, Will Z's 2015 solo album New Start (Mega Dodo) was inspired by Jain philosophy follows on from his collaborations with Juan Arkotxa and Leslie MacKenzie on The Book of AM and The Book of Intxixu.

Will Z

A TALE FROM THE BLACK MEADOW

When Mr Barrett first approached Roger Mullins to ask for information about the Brightwater Archive[1] I was unsurprised to learn that Mullins was not only unimpressed but very reluctant to help. He had fought the government to open the archive and he was not prepared to share his sensitive findings with anyone. Mullins was nonplussed by Barrett's celebrity.

At that time (in 1967) Barrett was making waves with his new band at UFO[2] but Mullins was very sniffy about "junkies trying to open the doors of perception."[3] However, Mr Barrett managed to persuade Mullins, who showed him some key features of the archive that are, even now, blocked from public view. Mr Barrett himself never spoke of the archive publicly, and it would seem that his later isolation enabled him to take any secrets that Mullins shared to the grave.

When I asked Mullins what had changed his mind, he told me that Mr Barrett had shared a story that Mullins had considered so useful that he was happy to give Barrett access to information relating to the land spheres[4], time slips[5], standing stones[6] and the disappearing village[7]. Barrett was reportedly also

---

[1] *The Brightwater Archive is an extensive collection of files gathered by Lord Brightwater and his team when he investigated the disappearances on the North York Moors in the 1930s. After his investigation was closed down, due to a lack of funding, the files were locked away. They were briefly re-opened for the University of York when Roger Mullins was conducting his research in the 1960s and 1970s. In 2013 the archive was opened again and elements of it are available to see online at thebrightwaterarchive.wordpress.com.*

[2] *UFO was a nightclub in London run by Joe Boyd and John Hopkins. The first bands to play there were Soft Machine and Syd Barrett's own Pink Floyd.*

[3] *Taken from Mullins' personal diaries – these are currently unpublished. The full quotation is found in an entry dated 5th March 1966 which is the day Barrett first approached Mullins at the University of York. "The gentleman was unkempt with dark eyes and a mess of black scraggy hair. He appeared to me to be the sort of man who was looking for another 'experience.' I really have very little time for these junkies trying to open the doors of perception. Why take hallucinogens when you have the Black Meadow to explore?"*

[4] *The Land Spheres have a very rich history of folklore attached to them. Giant black spheres were seen to float across the North York Moors on "Black Nights." Their origin was unknown. Sightings diminished when the RAF constructed the "early warning system" Radomes on the moors.*

[5] *Many who have walked the moors have reported incidences of missing time. Several folk tales allude to this. "The Coalman and the Creature" and "The Long Walk to Scarry Wood" explore the notion of time travel long before it was fashionable to do so.*

[6] *There are many standing stones on the North York Moors. On the Black Meadow there is said to be a stone that is covered in arcane spirals that can be used for occult purposes.*

[7] *The Disappearing Village is the most significant and prolific part of Black Meadow folklore. It is said that a lost village appears and disappears when the mist is high: "When the mist spreadsLike an unspooling ball of wool Threading over the landCan you see the smoke from the chimneys?Can you see the roofs above the clouds?And if the mist rises. If the mist rises*

very interested in the tales that Mullins had been collecting. Mullins added Barrett's own account to his collection of notes which I am very pleased to be able to publish for the first time.

There is a strange link between Barrett and Mullins. Both were searching for something, both had grand obsessions and both disappeared; Barrett from the public eye and Mullins into the mist.

Professor Philip Hull – University of York

The Audire
Mr Barrett - May 1967
(Adapted from Roger Mullins' notes by Chris Lambert)

There was a singer who visited the Black Meadow. He was something of a celebrity, from the flatlands to the east of the country, whose songs smacked of a delicious Englishness that the folk singers of the moors would have embraced.

Mr Barrett, like many artists before him, was drawn to the mysteries of the North York Moors. What is it about this place that calls so many into its fog ridden heart? He was looking for inspiration to help create a set of songs for his new band. He stayed the night at an inn in Sleights where he had a peaceful stay (as no-one knew who he was). In the early morning of a Saturday in late May he walked with two friends onto the mist-shrouded moor.

Like many artists of the current age, he had dabbled in mysticism, had experimented with herbs and medicines, tried to join obscure religious sects and had attempted to create music that went beyond the expectations of the everyday. He decided to seek out new experiences for himself. He had heard about the standing stones on the moors, as well as the great RAF Radomes[1] and the strange stories surrounding them.

As everybody knows, there are certain standing stones on the moors that require the visitor to take with them a sheet of parchment and some charcoal or wax crayon.[2] On locating the stone (after half a day of searching; he and his companions were not adept with an Ordnance Survey Map), he took a rubbing of a

---

The village will come The village has come." C. Lambert, *Tales from the Black Meadow* (Reading: Exiled Publications, 2013), p. 75.

[1] *The Radomes at Fylingdales were three 40-metre-diameter 'golfballs' or geodesic domes (radomes) which, according to the RAF, contained mechanically steered radar. They were constructed in 1962 and demolished in the 1990s.*

[2] *There is a detailed reference made to this ritual in "The Standing Stone". C. Lambert, Tales from the Black Meadow (Reading: Exiled Publications, 2013), p. 41.*

spiral that he found carved into the granite. His friends followed suit, before writing their worries and fears into the gaps between the spiral lines. The singer wrote in his concerns about his music, how he felt that he couldn't create what he envisioned. That task complete, they held the paper over a flame, watching their worries, concerns and hates disappearing into smoke and ash over the North York Moors.

Mr Barrett and his three friends felt jubilant and free. They ran across the moors singing and dancing. Stopping occasionally to look down strange holes or to roll in the heather. They made dens in the bramble. They ran into the mist trying to seek each other out by calls and chants.

In their delirious abandon, they found that they were drawing near to the RAF site on the North York Moors. Mr Barrett commented on the incongruity of the three spheres on the moors and encouraged his other two friends to see how close they could get to them. Not being tethered by the rules or mores of the establishment, they happily vaulted the high fences, making their way to the Radomes through a process of running, crouching and crawling.

They were prepared to walk nonchalantly, as though lost, if met by officious soldiers. On this day, they were not accosted and came close to the first of the three Radomes. They flattened themselves against the base of the sphere, before peering around the side to check for any movement. Surrounding the sphere furthest from them were soldiers and a collection of men and women in long white coats.

The soldiers were standing back whilst several of the scientists had their hands on the skin of the Radome. These scientists were standing still with their heads down. Mr Barrett assumed that they had their eyes closed. After a few minutes of stillness a scientist arched his back, falling into the arms of another scientist. A moment passed whilst the others flurried around, checking the scientist's pulse and waving smelling salts under his nose.

The scientist spluttered, jumped to his feet and began to pace and shout, gesticulating wildly. The others scribbled furious notes, listening carefully. The three travellers could hear snatches of words from where they watched. Cries of: "saw more… audire… father… vivid… audire…"

A few minutes after he had finished his explanations, another scientist collapsed and a near identical process repeated: revival, shouting, gesticulation and notes.

Mr Barrett was very excited by what he had seen. He slowly stood and, while his friends watched, he placed his hands on the surface of the Radome. He commented on the light buzzing he could hear, the vibrations under his fingertips. Mr Barrett lowered his head, closed his eyes and listened.

The birds and sheep seemed louder somehow. More vibrant. Sounds were loud and fast, like the strange affliction he had suffered as a child in moments of isolation. When he was seven years old, he suffering a prolonged illness, his hands seemed to expand inside, his skin became more sensitive and the voices of others grew acute and urgent, sounds had increased in volume, intensity and speed. He had forgotten all about that, but now it came back to him in a rush of images and feelings. He could hear his own heartbeat, the loud urgent breath of his two friends, he could hear the voices of the scientists.

"Just step through," one said. "I could just step through."

"I saw her," said another. "She was older, but I saw her."

"The dark and the fires," a third whispered. "All around. The dead air. The static. The fallen birds. The ruins."

He could hear another voice too.

"Have you got it yet?" It giggled. "Have you got it yet?"

The other voices, the sheep, the birds and the wind diminished into a static hiss.

"Have you got it yet?" The voice giggled again.

New sounds were heard. Cars outside. Children playing in the street. The slow ticking of a clock. The creaking of feet on floorboards. The skin of the Radome felt sticky, then soft. Mr Barrett pushed at it, allowing his arm to sink through the white custard membrane.

He pushed his face through, opening his eyes to gaze upon the room he had heard. The room was empty of furniture and objects save for a guitar and a wooden chair. Upon the chair sat a large man with a shaved head staring at the guitar in the corner. He turned his head to look at Mr Barrett who had now stepped fully into the room.

"Oh it's you," he said. "I thought it would be."
Mr Barrett looked about the room again. He found it hard to speak.

"You don't need to speak," said the large bald man. "I didn't. At least I don't think I did. My name's Roger."

Mr Barrett blinked, opening and shutting his mouth like a carp.

Roger got out of his chair, shuffling towards Mr Barrett. He peered at him through heavy set dark eyes. Mr Barrett stood stock still as Roger walked slowly around him.

"Have you got it yet?" he asked.

Mr Barrett found himself unable to speak. He was stiffening, his flesh crawling. He couldn't shake his head in response to the question.

"No you haven't," smiled Roger. "I didn't. Not until I woke up a few months ago."

Mr Barrett was finding it hard to breathe.

"Do you like what you see?"

The two of them stood staring at one another for an age. Mr Barrett could hear Roger's breathing, slow and deep. Could see the clammy sweat glinting on his face. Roger stepped away and walked towards the guitar.

"Do you play?"

Mr Barrett managed a nod at last.

"I don't think I do. I have been looking at it for some time, but I don't think I shall play it," Roger stated. "Will you?"

Roger picked up the guitar, strode over to Mr Barrett and passed him the instrument. Mr Barrett gasped at the feel of the wood in his hands, the delicate strings. He strummed a chord and began to play. Roger sank into his chair, slowly smiling. Mr Barrett played for several minutes and when he stopped, Roger took the guitar, thanking Mr Barrett gratefully for his efforts.
Roger walked back to Mr Barrett, who was standing stock still. Roger put his face close to Mr Barrett's. "You will remember this," he whispered. "You will remember this, it will help for a while."

Roger reached out his hand to touch Mr Barrett's cheek.

"So young," he smiled. "Good times. Good times. I wish I was there."

As Roger's finger brushed against Mr Barrett's skin, there was a surge of green light. The sounds of cars, children playing and the soft creak of footsteps on floorboards was replaced by the cries of birds, sheep, a soft breeze and the distant murmurings of scientists.

He fell. The room was gone, in its place was the vast sphere filling every part of his vision. His two friends helped him to his feet. They carefully made their way back to the fence, unnoticed by the groups of scientists and soldiers immersed in their work.

Inside the Plough Inn, Mr Barrett was taciturn. He drunk his one pint of ale and wandered off to his bed with barely a word, lost in thought. In the morning his friends were relieved to see him laughing and joking with the landlady, whilst he scoffed down one of her delicious cooked breakfasts. His friends pressed him to tell them again what he had seen but he told them it was all a blur. In fact, anything he did see was probably his imagination anyway.

Mr Barrett drove to Lincolnshire that day to play an incredible set with his new band and for a while, everything was wonderful.

JUST A WORD

For what should be very obvious reasons, this book could never have been written, or even contemplated, without the enthusiasm, encouragement and input of everyone involved.

So first - thanks to all the bands, musicians, label heads, shady Svengalis and aspiring oligarchs whose words have proved as entertaining over the last few months as their music has over the years.

To Gregory Curvey for the beautiful cover design...

To Chris Lambert for opening the Black Meadow archive...

To Keith Jones and John Blaney for making so many of the initial introductions...

To Amy Thompson for being here...

And to you for reading this far.

INDEX